WAIT
FOR
WHAT
WILL
COME

Also by Barbara Michaels

WAIT
FOR
WHAT
WILL
COME

BY BARBARA MICHAELS

DODD, MEAD & COMPANY, NEW YORK

Copyright © 1978 by Barbara Michaels
All rights reserved
No part of this book may be reproduced in any form
without permission in writing from the publisher
Printed in the United States of America

1 2 3 4 5 6 7 8 9 10

Library of Congress Cataloging in Publication Data

——————.

Wait for what will come.

I. Title.
PZ4.M577Wai   [PS3563.E747]   813'.5'4   78–18319
ISBN 0–396–07577–0

WAIT
FOR
WHAT
WILL
COME

 ONE

In summer, when the sun beams down from an azure heaven, the sea surrounding this rocky promontory has a smiling, innocent face. Golden gorse and purple heather nestle in the fissures of the caverned granite cliffs. The waves splash gaily onto the silver sands of the cove and play among the rocks, twinkling and winking. As the sun sinks slowly in the west, the vault of heaven resembles a painter's palette, splashed with sublime hues of crimson and cerulean blue, with a lone star pinned like a diamond upon the bosom of the night. In the dying hush of day, one may fancy one can hear the distant chiming of the sunken churches of Lyonesse.

—Diary of Caroline Tregellas, born 1762, died (?) 1780

Carla Tregellas—born 1952, and very much alive—was also thinking about the beauties of nature and the fabled cliffs of Cornwall as she approached the home of her ancestors for the first time. She was not stirred to rapturous appreciation. On the contrary, she muttered profanely under her breath and brooded on the disadvantages of living in a mechanized world.

Her rented Austin, inching its way through the streets of Exeter, was one in a line of similar vehicles, all emitting clouds of noxious fumes. The air was blue with exhaust and with the comments of frustrated motorists. She had the choice of leaving the car windows down and getting the full effect of the poisonous gases, or rolling them up and being overcome with the heat.

She had been naive to suppose that England in general, and Cornwall in particular, would be any different from the rest of the so-called civilized world. It was early June, and the Cornish coast was one of the playgrounds of England; she might have known that the traffic would be as bad here as it was between Boston and the Cape, or between Baltimore and the Bay resorts. Like those vacation centers of her native United States, Cornwall was a tag-end of land almost entirely surrounded by ocean, and therefore reachable by only a few limited routes. These were bound to be crowded with tourists.

The guidebook, and the man at the car-rental agency, had warned her to avoid Exeter, and she had had every intention of following that advice. But it wasn't easy to read road signs while concentrating on keeping to the left. And where had she gotten the idea that England was a cool, moist country? It was unseasonably hot, even for Cornwall, which is sometimes referred to by effusive tour guides as the English Riviera.

However, after she crossed the Tamar her sour mood improved, and she was forced to admit that even in the twentieth century Cornwall had its charms. The road followed the coastline, which was rocky, high, and rugged. From the top of the cliffs she had occasional breathtaking glimpses of the ocean and of little villages clinging picturesquely to the steep slopes. No wonder the towns built around these rock-bound harbors had prospered in the days of England's maritime glory. Falmouth and Plymouth, Penzance and St. Ives—the familiar names gave her a sense of homecoming. Some had been transferred by homesick emigrants to a similar landscape thousands of miles to the west, others familiarized by a literary tradition, from folk legend to Gilbert and Sullivan, that is the heritage of the entire English-speaking world. . . . But for her it was more than that. Her spirits quickened as the miles rolled out behind her, and she found her thoughts returning to the interview with the Boston lawyer, only a few weeks earlier. Yes, in the most primitive sense of the word, she was coming home.

II

"Roots?" Carla threw her head back and laughed. "No, Mr. Fawcett, I can't say I've ever had any wild desire to pursue mine."

The lawyer looked at her in surprised approval. She had a nice laugh, and the change of expression did wonders for her face. He had thought, when she first came into the office, that she was a solemn little thing, too grave and serious for a woman of twenty-six. The smile illumined her features, lent sparkle to her eyes, and emphasized the unusual delicacy of her bone structure.

Mr. Fawcett knew Caroline's age and other personal details, although this was the first time they had met. He had found her appearance unusual in several ways. Knowing that the family was of Cornish stock, he had expected that the strong Celtic strain would be visible.

3

He was a closet anthropologist, was Mr. Fawcett—and, although he would have denied it vigorously, something of a poet—and he now realized, with an unprofessional and not wholly comfortable thrill, that he was seeing an example of a racial strain far older than the Celtic, so old that its history had become the fabric of legend and folklore. The little dark people who had inhabited England in prehistoric times had been pushed back into the far corners of that island by the Celtic warriors, just as the Celts were to be pushed, in their turn, by later invaders. Into Cornwall, Scotland, and Wales, across the stormy gray waters into Ireland the beleaguered remnants of a dozen races had fled, and had stopped, their backs to the watery walls. There was nowhere else to go. Invasion came from the east, from the continent; and beyond the western limits of Britain was nothing but endless sea, and the Islands of the Blessed.

Some scholars claimed that there was a strong Mediterranean strain in the Cornish, and there was archaeological evidence to support the theory. The isle of Britain, lost in the cold mists of the northern seas, had been the goal of intrepid seafarers from the time of Odysseus. There are Minoan axes carved on the monoliths of Stonehenge, and Phoenician merchants had founded fortunes on the tin trade, jealously guarding their maps of the northern sea routes.

Seeing Carla Tregellas, Mr. Fawcett found these theories more plausible than ever. If he had not known better, he might have taken her for a Greek or a southern Italian, with her thick dark hair and warm coloring. Yet there was something in her face that was alien to those practical, earthy people: a hint of other wordliness in the wide-spaced gray eyes and sharply cut features. Her ears,

4

exposed by the short, tousled haircut, were small and delicate; Mr. Fawcett might have used the word "pointed" if his vein of poetry had not been so deeply buried. The little dark people, hunted like animals by the invaders, had gone underground; according to some scholars, they had become the pixies and elves of English folklore. . . .

Mr. Fawcett shook himself mentally, surprised and shocked at the track his thoughts were following. There was something about the girl that induced fantasy; the quality must be strong, to have such an effect on an elderly lawyer who prided himself on his common sense.

Certainly her manner did not support his wild ideas. Her tone was brisk and matter-of-fact, her ideas practical, as she went on:

"Of course I knew the family came from Cornwall. Where else, with a name like Tregellas? 'By Tre, Ros, Pol, Lan, Caer and Pen, you may know most Cornishmen.' I've read a few novels about the country, seen things on TV—but I never did any genealogical research. I mean, why should I? I suppose I took it for granted that the family was poor and obscure. I know many Cornishmen came to this country in the nineteenth century, after the tin mines failed and they couldn't find work."

She paused, waiting for him to comment, and Mr. Fawcett started guiltily. He had been fantasizing again. But really, those eyes of hers were quite remarkable. So dark a gray that in a certain light they looked black; but at times—when she smiled, for instance—they became a luminous silver, reflecting every emotion.

Come, now, Mr. Fawcett told himself sternly. This won't do. Whatever is the matter with you?

5

"Your attitude is understandable," he said primly. "Until the success of the book to which you referred, genealogical research was a hobby of the middle-aged. Young people are not usually concerned with the past. And there is some truth in your surmise that the family —your branch of it, at least—was poor and of little consequence."

"I didn't say they were of little consequence," Carla said. "The word I used was 'obscure.'"

"What? Oh—oh, yes. I see what you mean. Er—are you at all interested in the history of your family?"

"Not much."

"You are an outspoken young woman, aren't you?"

"I've been told so." Carla smiled at him, and his momentary pique evaporated. "I'm sorry," she went on. "Tell me what you think I need to know. I guess I can't get out of this situation without taking some action, and I may as well have all the facts."

"Quite right. Very well, then, you must understand that your great-great-grandfather, William Tregellas, was the proverbial younger son. There is some story of a quarrel with his father, which resulted in his being disinherited. In fact, there was little for him to inherit at that time. The family is very ancient, actually, but it fell into decline after the Civil War—the English Civil War, that is, between—"

"I know about the English Civil War," Carla said, with a faint smile. "Cromwell and King Charles. I suppose my family supported the king? Stupid of them."

"Quite so," said Mr. Fawcett, unreasonably irritated by this cynical observation. Cynicism did not suit those wide gray eyes. "Hmph. In any case, it was not until the nineteenth century, after William had left for America,

6

that a cousin of his restored the family fortunes. For a time there was a great deal of money. However, modern taxation has accomplished what war and disaster did not do. The money is gone. There is nothing left except the house and a few acres of land."

"So my hunch was right," Carla said calmly. "It is a hoax."

"Hoax? Hoax? My dear Miss Tregellas—"

"Oh, I didn't mean that you—" Carla's apologetic exclamation was quite genuine, but Mr. Fawcett caught a glimpse of something in the gray eyes, like an imp laughing. "You must excuse me," she went on contritely. "I'm one of those horrible people who speak before they think. I'm not proud of it. I'm trying to cure myself, but it seems to be a deep-seated trait. As soon as I saw your office, I knew everything was all right, but. . . . Really, it is an improbable situation, isn't it? Long-lost heirs, ancient family, a castle on a headland overlooking the sea. . . ." Her smile invited him to share the joke, and unwillingly Mr. Fawcett smiled too. "I'm a very practical person, Mr. Fawcett," she finished. "It's just as well, isn't it? Because the great inheritance isn't much, after all."

"Essentially, that is correct. I am happy to see that you do not entertain ideas of rushing off to England and establishing yourself as lady of the manor—"

"Good Lord, no. I like it here. I've got a good job; I'm doing post-grad work at night, and in a few years I'll be in line for a position as dean or headmistress at a top school. No lady-of-the-manor stuff for me."

"That is just as well, because the option is not open to you," Mr. Fawcett said, wondering how he could have mistaken this brusque, unsentimental young female for a creature of romance. "There is no capital remaining with which to maintain the house. I take it, then, that you wish me to notify my colleague in Truro that he is to put the estate on the market?"

"Yes, please." Carla was silent for a moment. Then she burst out, "I still don't understand this. If there's no money, why did my cousin's lawyer spend what must have been a tidy sum tracing me? Why not just let the place revert to the Crown, or whatever it does?"

"Because those were the instructions of your cousin's will," said Mr. Fawcett patiently. "Actually, Mr. Walter Tregellas was the direct descendant of your great-grandfather's elder brother, which would make him your—"

"Cousin will do," Carla said. "Weren't there any closer heirs?"

"Strangely, there were not. The will was most specific: the lawyer was directed to trace the nearest surviving blood relative who still bore the family name. Even with that qualification one would expect nearer heirs to exist, but it seems that the family has completely died out in England. Walter himself died without issue, and he was the only son of his father. His uncle's children—"

"Wait a minute. You mean, if I had been married I wouldn't have inherited?"

"Presumably not," Mr. Fawcett said thoughtfully. "It really was a most impractical will, now that I think about it. And I fear that it means more trouble than gain for you. The chances of an advantageous sale seem remote. I am told that the estate is run down and isolated, the house too large to appeal to the average purchaser. Yet you really have no other option—"

"Yes, I see that. The house will have to be sold—if it can be sold. The sooner, the better."

"Very well. I will need your signature on these documents." He opened the file folder that lay on the desk and began sorting through the papers in it. He selected one and handed it to Carla.

"You may be interested in seeing what the place looks like."

The document was a photograph. Carla took it, inwardly amused, for she was not unaware of the old lawyer's reaction to her pragmatic comments. He looked like the original Proper Bostonian—tall and lean, dark suit and vest, rimless pince-nez—but he must harbor a streak of well-hidden romanticism. Her blunt, matter-of-fact acceptance of the situation had irked him a little. Poor old thing, she thought tolerantly; old people are all sentimentalists. The young are the only realists.

Then she looked at the photograph, and her smug platitudes shattered. A month later she was on her way to England.

III

Now, in the stormy sunset of a summer evening, she sat looking at the original of the photograph. She had had second thoughts about her decision, not once but a dozen times during the intervening weeks, but something had driven her on. It was not such an illogical decision, really; even before the interview she had been thinking of taking the summer off to travel. She had worked hard for four years after leaving college, and since she was paid on a twelve-month schedule, there was enough money for a cheap tour. As Mr. Fawcett had pointed out, when she expressed her interest, there was no hurry about putting the house on the market. She may as well have a look at it before it went out of the family forever. At least she could count on free board and lodging while she was in England, since Walter Tregellas's will had specified that the servants were to be kept on, and their wages paid, until the house was sold—or the money ran out.

Yes, the decision had been reasonable, and it had pleased Mr. Fawcett. The old romantic, Carla thought, with affectionate contempt; he knows I can't keep the house, but he wants me to snuffle and moan about it. She had no intention of moaning, or regretting what must be; but as she studied the tall towers and ivied walls, she felt, intensified, the same strange pang that had struck her when her eyes first fell on the photograph.

She had stopped the car outside the stone wall that formed a boundary between the estate and a leafy country lane. There were trees around the house; on the high western cliff, with winter winds blowing clear across the Atlantic, such shelter was imperative. But the front of the house was open; she could see it clearly down the length of what had once been a well-tended drive.

The main building material was gray stone, perhaps the same granite of which the cliffs were formed. The house faced east, its back to the threatening west, but it did not give the impression of cowering away from storm and gale. Solid and sullen, it endured, having outlasted centuries of the worst the Cornish weather could hurl against it. The setting sun gave the walls an illusory wash of pale gold; windows and doors were dark squares against its glow. Although the photograph had been in black and white, it had given a good impression of the original. What astonished Carla was its size. Originally it had been a Tudor manor house, but over the centuries it had thrust out wings into the trees that surrounded it on three sides. It stood on a slope, so that from where Carla was parked there seemed to be nothing behind it but a vast gulf of empty sky. The sullen heat of the day had presaged rain, and the storm was forming now; clouds streaked with violent sunset colors formed a backdrop of savage beauty for the massive walls.

A bank of cloud engulfed the sun, and it was as if a spotlight had been switched off. The landscape went gray. The house was like a prison now, all light lost from the black walls and irregular chimneyed roofline. As Carla watched, a single light appeared in one of the upper windows—a dim, gray-yellow light that blinked once or twice and then went out.

A huge drop of rain spattered on the windshield. Carla shivered. The breeze was suddenly cool; but that was not the only reason why she felt chilled. She started the engine and turned the car into the narrow drive.

By the time she reached the house, the rain had become heavy. There was no porch before the entrance, but the door was deep-set, in walls of great thickness, so that it provided some slight shelter. She was soaked by the time she reached it, however, having delayed to extract her suitcases from the car.

The portal was large and imposing—a carved barricade big enough to admit a grand piano—and was adorned with a curious brass knocker, so tarnished that it was only slightly lighter than the aged panels. Carla studied this device with interest. It shone greasily in the dimming light, as if it had been dampened by oily water. It was evidently meant to represent some kind of sea creature; she could make out the curve of a long forked tail and a curiously misshapen head. A gust of wind blew

II

rain against her back, and she decided to postpone antiquarian research till a more favorable time. Seizing the knocker firmly, she raised it and let it fall.

The sound seemed to die, as if the wood had absorbed it. She pounded again, and again. There was no sign of life, human or otherwise, and no sound except for the whine of the wind and a far-off susurration, which must be that of waves breaking on the rocks beyond the house. She was just about to get back into the car and see whether the back of the house was more hospitably inclined, when the door opened.

The grounds might appear neglected, but at least the hinges had been oiled; the heavy door made no noise as it moved. It opened onto a surprisingly pleasant vista of lighted hallway, carpeted and paneled, with a lovely Tudor staircase in its center. Framed in the open doorway, dwarfed by its dimensions, was a little old lady. Her smiling, rosy face and masses of snowy hair, her delicately veined hand and black dress made the noun "lady" inevitable. The adjective was equally imperative; if Carla was any judge, the woman was nearer eighty than seventy.

The lawyer had told her that Walter's housekeeper, Mrs. Pendennis, was in charge of the establishment, but Carla would have known her occupation without this. She looked exactly like a housekeeper in a novel—not the grim, malevolent type of housekeeper, but the sweet, amiable sort, like Mrs. Fairfax in *Jane Eyre.*

It was nice to be greeted with a smile, good to know her arrival had been expected. An answering smile was forming on Carla's lips when the curved mouth fell open, and the sweet little old lady's eyes widened till the whites showed all around the pale-blue pupils.

"Heaven save us," she gasped, extending trembling hands as if to ward off some terrible apparition. "It's Lady Caroline—come back from the dead!"

IV

Carla's immediate reaction was one of pure annoyance. She was wet and tired, and the warmly lit hall looked charming—the sort of place that would lead to an equally charming drawing room, where silver tea-things would be set out on a polished mahogany table. Picking up her suitcases, she slipped neatly past the old lady, who had retreated several steps, and closed the door.

"Now stop that," she said sharply, in the tone that had proved useful with hysterical students. "I've come from the States; and although some people consider it next door to hell, it is definitely part of this earth. You knew I was coming, surely. You are Mrs. Pendennis, aren't you?"

The housekeeper nodded, in a mesmerized fashion.

"And you know who I am," Carla went on, reluctant to mention the name that was so similar to the one the housekeeper had pronounced. "I've driven all the way down from London today, and I'm rather tired. Will you show me to my room, please?"

"London," Mrs. Pendennis repeated. Her eyes moved from Carla's dripping hair to her sandaled feet. She seemed to gain reassurance from what she saw. "Yes . . . yes, of course, you must be tired. There is tea ready in the drawing room; would you like a cup before you go up to your room, or shall I have the maid take it to you?"

"No, that's not necessary. Thank you. I'll join you in the drawing room."

Mrs. Pendennis nodded. Folding her hands in front of her, she turned and led the way toward a doorway at the left.

The drawing room had once been lovely. It was still a beautiful shell, with gracious proportions and the remains of handsome oak paneling. But the rug that covered only half the long floor was a shabby wreck, and the furniture was cheap modern stuff. Light-colored squares on the walls showed where pictures had once hung. Incongruous in the decay were a few remaining antiques —a rosewood desk under the long windows that faced east, and a silver tea set on a low table. Carla eyed this last item, and the steam rising from the hot-water jug, with some trepidation. How had Mrs. Pendennis known the time of her arrival so accurately? She would not have been particularly suprised to hear the housekeeper refer casually to her crystal ball. She was relieved when Mrs. Pendennis remarked innocently,

"Mary saw your automobile from an upstairs window. She spends most of her time staring out of the window, I suspect, although I can never catch her doing it. These modern young women make wretched servants, don't they?"

"So I am told," Carla said. "But I'm glad she was watching this time; I'll be grateful for something warm. I had no idea the weather could change so abruptly. The wind was absolutely chilly just now, and I've been sweltering during most of the drive."

"The sea breeze is always cool," Mrs. Pendennis said.

"But we are due for a storm, I fear. I hope it won't be a severe one. I would be sorry if your first impression of Cornwall should be frightening."

"I'm not afraid of storms." Carla sat down in one of the shabby chairs and gestured toward another. She knew, from the way Mrs. Pendennis was hovering, that a woman of her generation would remain standing until the "lady of the house" had seated herself. "Please, won't you join me?"

Mrs. Pendennis beamed. She had the sort of face that might have appeared on a lace-edged Mother's Day card —soft and crumpled, sweet and rosy. But Carla noticed that she was reluctant to look her directly in the face.

"Thank you, my dear. Shall I pour, this first time? I'm sure you must feel a little strange, and you must have many questions about the family."

Her dainty wrinkled hands moved neatly over the cups and plates. Carla accepted a bread-and-butter sandwich and a steaming cup, refused lemon and milk. She was about to speak when the door at the far end of the room opened and a girl trotted in, carrying a tray. She was young and overweight, her robust charms amply exposed by a tight-fitting skirt and knit top. Her face was round and red, and her small black eyes fastened on Carla with greedy curiosity.

"Excuse me, ma'am," she said breathlessly. "But I forgot the scones and cream; and I thought the young lady might like to try them, being hungry, as you might say, after coming such a long way."

Carla returned the frank grin directed at her. She knew that curiosity rather than consideration had prompted the girl's gesture, and she was in complete sympathy.

"Thank you," she said. "You must be—"

"Mary. I hope you enjoy your tea, miss. We had the kettle on the boil since three, and as soon as I saw your car, I said to Mrs. Pendennis, I said—"

"That will do, Mary," Mrs. Pendennis interrupted. "Thank you."

As soon as the door had closed behind the maid, Mrs. Pendennis shook her silvery head.

"It is impossible to train these girls properly!"

"Naturally she was curious about me," Carla said. "And I appreciate the food. I must admit I'm starved. Is this the famous clotted cream I've heard about?"

"Yes. Mary is addicted to it, as you can see from her figure."

The famous clotted cream didn't look particularly delicious. It resembled pale whipped butter, with little lumps in it. Carla piled it onto a scone, topped the heap off with a teaspoonful of strawberry jam, and took an experimental bite.

"I sympathize with Mary," she said, and finished the scone with more appetite than elegance.

Mrs. Pendennis had followed her example. She patted her thin lips delicately with a tiny napkin; her blue eyes twinkled.

"I must admit to a certain partiality for it myself," she said.

After that display of vulgarity the mood relaxed, and Carla began to enjoy herself. Mrs. Pendennis appeared to have forgotten her initial qualms, whatever their cause; she chatted cheerfully about Cornish food, Cornish habits, and Cornish weather. Her comments about the latter phenomenon were apologetic, and indeed Carla felt she was getting an admirable display; the clouded sky was almost as dark as night, and in spite of the thickness of the old walls she was uneasily conscious of the wind. Rain splashed against the windows as if it had been flung from a pail by a muscular arm. The lights dimmed and flickered and finally went out altogether. Mrs. Pendennis clucked disgustedly.

"I was afraid that might happen. It sometimes does when we have a high wind. Sit still, my dear, and Mary will bring candles in a moment."

Carla had no intention of moving. She could hardly see the teacup she was holding. After a few moments the door opened and Mary appeared, shielding a candle that cast insane shadows over her face.

"They've gone out," she announced unnecessarily. "The electric cooker has gone too, ma'am, and Mrs. Polreath says as how she cannot prepare a decent meal on that old black horror, and so she will be going now, ma'am, before the storm worsens."

"Nonsense," Mrs. Pendennis said sharply. "Mrs. Polreath agreed to stay until eight, and stay she must. I shall speak to her."

"There's no need for her to cook a big dinner," Carla exclaimed. "I'm too tired and too full of scones to do it justice. But the storm is so bad. . . . Shouldn't Mrs. Polreath—and you, too, Mary—stay the night?"

Mary let out a gasp.

"Stay the night? Oh, no, miss, I wouldn't spend the night in this house for anything you could offer me!"

"Let us have no more of that," Mrs. Pendennis ordered angrily. She stood thinking for a moment, and then said in a vexed voice, "I suppose we shall have to make do with a cold supper, then. Perhaps, Miss Tregellas, you would like to have it in your room? Mary shall bring you a tray before she leaves. Then you can rest, and go to bed early, if you like."

"With the lights out, and no telly, there's not much else to do," Mary said cheerfully, ignoring the quelling glance the housekeeper gave her.

"That will suit me fine," Carla said. "But I can get my own tray, if Mary wants to leave now."

She had forgotten her place. She was reminded of it by a glance of freezing disapproval from Mrs. Pendennis and an amused giggle from Mary, so she did not pursue the matter, but followed the housekeeper's diminutive, stately figure out into the hall and up the stairs. Carla carried her own candle; the light produced by this, and by the housekeeper's, was barely sufficient to let her see her way. She caught tantalizing glimpses of dim old portraits and bits of fine carving as she climbed the stairs, but she was too busy concentrating on her footing to see very much. The uncarpeted stairs were so worn in the center that each step had a perceptible dip. Carla felt a thrill run through her at this mute evidence of age. In the shadowy light it was not difficult to imagine that she had gone back several centuries in time; the ravages of age and poverty were concealed by darkness, and the basic atmosphere of the house was revealed—the smell of centuries of dust and polish and drying wood, the creak of boards underfoot and the muted howl of the wind outside, the rattle of window frames and shutters. . . .

Suddenly Mrs. Pendennis stopped, with a stifled exclamation, and Carla jumped, as something flung itself down the stairs and ran past her. She had had no warning, for the creature had not made the slightest sound; but she felt it brush her leg as it went.

"Good heavens," she gasped, modifying the expletive

out of deference to Mrs. Pendennis. "What was that?"

"It was the cat," said Mrs. Pendennis, through tight lips. Carla was seized with a sudden ungovernable impulse to laugh.

"I'm sorry," she gurgled, as the housekeeper stared at her in well-bred surprise. "I was reminded of Gilbert and Sullivan. *Pinafore*—do you know it? 'Goodness me, why, what was that? Silent be—it was the cat. . . .' "

"I am familiar with the reference," said Mrs. Pendennis, looking like Queen Victoria when some unfortunate courtier tried to amuse her. "I am happy to know that their fine operas are still known in the States. Unfortunately, the wretched creature is more of a nuisance than a source of pleasure to me. It is the kitchen cat. It is not allowed to go upstairs."

"I have found," said Carla, with equal gravity, "that it is difficult to convince a cat that he is a second-class citizen. Why do you keep a cat, Mrs. Pendennis, if you dislike them?"

"I don't dislike a decent, well-behaved cat," said the housekeeper. "But this creature. . . . He is, however, an excellent mouser. I hope, Miss Tregellas, that you are not disturbed at the idea of having mice in the house? A place of this size and this age. . . ."

"I'm not crazy about mice, but they don't bother me."

"Excellent. Shall we proceed?"

When the housekeeper had turned and resumed her dignified progress, Carla could let the corners of her mouth relax. She was grateful for the moment of mild comedy, for the atmosphere of the house was far from cheerful, particularly on a stormy night. The upper hallway stretched out like a long dark tunnel, with closed doors and an occasional gloomy picture to break the monotony. Mrs. Pendennis marched the full length of it and turned into a side passage. Her heels echoed hollowly on the bare floor. Finally she stopped before a door and threw it open. A draft of cold air came out, setting Carla's candle flickering wildly. Mrs. Pendennis, wiser in the ways of the old house, had shielded hers with her hand, and now she moved into the room, preceding Carla.

"I have taken the liberty of giving you the Green Room, Miss Tregellas. It is not the master bedchamber, but I thought you might prefer to be in this wing, near my own room, rather than be isolated in the front of the house—especially now that the electricity has failed!"

"Definitely," Carla said heartily. "It—it's a very nice room, Mrs. Pendennis."

That was what she said. What she thought was: Shades of Charlotte Brontë!

There were no bits of homey modern shabbiness here. The room, a drafty, high-ceilinged chamber with dark-paneled walls, was furnished with heavy old antiques, including a four-poster bed hung with dark-red curtains. Velvet draperies had been drawn over windows on the west wall; thick as they were, they moved unquietly in the draft. Another damp breeze came from the fireplace, which had a beautifully carved stone surround. The carpet was threadbare, but it had once been a fine Bokhara.

Carla realized that Mrs. Pendennis must have culled the best of the remaining furniture from the other rooms of the house to adorn this one. Most of the valuable pieces—furniture, paintings, and the like—had been sold; and Carla had a hunch that the household was being maintained on the things that remained. The silver tea set might have poured for a Tregellas for the last time. It was worth several thousand dollars, if she was any judge—enough to pay the wages of the staff for a good long time.

The Green Room was certainly impressive, in a grim, old-fashioned way, for the poor light masked its deficiencies. Carla found it a little pathetic, too. The housekeeper had tried so valiantly to conjure up a shade of the prosperous past. . . .

Mrs. Pendennis lit several other candles. From their presence, Carla deduced that the failure of the electricity was not uncommon. The room was adequately lighted now, and the housekeeper inspected it critically.

"My own room is the last on this corridor," she explained, running a finger over the edge of a table, and nodding with satisfaction. "The bathroom is across the hall. I hope you will find everything you need. For once, Mary seems to have done a reasonably satisfactory job of cleaning. If you should require anything else—"

"I'm sure everything will be fine," Carla said.

Then she realized that the housekeeper's pause had not been one of courteous anticipation.

Candle held high, Mrs. Pendennis was staring fixedly at the wall above the table. Her eyes glittered eerily in the reflected light. Carla followed her gaze. There was a picture on the wall. It was so darkened by time and shadows that from where she stood Carla could not make out its details. She could hardly believe that it was responsible for the housekeeper's horrified shock; surely Mrs. Pendennis must have supervised the placement of every object in the room.

The housekeeper began to back away, muttering to herself.

"How? I told Mary to put the hunting print there. How did it—"

She stumbled over a bare spot in the carpet, and Carla jumped to catch her arm as the candle swayed and dripped. Mrs. Pendennis transferred her ghastly stare to Carla, and let out a little scream.

"What's the matter?" Carla asked.

"Nothing. Nothing at all. Mary must have misunderstood my orders. It is of no consequence. Sleep well. That is, Mary will bring your supper. . . . I trust everything will be satisfactory."

She wrenched her arm from Carla's grasp and left the room as fast as her elderly legs would take her. The door closed with a slam.

Carla went at once to have a closer look at the picture, but she could see nothing that would account for the old lady's terror. The picture was a portrait, and a very bad one. No wonder it had not been considered valuable enough to sell. It showed the head and shoulders of a woman. The shape of the lace framing her throat, and the coiffure, suggested a date somewhere in the eighteenth century.

Carla turned away with a shrug. Her most immediate requirement was the bathroom across the hall.

It was surprisingly modern and well appointed. Or perhaps not so surprising; bathroom fixtures could not easily be ripped out and sold. But when Carla started to run water into the tub, it ran cold and remained cold. Either the system was controlled by some complex mechanism she did not understand, or the water was heated by electricity. So she abandoned the idea of a bath

—no Spartan, she—and sponged herself off quickly before slipping into a nightgown and her warmest robe.

When she returned to her room, Mary was there with a tray. She started when Carla opened the door.

"I wondered where you'd gone," she said, depositing the tray on a table. "Will there be anything else, miss? If not, I'd like to be on my way."

"This looks fine," Carla said, with an admiring glance at the contents of the tray. The unknown Mrs. Polreath had managed to heat water for tea. Another covered container suggested soup. If this was the cook's version of a slap-dash cold meal, Carla was curious to see what her best might be. "You go on, Mary. I hope you don't have far to go. Just listen to that wind!"

Mary gave her a rather sickly smile.

"Yes, miss, it's fierce. My old granddad used to say, when the wind blows, a man needs two other men to hold his hair on his head."

"Really, I think you ought to stay here tonight."

"Oh, no, miss!" Mary swallowed convulsively. "I wouldn't—that is, miss, I haven't far to go, just to the village, and my mum and dad would worry if I didn't get back. I'm used to it, miss, we all are hereabouts."

Carla had a strong impression that the girl had started to say something, and had changed her mind. Perhaps Mrs. Pendennis had lectured her about expressing her real feelings; but they were quite apparent. She was afraid to stay in the house at night—so afraid that she was willing to risk a southwesterly gale rather than do so.

Carla was tempted to pump Mary. The girl wasn't overly bright, and a little persuasion would probably elicit some nice gruesome tales of ghosties and ghoulies.

But she hadn't the heart to delay Mary any longer—and besides, she wasn't too anxious to dwell on horrors, not with the prospect of sleeping in that grim old bed before her.

"Hurry, then, if you must go," she said. "And thank you, Mary. Be careful."

"Yes, miss, I will. Thank you, miss. Good night."

Then she, like Mrs. Pendennis, backed out of the room. She did not look at the portrait; Carla had the impression that she was watching it out of the corner of her eye, as a man will watch a dangerous animal, alert for its slightest threatening movement.

 TWO

WHEN Carla awoke the next morning, it took her several minutes to realize where she was. The room seemed very dark. Surely it couldn't be that early in the morning. . . . Then she realized that the bed curtains were drawn. Yes, she had closed them last night, in a slightly more sophisticated version of the cowardly old custom of burying one's head under the covers.

She flung them back and leaped out of the bed—and fell sprawling, having forgotten that this bed was a foot or two higher off the floor than the ones she was accustomed to. Picking herself up, she hobbled to the window.

The heavy draperies were still closed. They were thick enough to darken the room quite effectively, but streaks of light penetrating through and around them were hopeful harbingers of a fine day. Carla pushed them back and blinked in a flood of dazzling sunlight. The windows were not really windows, but French doors. She opened

25

them wide and stepped out onto a small stone-railed balcony.

Behind the house, in the east, the sun was rising. The western sky reflected its glory in shining pastels, rosy pink and pale azure, puffy clouds edged with gold. Sky blended with sea in a shimmer of light. The horizon was unbounded.

An enclosed area of perhaps three acres stretched out from the base of the house to the precipice, but from her lofty perch Carla felt as if she were surrounded by ozone, or something equally healthy and inspiring. The light was so clear she could see each leaf on the trees below. The air was nippy. Still she lingered, clutching bare arms with her hands in an effort to warm them, reluctant to leave that spectacular view. Mingled with aesthetic appreciation was a new and reprehensible sense of possessiveness. It was all hers—only for the moment, soon to be lost—but while it lasted, hers. The house, the grounds, the vista of sea and sky.

She was roused from her reverie by a knock at the door. Shivering, she trotted back into the bedroom in time to greet Mary as the maid entered with a tea tray.

"Good morning," she began, and then shook her head disapprovingly as she saw Carla's scanty nightgown. "You'll catch your death in that, love. Hop into bed and I'll close the window."

"No, please don't." Carla had followed her advice; wriggling chilled toes under the blanket, she accepted the tray Mary put on her lap. She was tempted to warm her hands over the steam rising from the spout of the teapot; but she could not bear to shut out the sunlight and the chill, winy air.

"I'll be warm enough now," she went on. "The fresh air feels good. And the tea looks marvelous. How did you know I was awake?"

Then she remembered her undignified exit from the bed. Catching Mary's twinkling eye, she began to laugh. "Did it make that much noise?" she asked.

"Sounded as if the ceiling was coming down," Mary answered, grinning. "I told Mrs. P. that damned old bed would break your leg, but there's no arguing with her when she gets a notion, bless her heart. She wanted to do you honor."

"I know. The room looks fine, Mary. I think you deserve much of the credit for that."

"It's my job. To be honest, I can't abide this nasty dark old furniture. Give me a nice bit of chrome and vinyl, something cheerful. But it's clean, miss; I'll vouch for that. Well, if there's nothing else—breakfast in half an hour?"

She left, with a nod and a wink. Propped up against her pillows, Carla sipped scalding tea. The fresh air smelled like heaven, the sunlight poured into the room, the hot liquid warmed her clear down to her toes. From somewhere below—could she possibly smell bacon, all this way from the kitchen? Her stomach rumbled hopefully, and she succumbed to an attack of sheer euphoria. To think she had intended to let this place go, unseen and unvisited!

Then a sheepish, self-conscious smile curved her lips as she recognized one of the reasons for her feeling of well-being. Luxury was awfully seductive. In her youth she had been a fiery radical, waving placards and demanding social justice. It was still the right way, of course. . . . But now she began to understand why the lords and ladies of the manor fought so hard to retain their unjust privileges.

In daylight the room was so unlike the gloomy chamber of the previous night she could almost believe she had been transported, in her sleep, to another place. True, the sun was merciless in exposing the worn spots on the carpet and draperies, but the shabbiness was so genteel, it almost looked good.

Carla shook her head wonderingly. What a coward she had been the night before! It was a facet of her character of which she had hitherto been ignorant, and she found her fear hard to comprehend now. Before her visit to Mr. Fawcett, she would have described herself as unimaginative to the point of dullness, without the slightest taint of superstition. Her friends' foibles—the lucky pieces, the astrological columns, the avoidance of black cats, ladders, and broken mirrors—had aroused in her only amused disgust. She didn't even enjoy a good ghost story.

And now she seemed to have landed in the middle of one. Despite her lack of familiarity with the genre, she had no doubt as to the general outlines of the plot. It must center around an earlier Caroline Tregellas, now deceased—very much deceased, if the lady in the portrait represented that Caroline, for her costume suggested the late seventeen hundreds. Carla stared at the portrait, now clearly illumined by the bright sunlight. Mrs. Pendennis had better eyesight than she did, or a better imagination, if she saw any resemblance between the blurred features and those of her new employer. The painted woman had dark hair and eyes, but there the coincidence stopped. It was impossible to make anything particular out of the rest of the face.

Some people might have found it surprising that the family ghost story should have been accepted by such disparate personalities as the refined elderly housekeeper and the cheerful, slightly vulgar maid. However, Carla knew that superstition is not a weakness of the uneducated. A resident family ghost gave an old mansion prestige; the residents might be frightened of it, but they were also secretly proud of the distinction. Then she thought, with a sharp mental shock: Good Lord, it's my ghost too!

The idea, and the surge of incongruous fascination it produced, made her smile. Last night she had barely taken time to wolf down her supper before climbing into bed and pulling the bed-curtains shut against the shifting shadows of the big, drafty room. The subtle, continuous motion of the draperies would have furnished subject matter for a few nightmares all by themselves, and the howling of the west wind had sounded like an army of lost souls wailing for the unattainable joys of Paradise. But in the sunny morning it was impossible to take such ideas seriously. In fact, Carla found that she was looking forward to getting the story out of Mrs. Pendennis. A resident ghost of one's own. . . . With that added attraction, maybe she could sell the house to a rich fellow American.

Electrical service had been restored. There was hot water in the bathroom. Carla hurried through her ablutions, dressed, and went downstairs. The smell of bacon led her to the kitchen.

She fell in love with the room at first sight. Geraniums bloomed along the wide windowsill, and the flagged floor had been scrubbed to perfection. From the beamed ceiling hung bundles of herbs and vegetables, and a huge black country ham. An electric stove and refrigerator were the only touches of modernity. The old cookstove still occupied a place in one corner, and although it added to the charm of the room, Carla didn't blame Mrs. Polreath for refusing to cook on it.

The plump young woman who was standing at the sink was obviously the cook. Carla wondered if all the residents of Cornwall suited their stereotypes as well as the ones she had met thus far. Mrs. Pendennis might have stepped out of *Jane Eyre*, and the cook was round and pink-faced, a living testimonial to her art.

"Good land, miss, you gave me such a start," she exclaimed, pressing her hand against her ample bosom.

Carla apologized, admired the kitchen, and introduced herself—an unnecessary but amiable formality, which seemed to please the cook. She wiped her hands on her apron before accepting the hand Carla extended. Carla would have been delighted to eat breakfast at the huge oak table, so solid and massive that it looked as if it had grown up out of the floor, but the cook directed her to the breakfast room. She decided not to make an issue of it, although the situation struck her as more than a little absurd. Two servants—three, if you counted Mrs. Pendennis—to wait on one healthy young female in a decaying house whose furniture was being pawned to pay their wages! Ah, well, she thought, when in Rome. . . . It would only be for a few weeks.

Mrs. Pendennis was finishing her breakfast. They chatted for a while, commenting on the weather—always a useful topic and, in Cornwall, a pertinent subject—while Mary brought bacon and eggs and fresh toast and coffee. But Carla was conscious of the housekeeper's sidelong glances, and when Mary had left, she decided to have the matter out.

"Who was Lady Caroline?" she asked abruptly.

Mrs. Pendennis sighed. "Oh, dear. Really, I am ashamed. I ought not to have blurted it out so crudely, when you had barely arrived. Yet I don't know; perhaps you ought to be warned. . . . And the resemblance is really quite astonishing."

"If the resemblance you are speaking of is to the portrait in my room, I can't see it," Carla remarked coolly.

"Of course not," Mrs. Pendennis replied, with equal sangfroid. "One never has an accurate mental picture of one's own features, my dear. Reflections are misleading; they reverse everything, don't they?"

Carla was a trifle disconcerted. Mrs. Pendennis was a funny mixture of superstition and shrewd common sense. All the same, she was not prepared to admit that the resemblance existed anywhere but in the old lady's fertile imagination.

"Well, suppose you tell me the story," she said. "Why did you say I ought to be warned?"

She had anticipated a good, gruesome ghost story, and had expected to find it amusing, in the cheerful light of day. But Mrs. Pendennis was an excellent raconteur, and the fact that she obviously believed every syllable of the demented tale she proceeded to relate gave it a force that wiped the tolerant smile off Carla's face and caused her to neglect the remainder of an excellent breakfast.

As she had deduced, the Lady Caroline of the portrait was an eighteenth-century maiden, the only daughter of the Squire Tregellas then in residence.

"The loveliest maiden in the Duchy," said Mrs. Pendennis dreamily. "Hair like black silk, skin as fair as a white rose petal, lips like flowers. When she walked through the garden it was like watching a bird in flight. Every young nobleman in the south of England sought her hand, and she was to marry the richest and handsomest of them all. Lord William was his name; he was tall and gallant, with a laugh ever on his lips and a cap of shining golden hair like a king's crown. He was here that night, the eve of their wedding. They sat on the sofa in the parlor, their hands entwined, whispering together, while her mother drowsed by the fire; when suddenly she pulled her hands away from his grasp, and rose. Her eyes were fixed and glassy, like those of a sleepwalker; when he spoke to her she did not answer, but glided from the room. He saw her begin to mount the stairs, so he did not follow. It was the last time he or any other man saw Caroline Tregellas—alive or dead. She vanished from the face of the earth that night."

She took a sip of coffee and looked challengingly at Carla.

"Well!" said Carla. "Well, that is really quite a. . . . I suppose the family looked all over for her? Yes, of course. So she wasn't in the house. She must have gone out. Maybe she felt the need of fresh air, and went for a walk. If she walked along the cliffs in the twilight—she fell, that's what happened. I've heard about the currents off this coast; her body might have been swept out to sea and never found."

"That was the story that was put about," said Mrs. Pendennis, now refreshed and ready to continue. "But of course all the neighborhood knew it was not true."

"Oh, they did, did they? How did they know?"

"The story was an old one." Mrs. Pendennis's voice

became soft and compelling. Her eyes, fixed on the ceiling, had the same glassy stare she had attributed to her lost heroine. "But it had been forgotten. They were not scholars, the Cornish gentry of the eighteenth century. They lived for hunting and drinking; they did not read the crabbed old histories of their houses. And it had been two hundred years. . . . The knowledge might not have saved her. But it would have saved Lord William. He thought as you did, of course. When she failed to return, and the aroused household could discover no trace of her within, he insisted that the grounds be searched, and went out himself to help. A gale was rising, and the seas were high; but the searchers were local men, who knew every inch of the terrain. They searched for hours, until clouds obscured the moon and they could no longer see. They did not find Lady Caroline; but they found her lover, by the western gate. His body was cold and stiff. His eyes—"

"Were fixed in a stare of horror," Carla interrupted rudely. "Really, Mrs. Pendennis—"

"No, his eyes were not open," the housekeeper corrected. "They were covered by a long strand of seaweed, like a blindfold. The dripping weed wound round his mutilated body, which was broken as if by the grasp of a great beast. He had come too soon, you see. If he had been a moment later, they would have been gone, down into the sea from which *he* came to fetch her. But Lord William was there in time, and he tried to stop them.

"The searchers carried him back to the house and, to their astonishment, found he was not dead. It would have been better if he had died. His beautiful golden hair had turned snow-white. The scars on his body healed, but those on his mind did not. He died many years later in the madhouse at Bodmin. He never spoke a sensible word; but he raved often, in his spells, of the dark slimy thing that had crushed him in its boneless arms while his sweetheart stood watching with wide, unwinking eyes."

She refreshed herself with another sip of coffee.

This time Carla had no comment. She really couldn't think of anything to say. When the housekeeper resumed, her voice was no longer an eerie whisper, but the dry, brisk voice of a researcher recounting facts.

"The story was hushed up, but of course, my dear, one cannot keep people from talking. It was Caroline's brother, Squire Thomas, who discovered the truth of the legend. He had been a small child when his sister disappeared, but he had heard the servants whispering, and had seen his mother fade into the decline that eventually ended her life. He found the manuscript that explained his sister's fate. Afterwards he became a recluse, hoping, by mortifying the flesh, to exorcise the curse that afflicted his house. Whether he succeeded or not. . . .

"He learned that his sister was not the first Tregellas maiden to fall into the clutches of the sea demon. Every two hundred years the sacrifice was made, all the way back to the Dark Ages after the decline of Roman Britain. The first victim of the monster was a Roman princess, the ancestress of the family, whose father had a villa on this very spot. You will find traces of Roman mosaic in the garden, my dear; it bears images of sea creatures, dolphins, fish, octopi, and the like. The ancient manuscript was, unfortunately, incomplete, so one does not know for certain what brought the curse upon the house. There are several possibilities. The Roman lady might have been a priestess of some sea god, such as Dagon or Poseidon, who developed a monstrous passion for her master. Or perhaps—you have heard the legend of Lyonesse? No? It was a lovely country west of Land's End, filled with homes and churches and pastures; but it sank down into the sea on the day of the last battle, when Arthur received his death wound at the fight of Camlann. The princess had a lover in Lyonesse, they say, who drowned when his city sank fathoms deep. By her sorceries she called him from his watery bed, and he came. He is immortal; and his mortal brides must die. So, every two hundred years. . . ."

She ended with a quaint little shrug, her wide blue eyes fixed innocently on Carla's face; and the latter came out of the paralysis of incredulous fascination to which she had succumbed. The blend of brisk narrative and Hitchcock horror in Mrs. Pendennis's story was like nothing she had ever encountered, on or off the silver screen.

"Amazing," she said. "I must say, Mrs. Pendennis, I'm proud to be a member of a family with a curse like that. Why, it puts banshees, and White Ladies, to shame. I've never heard such a wild story."

"I will show you the original manuscript and Squire Thomas's commentary," said Mrs. Pendennis calmly. She seemed much relieved in her mind now that she had told the tale.

"I'd like to see it. Especially since—if I follow the implications—I am next in line to be gobbled up by the demon. Every two hundred years, you say? Our merman isn't very passionate, is he? But of course he's a cold-blooded mammal. . . . And me the living likeness of poor Lady Caroline!"

"You may laugh about it if you like," said Mrs. Pendennis. "But I must insist, my dear, that you leave the house before Midsummer Eve."

"That's the fatal date, is it?"

"I can't blame you for not believing me," Mrs. Pendennis said. She leaned toward Carla, her cheeks flushed, her eyes intent. "But it won't hurt, will it, to indulge an old woman's fancy? Midsummer Eve is several weeks away; you planned to come for a brief holiday only. The house must be sold, you can't intend to remain long—"

"I had meant to stay only a few weeks, yes. But I must speak to my lawyer in Truro before I decide what I'm going to do. If there is enough money for me to hang on for a little longer, I can't see why I shouldn't stay all summer. It's a fascinating old house, and I love what I've seen of the country—"

"You mustn't, you really mustn't," the old lady exclaimed. "I tell you, the sacrifice must be made! It is two hundred years, almost to the day—"

"I assure you, I have no intention of wandering the cliffs on Midsummer Eve," Carla said, with mounting irritation. "No watery monster is going to lure me—"

"You don't understand! It isn't a monster; I should not have given that impression. Haven't you heard of the Silkies, and mermen, who have won the love of mortal women?"

"Not since sixth grade," Carla said. "Mrs. Pendennis—"

"He is beautiful, in his own fashion," the housekeeper went on, unheeding. "Tall and virile and irresistible to those over whom his spell is cast. . . ."

Carla rolled her eyes and managed not to utter any of the sarcastic comments that came to her mind. Mrs. Pendennis was immune to irony. She was pathetic, not vicious.

"Honestly, Mrs. Pendennis, it will be all right. I'm not that easily spellbound. I don't care how gorgeous your merman is, I won't—"

"But you won't be able to help yourself!" Mrs. Pendennis's cultured voice rose to a shriek. "You still don't understand! They are all the same—you, and Lady Caroline, and the others—the same undying soul is alive in all of you, the soul of the Roman princess. She lost her soul, for loving a soulless creature; she is doomed to repeat her crime, and her doom, until the curse is broken. When the time comes, you won't be able to resist. Her mind will come alive in you, and she will take your body down into the sea, in the arms of her demon lover."

 THREE

CARLA got out of the room, and the house, before she yielded to her urge to do something reprehensible—laugh, or swear, or throw her cup at Mrs. Pendennis's venerable white head. She stamped up and down the driveway for a while until common sense conquered impatience, and then she was able to laugh, albeit somewhat sourly.

Nothing could have been more destructive to Mrs. Pendennis's outré legendry than the view before her. The wilderness of the untended grounds had the bucolic charm of a meadow; wild flowers, their bright blues and yellows unfamiliar to her, bloomed luxuriantly under the hedges, and birdsong filled the air with melody. Carla drew in a deep breath of fresh air and began to walk, exploring her domain.

She came almost at once to a wall of crumbling stone. The gate hung by rusted hinges. The area beyond was in an equally disreputable state. Weeds had grown up between the cracks in the paving stones, and the buildings on the far side of the court were disintegrating. The roof of one had completely collapsed. Another structure had obviously been the stable. It now sheltered an ancient Mercedes and her rented Austin.

Carla stared at the car. She had left it in front of the steps the night before, and had forgotten all about it. How had it gotten here? The hood was dry; obviously someone had driven it into the relative shelter of the old stable the night before. Who?

She dismissed this minor mystery with a shrug and proceeded with her exploration. It was a depressing process. What had once been the extensive service area of a large country estate was now a decaying ruin. Hardly a building remained whole, and weeds shrouded everything. Of course a place this size required constant maintenance, and maintenance cost money. Even more than the threadbare condition of the house, this area brought home to her the decay of a once prosperous family.

She passed through a gate on the far side of the stable-yard and stopped short with a start of surprise.

The garden was of considerable size. Her city-bred mind measured it as about the size of a square block. She knew enough, despite her breeding, to recognize the amount of labor required to produce those neat, straight rows of green sprouts, and to realize that this was no pleasure garden. The lettuce was already big enough to harvest; tomato vines were fruited, and the feathery sprouts of carrot were inches high.

She was wearing sneakers. Not until the gate had swung shut behind her, with a squeak of hinges, did the gardener realize she was there. He straightened up from behind the row of vines that had shielded him; and for a moment, silenced by mutual surprise, they gazed at one another.

Carla's sense of humor, momentarily beaten down by Mrs. Pendennis, reasserted itself. It was lucky she wasn't susceptible to horror stories, or she might have been tempted to regard this man, whose lower extremities were still concealed by the plants, as a land-locked merman.

He was bare to the waist; his body, heavily tanned, was streaked with perspiration so that it shone in the sunlight. His thick dark hair was damp too. It grew down on his forehead in a distinct widow's peak, whose double-arched shape was echoed by slanting eyebrows. The eyes, narrowed into faunlike slits, were an unexpected greenish brown, like river water with light slipping through it. Everything about him, from his high cheekbones to his long, lean body, was faintly exotic, and the look with which he regarded her, his head tipped a little to one side, was as wary as that of a startled animal. Carla spoke softly and slowly, as she would have spoken to a strange dog.

"Hi, there. I'm sorry if I startled you. I'm Carla Tregellas. . . ." And then, when he did not respond, but continued to stare, she added, "What a beautiful garden. You've done a splendid job."

The faun straightened and placed muddy fists on his hips.

"Quite the lady of the manor, aren't we? Sorry I haven't a forelock to pull, you must take the gesture for granted."

This offensive speech, pronounced in what was obviously a savage imitation of the local accent, roused Carla's temper.

"Well, what the hell did you expect me to say, with you standing there gaping like an idiot? At least I was taught to be civil to people."

"Aow, aow, don't speak so sharp, miss." The faun threw up his hands and ducked his head in a gesture of burlesqued terror. The movement—economical, controlled, beautifully effective—gave Carla her clue.

"You're an actor," she exclaimed.

"Dancer."

"Yes, of course." Carla nodded. The combination of muscle and grace might have been found in several of the athletic professions; combined with the man's histrionic talents, it could only mean one thing.

"What are you doing in my vegetable garden?" she asked.

Her tormentor grinned and relaxed.

"Weeding."

"I meant—"

"I know." His accent was educated now, with no trace of the twangy Cornish vowels. "I'm—resting, I believe, is the proper term. There isn't a great demand for my talents at the moment."

"Really? That surprises me. I thought good male dancers were hard to find. Of course, you may not be good."

"That is certainly a reasonable hypothesis," was the affable reply. "Another possibility is that I have become critical of my effete and purely ornamental profession, and have decided to turn my talents to something practical. Back to the earth, so to speak."

"I guess vegetables are practical."

"More than you realize." The man wiped perspiration off his upper lip with the back of his hand, leaving a muddy streak. "Not only will we eat this summer, but I hope to peddle a few pounds' worth of produce in Truro."

"How art the mighty fallen," Carla murmured, looking from the neat, thrifty rows of vegetables to the battlemented walls of the house.

"Fallen, hell. This is a distinct step upward." As Carla continued to contemplate the decaying home of her ancestors, the faun continued irritably, "You're a Tregellas, all right; the family face is unmistakable. I had hoped, however, that being an American, you might have risen above the sappy sentimentality that ruined your kin."

"It's not a family weakness, it's endemic to the area," Carla said nastily. "I have just been listening to a dippy old lady telling me the most absurd story I have ever heard. If she weren't so obviously weak in the head, I would think she was trying to frighten me into leaving. Anyhow, who are you to lecture me?"

The faun straightened to his full height. He was taller than she had thought.

"I'm the grandson of that dippy old lady," he said gently. "One of the reasons why I am wasting my genius in the dirt of your garden is to help the dippy old lady keep this worthless ruin going for a few more months, so that you can reap a bit of money out of the disaster. The trait is called loyalty. I don't suppose you've encountered it before." And, as Carla gaped speechlessly, he added, "Don't thank me. I tried to convince her to chuck the whole mess years ago."

"What is your name?" Carla demanded.

"Mike," said the faun sulkily.

"Nonsense. Mike is a ridiculous name for a ballet dancer."

The young man's grim mouth relaxed a little. "I called myself Michel Penkowsky."

"But I've heard of you." Carla forgot the verbal riposte she had been composing. "I read a review, last year—you did *Afternoon of a Faun* when the star was taken ill. They said you were sensational."

For some reason this remark turned Mike's face back into solid granite.

"How ducky," he snarled. "A ballet aficionado, as I live and breathe."

"I don't know much about it, I just know what I— Oh, you're impossible. I'm sorry I insulted your grandmother. But how the hell was I supposed to know about her noble qualities? If you had heard the crazy stuff she was giving me just now—"

"I've heard it." Mike shifted his feet and looked uncomfortable. "The abandoned merman and the family curse? So she has a little quirk. Most people have more than one. Hers is perfectly harmless, she just—"

"Harmless, my eye. She could scare a nervous person into hysterics. Oh, go back to your parsnips. I'm sorry I disturbed you."

"Go around that way," Mike said, as she started forward. "Don't tread on the beets."

Carla obeyed, her shoulders stiff with outrage. She had reached the far end of the garden when he called out again.

"Don't go near the cliff, love. The goblins will get you if you don't watch out." As she glared, he put his hands behind his head, fingers outspread to simulate horns, and contorted his thin face into a hideous grimace.

Once she was out of sight, Carla let her scowl relax. It would never do to admit it to such a cocky young man, but she didn't mind his rudeness. Her own blunt nature found candor much easier to deal with than smooth hypocrisy—or the crazy vapors she had found in Mike's grandmother. She couldn't yell at Mrs. Pendennis, that wouldn't be nice; but Mike was fair game.

The nickname didn't suit him. Michael was better. She would call him that; and if he didn't like it, too bad. He hadn't mentioned his last name. It would be Pendennis, of course, if his father had been the housekeeper's child; but perhaps he was related to the old lady through a daughter. Whatever his name, Carla was willing to bet it wasn't Penkowsky. How strange that he should be the young dancer she had read about. She had been characteristically honest when she told Michael she liked ballet, but was not an expert. She would never have heard of him if he hadn't been outstanding.

His profession made his present occupation even more incongruous. Did dancers take long vacations? Surely they had to practice daily, whether they were employed or not. She could understand why Mrs. Pendennis might want to stay on till the last possible moment in the house. According to the lawyer, the housekeeper had come to Tregellas House as a young widow; it was home to her now, no wonder she hated to leave it. But her grandson was something of a saint if he was willing to give up a promising career, even temporarily, to cater to an old woman's whim. He didn't look like a saint.

Finding herself ankle-deep in a mud puddle, Carla dismissed the Pendennis family from her mind and started to pay more attention to where she was going.

The hot sun was burning off the remains of the night's storm, but there was still considerable moisture under the trees. They were evergreens, the same ones she had noticed the day before, forming a somber backdrop to the house. Stunted and twisted by the sea wind, they provided some protection from the elements—but not much, to judge from the way the gale had battered her windows last night. Fallen pine needles carpeted much of the ground, mulching it against underbrush, but weeds and wild flowers had straggled through in some places.

Passing through the belt of trees, Carla found herself in a sunlit open field that ended, several hundred yards away, in a stone wall. The wall was high; she could see nothing beyond it except blue sky. Pushing through the tall grass, she made her way to the gate. It was a rough wooden structure, relatively new, but in bad repair. The catch was rusted. It had been reinforced by a strand of wire looped over the gatepost. Carla removed this, pushed the gate open, and stopped, transfixed.

There was a path beyond the wall—a narrow track of beaten earth scarcely two feet wide. Beyond the path was a sheer drop, ending in rocks like pointed teeth, where waves creamed into spun-silver spray. The color of the water was a deep blue; obviously the depth at this point was considerable.

Her fingers were cramped. Involuntarily she had grabbed hold of the gatepost and was hanging on for dear life.

It was sheer reflex; she couldn't possibly fall unless she walked deliberately over the edge. But she thought she knew now what had happened to the unfortunate girl who had vanished on Midsummer Eve two hundred years before. No doubt the distance between gate and cliff had been greater then. A coastline like this one was constantly being eaten away by the sea. Even so, it would not have been difficult to miss one's footing on a windy, dusky evening, while walking along the cliff.

And why would a girl leave her lover on their wedding eve, to walk in the twilight alone?

Carla shook her head angrily, as if she could shake the story out of her mind. It had happened centuries ago; no one would ever know the truth of it.

She closed the gate behind her and turned to the left, keeping close to the wall. After a short distance the grass verge widened out into a narrow promontory, and Carla relaxed. The view of the ocean was magnificent. She had never seen such shades of blue, from a clear sparkling translucency like the best aquamarine to a profound and exquisite lapis lazuli. The sides of the cliff were dotted with clumps of vivid emerald green, where a few hardy plants had found a footing. There were even a few trees, strange dwarfish shapes that had a macabre charm.

The path turned abruptly, following the wall. Carla followed it too. She was not altogether reluctant to turn her back on the deceptively smiling water.

Inland, to her left, was civilization, in the form of a narrow dirt road and, a mile or so distant, the clustered houses of a small settlement clinging to cliffs so steep that the chimneys of one cottage were on a level with the doorstep of the one above. The houses were of stone, some of them whitewashed, and at this distance they looked gay and tidy with the shining azure water of a small bay behind them; but they lacked the deliberate charm of tourist villages such as St. Ives and Mousehole.

46

There were no quaint blue doors or window boxes full of flowers.

The civilized world to her left; to her right, not only the untamed savagery of the ocean, but mute evidence of the savagery of primitive man. The rough stones were taller than she—massive, rough-hewn. There were only two of them, leaning inward so that they formed a crude arch, an open pyramid shape. The flowering weeds around their bases did nothing to soften the grim, dark granite.

As she approached, Carla saw that there were other stones lying around. Some were as large as a banquet table and so thick that, even prostrate, their fallen surfaces were as high as her waist. An elusive path, no more than a vague break in the tall grass, led toward the two standing stones and passed under them. Carla did not do so. No doubt the stones had stood for centuries in their present positions, and would stand for hundreds of years more, but they looked unstable, leaning at such an angle.

As she stood admiring the blended blue tapestry of sea and sky framed by the arch of stone, she realized that someone was sitting on one of the fallen monoliths. He sat so still that for a startled moment she fancied she was imagining him; the sunlight shone on a cap of disheveled fair hair, just like Mrs. Pendennis's description of the unhappy lover of Lady Caroline. Even after she had blinked a few times, the figure refused to disappear, so she cleared her throat noisily. The golden head turned.

"Good God," said the apparition, bounding to his feet. Fantasy died a-borning; this was no slim, drooping hero of romance, but a very large young man with a sunburned nose and bushy blond eyebrows. An expression of utter panic came over his face as he squinted at her, and Carla realized that with the sun behind her he probably couldn't see clearly.

"I'm sorry I startled you," she said, wondering how many more times she would have to apologize that morning. "I'm Carla Tregellas."

She went toward him, giving the leaning stones a wide berth, and reflecting on the fact that in this region her name was sufficient identification to most of the strangers she might meet—not a mere label, but a complete genealogy. It gave her a new and rather pleasant feeling of stability and pattern.

The large young man jumped clumsily to the ground and extended his hand. His mouth had opened in a wide grin.

"Of course you are," he said. "I do beg your pardon for gaping. My name is Tremuan—Simon Tremuan. I was deep in my book, and with the sun making a halo around you, you looked like one of the elf people, sprung up out of the ground."

Carla found this pretty flight of fancy hard to reconcile with the round sunburned face and the warm hand that had enveloped hers. She glanced at the book.

"*Cornish Legends,*" she read, and laughed a little ruefully. "I'm afraid I've had my share of them this morning. But if you are interested in the subject, I can give you a good one."

Simon Tremuan grinned more broadly.

"Don't tell me, let me guess. Mrs. Pendennis? My poor girl. I had hoped she wouldn't hit you with that story on your first day here; it really has become an idée fixe with the dear old soul. Oh, now, please don't look so offended. I assure you she doesn't babble to the countryside at

48

large. We're old friends, she and I, and since I am the family doctor, she is inclined to confide in me."

"You're a doctor?" Carla asked, and then made an apologetic gesture. "I didn't mean to sound surprised."

"The village quack," said Simon cheerfully. "No reason why you shouldn't be surprised; I'm not really a very good doctor. I fell into it, as you might say. Took over my father's practice."

"But you're more interested in folklore."

"I'm interested in too many things," was the candid reply. "If you want trivial information on any useless subject, ask me."

Carla laughed. "All right, I will. What are these stones?"

"Lucky you, you've struck one of my hobbies. But won't you take a seat? I am apt to lecture at length."

Carla looked helplessly at the stone the doctor indicated. Before she could speak, he had taken her by the waist and lifted her up onto the flat surface. He swung himself up beside her and looked at her complacently.

"This is the remains of a very fine stone circle," he explained, with a sweeping gesture. "The stones were all standing originally—that being at some time in the eighteenth century B.C. Only the two largest monoliths have remained upright, but not very upright, as you can see."

"You mean this place was like Stonehenge?"

"Well—something like it. Stonehenge seems to have had something to do with sun worship. It may even have been a kind of astronomical observatory, though I'm skeptical about the grandiose claims that have been advanced for it."

"Was it a temple, do you think?"

"Stonehenge, or this circle? The answer is probably

yes to both; though I think archaeologists are rather too prone to claim an object has a religious function when they can't think of any other purpose for it. Of course Stonehenge is much larger and grander than your monument, but Cornwall has more prehistoric remains than any other part of England—standing stones, pierced stones, monoliths, even a prehistoric village or two."

"You do know a lot about the subject," Carla said admiringly.

"Not really. I'm much more intrigued by local legends than by archaeological fact. It's amazing what weird stories our ancestors invented to explain these—to them—mysterious structures. Names such as the Giant's Punchbowl, the Devil's Table, the Pixies' Circle give you some idea of the traditions that have grown up around them. There's a stone circle near Penzance that is called the Nine Maidens. Supposedly the girls did something frivolous, like dancing on the Sabbath, and were turned to stone as a punishment."

"Their God was a terrible person, wasn't he? To think he would punish people for such trivial sins. . . ."

Her companion leaned forward and looked into her averted face. The position looked ludicrous, for he was wildly overbalanced; but his expression was quite serious.

"Does it bother you?"

Carla didn't have to ask what he meant.

"I guess it does," she said, in surprise. "What kind of doctor are you, a psychiatrist? You're digging up feelings I didn't even know I had."

"I thought I detected the symptoms of a sudden attack of ancestral consciousness, that's all. I've often wondered what it would be like to be free of all that—rootless, unbound by the past, as you must have been. Then to find yourself suddenly plunged into a tradition that goes back hundreds of years—to be part of that fixed, unalterable pattern. . . . It wouldn't be surprising if you were more sensitive to suggestions simply because they are so new to you. You haven't been immunized by experience."

"I was thinking along those same lines just a few minutes ago," Carla admitted. "But about the advantages rather than the difficulties. It's rather comforting to feel that you have a place in some larger order of things. . . . I never thought I'd feel this way. I always prided myself on my independence. But since I got here. . . . Do I—I don't really look like her, do I?"

"Lady Caroline?" The answer was slow in coming. "You have the family features, certainly. But, my dear girl, I haven't seen that old portrait for years. I thought Mrs. Pendennis had banished it to the attic."

"She had," Carla said grimly, and went on to tell him about the housekeeper's shock at finding the portrait in her room. Simon listened intently, a frown wrinkling his broad forehead; but when she had finished he said lightly,

"I expect the maid fetched it, to cover a stain on the wall, or something equally harmless. Don't worry about it. After all—even if the resemblance does exist, such genetic coincidences often occur. There's nothing supernatural about it."

"You're right. Thanks for the therapy. I guess I'd better be getting back now. I walked out on Mrs. Pendennis while she was telling her ghost story, and she may be wondering where I've gone."

Simon helped her down, his hands lingering.

51

"Could I possibly persuade you to come and have your elevenses with me? The village isn't far, and we can ring Mrs. Pendennis if you think she will worry about you." Carla hesitated, and he added persuasively, "You really shouldn't explore on your own. I could point out some of the dangerous spots."

"I assure you, I won't take chances. I'm not the adventurous type. But," she added, as his face fell, "I'd love to come."

"Wonderful." He took her arm. "There is one place I must show you. It's just down here."

Carla hung back as he led her toward the end of the promontory.

"I have a poor head for heights," she confessed. "Don't go too near the edge. . . ."

"I wouldn't let you fall. Not that there is much danger; this part of the cliff is comparatively stable. I only wanted to show you your private bathing beach."

He put his arm around her as she continued to look doubtful, and Carla was glad to lean back into its sturdy strength. The faint path she had observed led straight to the tumbled granite of the cliff, and continued vertically downward, winding back and forth between the rocks in miniaturized switchbacks. Far below, enclosed between curving points of rock, was a small bay and a sweep of shining silver sand. The water was a soft jade-green; little waves washed gently onto the sand from the shallows.

"The path is actually quite safe," Simon said. "In daylight, at any rate; I wouldn't risk it after dark if I were you. And if you stay within the bay the water is safe too —no currents, no undertow. Are you a strong swimmer?"

"Not that strong."

"Naturally you mustn't swim alone. That's foolish anywhere. But it's a lovely spot for a bit of private sunbathing. If you are addicted to basking in the altogether, I'll not approach without giving a loud shout."

He grinned down at her, and Carla smiled back.

"It's a tempting thought," she said. "I don't suppose many people come here."

"The place is on your property. I trespass occasionally, and so do a few others, but the villagers prefer the public beach. I won't say you might not find a pair of lovers now and then. . . ."

"They're welcome to it." Carla turned away from the awesome view. "Don't worry, I won't come alone, even to sunbathe. I told you, I am a depressingly practical person."

"You don't look practical."

Standing close, still in the circle of his arm, she realized how very big he was. Her head barely reached his shoulder. One of his hands lifted the hair away from her ear and his finger traced its contours with a touch so delicate she scarcely felt it. After a moment he let her go, and said jokingly, "You have pointed ears. I knew you would. Are you sure you aren't one of the pixies?"

The hand that took hers, to lead her back from the cliff, was warm but impersonal. Carla wondered if she had imagined the intimacy implicit in the subtle, imaginative caress.

"I thought pixies were little men with long beards, wearing red hats," she said.

"No, no, you're thinking of brownies or dwarfs. Some authorities think they are related, but I'm convinced that our local pixies are of a different species altogether. They were here from the beginning—before the Romans, before the Celts or even the Phoenicians. They never were quite human; and millennia of savage oppression turned them into something rather dangerous. Their crude stone weapons had no chance against the bronze and iron spears of the newer races, who hunted them like animals. Living underground, they became squat and dark and gnarled—"

"I thought underground creatures became paler," Carla interrupted. "Like the blind albino fish in subterranean pools."

Her companion threw his head back and roared with laughter.

"Damn it, young woman, how dare you throw the cold water of biological fact on my poetic fancies? Don't you believe in fairy tales?"

"I think you do," Carla said breathlessly. The doctor's long legs made it hard to keep up with him. He heard her gasp, and slowed, as they turned onto the road.

"The main road goes round the other side of the village," he explained. "This is only a cart track. . . . Do I believe? No; but I wish I could."

They had reached the outlying houses of the village before Carla could think of an appropriate reply to this plaintive comment. The path became a cobbled street, plunging downward at a steep angle. At the bottom she saw the gleam of water and a flotilla of small boats drawn up on the shingle. A squat stone tower lifted up over the roofs.

"It's a pretty town," she said.

"There's not much to see: a few shops, the church, an inn—we're not one of the quaint tourist centers, but we get a certain number of trippers, mostly the young ath-

54

letic ones with packs on their backs. Ah—good morning, Mrs. Marion. Fine day, isn't it?"

The woman he addressed had just come out of her house. Carla suspected that the broom she carried was only an excuse, but her curiosity was not rewarded. The doctor did not stop to introduce Carla. He took her arm as the street became even steeper. Finally they reached a house that was slightly larger than its neighbors.

"Here we are," he announced, and sniffed appreciatively as a warm rich smell of baking came from the opening door. "Ah, we're in luck. Mrs. Chynoweth has made rock cakes."

The house was very dark. Carla thought it a pity that there were no large windows, to take advantage of the stunning view toward the bay, but she realized that dwellings exposed to the coastal storms could not afford such luxuries. Her eyes were still adjusting to the change of light when Simon led her through a door on the right of the narrow hall, and raised his voice in a shout.

"Mrs. Chynoweth! I'm back, and I've brought a guest. Fetch out the good china."

Carla took a chair and looked curiously around the room. It had two small windows looking out onto the street; they were covered with machine-made lace curtains. The furniture was old and dark—a heavy sofa upholstered in worn maroon plush, two matching chairs flanking the fireplace, and a table covered with books and magazines. The mantel and the glass-fronted cupboards on either side of it were covered with a miscellaneous assortment of bric-a-brac, framed pictures, and shells. Simon seated her in one of the chairs. The other was occupied by a large malevolent-looking tabby cat.

"That's Tristan," Simon explained, waving at the cat,

which showed no signs of being moved by the introduction. "Very appropriate name. His amatory and pugilistic habits resemble those of his namesake."

"One does think of Tristan as a great lover," Carla said, amused. "But surely he was also a perfect gentle knight—one of the Round Table types."

"You're thinking of the glamorized Tennyson version," Simon replied. "The original knights weren't particularly genteel. Tristan was a Celtic tough guy; his real name was Drustans. He came from these parts, you know. There's a memorial pillar near Castle Dor with a Latin inscription to Tristan, son of Mark."

"Son of Mark? I thought he was his nephew."

"He was, in the standard versions of the story. Actually, it makes a better yarn if he was his son, don't you think? Frightfully Freudian, seducing his father's young bride, and all that sort of thing."

"I don't know about the Freudian part, but it does make sense," Carla admitted. "Those tough medieval warriors must have worn out a lot of wives. They married girls of fifteen or sixteen; the girls had no choice in the matter. Married to scarred old men, buried in remote castles—if there was a good-looking young son of a former marriage hanging around, who could blame them for taking advantage of the situation? There were a lot of cuckolded kings in those legends, now that I think of it."

"It's a frequent theme," Simon agreed. He looked dubiously at Tristan, who was still occupying the only other comfortable chair; and Tristan stared back at him with cold contempt. Simon pulled up a straight chair and sat down. Carla laughed.

"Chicken," she said.

"I wouldn't disturb him for the world. We exist in an uneasy truce as it is; if I annoyed him, he might turn back into a Celtic knight at the full of the moon, and cut my throat."

The door opened and a woman entered, puffing under the weight of a heavy tray. Simon got up to take it from her, and she shook hands with Carla, smiling broadly.

"This is a pleasure, Miss Tregellas. I had not hoped to see you here so soon. If I had known you were coming I would have cooked something better." Carla looked speechlessly at the tray, which held enough food for two strong men, and the housekeeper went on proudly, "Fortunately we did have some clotted cream on hand. Mary said as how you were fond of it."

Carla responded appropriately; but after the housekeeper had gone she shook her head despairingly.

"I can't go on eating like this. I won't fit into any of my clothes."

"You're going to be wined and dined, whether you like it or not," Simon said. "The Cornish are the most hospitable people on earth, once they accept you; and you are one of their own, the long-lost heir returned."

"I hope they don't expect me to play lady of the manor." Carla accepted a rock cake, thick with currants and still warm from the oven. "I'm not the type, even if I had the money to do it right."

"I'm not so sure about that." Simon studied her thoughtfully. "I think you'd do an excellent job of it, if you ever decided to take it on."

"But I can't. I'm just passing through."

"Then we must make your stay as pleasant as possible. Here, you must finish the clotted cream, or you'll hurt Mrs. Chynoweth's feelings."

"Impossible. I'm so full I won't be able to eat lunch. Which reminds me, I forgot to call Mrs. Pendennis."

"There's a phone in my office."

The doctor's surgery and tiny office were across the hall. The surgery had the usual equipment, scrubbed till it shone, but showing the scars of long usage.

"I'm not awfully up to date," Simon explained. "There's a good hospital in Truro; serious cases go straight there. All I really do is lance boils and splint broken arms. It keeps me busy, though, especially in summer, when the hikers walk along the cliffs in high heels. I'll just tell Mrs. Pendennis you're on your way, shall I?"

"Please." Carla waited while he made the call. She heard only his side of the conversation, but from the long silences, and the amused, rueful smile he gave her, she deduced that the housekeeper was irate at her disappearance.

"She's waiting lunch," Simon reported, hanging up the telephone. "Can you find your way? I'll go with you if—"

"No, I won't get lost. But I won't be able to eat lunch!"

"Run, and work up an appetite."

"Thanks, I will. And thanks for this. I enjoyed it."

"You'll see me soon," he promised, holding her hand a little longer than courtesy required. "We get very bored with one another here. It's nice to have a new face to look at—particularly one as worth looking at as yours."

It was not a particularly clever compliment, but Carla liked it. She also enjoyed the nods and smiles she received from people as she climbed up the street. Every housewife along the way had decided to sweep her steps at the same hour. When she reached the road, she took Simon's advice and began to run.

Mrs. Pendennis was aloof and obviously offended when, panting and perspiring, Carla trotted into the house.

"I couldn't think where you had gone," she said stiffly. "No, that is quite all right, Miss Tregellas. Will five minutes be sufficient for you? Thank you, Miss Tregellas. I will give instructions to the cook."

She swept out. Mary, leaning on her mop, winked at Carla.

"It's only a cold lunch," she whispered. "Take your time, love, and don't let the old girl upset you. She likes to fuss."

All the same, Carla hurried, and when she entered the dining room in less than the five minutes she had been allowed, Mrs. Pendennis forgave her with a gracious smile. Lunch consisted of cold salmon and a salad, plus a chilled white wine of such surpassing excellence that even Carla's untrained palate was impressed.

"That was Mr. Walter's one indulgence," Mrs. Pendennis said, when she expressed her appreciation of the wine. "Or perhaps I should say his greatest indulgence; he was—er—something of a hedonist. At one time his cellar was the finest in Cornwall. Some of it remains—"

"No thanks to him," said Mary, offering mayonnaise. "Poor old soul, he was cut off before his time. He'd calculated it would take another year to finish off the drink."

"That will do, Mary," said Mrs. Pendennis severely. "We will wait on ourselves now. I will ring when I want you."

Mary went out, whistling, and Mrs. Pendennis sighed.

"These modern girls. . . . Did you have a pleasant morning, my dear? I meant to warn you about walking alone. There are dangerous places—and not all of them marked, I am afraid. Mr. Walter felt—"

"I wasn't alone. I met Doctor Tremuan, and he showed me some of the sights."

"A charming young man. I have the greatest confidence in him. His family is one of the oldest in the neighborhood; and he himself is quite a scholar."

"Yes, I know. He seems very nice. I met your grandson, too."

"Michael?" Mrs. Pendennis flushed. "I do hope. . . . That is, where did you find him?"

"Working in the garden. It looks just fine. I don't know many men who would give up their own work to help out as he is doing. It's because he's so fond of you, I'm sure."

"He has nothing else to do," said Mrs. Pendennis; and, as Carla stared at her in surprise, she flushed more deeply and added, "Nothing worthwhile, I mean. Don't think I do not appreciate his assistance, Miss Tregellas. But you must not feel under any obligation. He has his board and lodging, you know, and a chance to have a nice long rest."

Carla murmured something noncommittal and sipped her wine. She had struck a sore spot, but she had no idea what it was. Certainly she would not have described gardening as a nice long rest.

"I am glad you enjoyed your visit to the village," the housekeeper said. It was obvious that she didn't want to discuss her grandson. "You missed a caller while you were out. Young Mr. Fairman. He came all the way from Truro with the expectation of seeing you."

60

"Who is— Oh, I remember. The lawyer."

"He was Mr. Walter's solicitor. I am sure he will want to discuss your affairs."

"He shouldn't have come without telephoning," Carla said, unwilling to accept the implicit criticism. "I'm sorry I missed him, but it was his own fault. Am I supposed to call him?"

"He said he would ring you this afternoon."

"Then I'll stick around for a while. I'm anxious to see the house anyway. Perhaps I can explore this afternoon."

"I had anticipated that you would wish to do so. I am at your disposal."

Carla groaned inwardly. She didn't want a guided tour. She wanted to prowl and linger, soaking up atmosphere. Later it would be fun to hear something of the history the old lady seemed to know so well. But not now. However, she hadn't the heart to refuse the offer. She had already offended Mrs. Pendennis once that day.

So, after a raspberry tart that strained Carla's appetite to the limit, they set out to look over the house.

As the tour progressed, Carla realized that it was a good idea to see it for the first time in the company of someone who knew the purpose and history of every stone in the walls. It was a pity she couldn't turn the place into a Stately Home, with Mrs. Pendennis guiding the tourists. The old lady's appearance and accent would justify adding an extra fifty pence to the price of admission.

However, she had to admit that the house was not the stuff of which historic mansions are made. According to Mrs. Pendennis, the foundations had been laid in 1485, but almost nothing of the medieval manor remained.

The Great Hall had been gutted by fire in 1740 and had been torn down by a tasteless Tregellas; the chapel, gatehouse, and other fifteenth-century features had also succumbed to disasters natural and aesthetic. Much of the inhabited portion dated from the most recent period of affluence—the mid- to late-nineteenth century—and although it appealed to her peculiar tastes, a purist would have considered the place an architectural nightmare. Some rooms, like the library and master bedchamber, were gaudily neo-Gothic, inspired, as so many works of the period were, by the medieval romances of Sir Walter Scott. Stone balconies jutted out in inappropriate places, turrets and battlements sprouted like mushrooms, serving no useful purpose. The casements (no one would ever dare to call them windows) were leaded, the ceilings were not only beamed but gilded and carved as well. Carla won Mrs. Pendennis's heart by her fulsome admiration.

The house was a tragedy, though. It was dead and rotting. Some of the fine old paneling had already been torn out and sold. Carla sympathized with Walter Tregellas's decision to vandalize his house so that he could go on living in it, but his methods seemed rather haphazard. She would have pawned the tea set before she ripped up the walls.

Another depressing fact became evident as she saw more of the house. It would not be easy to sell. Few people could afford to keep up a house of that size, and those who could would undoubtedly prefer something more impressive and in better repair. Yet she became more and more saddened at the idea of giving it up. What fun it would be to redecorate and restore, to scour antique shops for furniture of the right era, to have tea parties on the stone-paved court, and watch the sun set into the Atlantic from her own private balcony.

They had examined the main portion of the house and one wing when an alien sound shook the dusty air. It reminded Carla of a late-night horror film, and she felt a faint chill run through her as Mrs. Pendennis continued her placid lecture, apparently unaware of any noise. Finally the housekeeper's old ears caught the sound, and she broke off in midsentence with a disgusted cluck.

"That girl! She will never learn."

By that time Carla had recognized her own name, shouted at the loudest pitch Mary could produce.

Finally Mary herself appeared at the top of a flight of stairs. She caught sight of her quarry and broke off in mid-shout.

"Miss Tre—— oh, there you are, miss. I've been running about shouting for ever so long."

"So we noticed," Mrs. Pendennis said.

"There's a telephone call, miss. It's Mr. Fairman."

Carla followed the maid through corridor after corridor, down innumerable steps, to the telephone, which was in an uncomfortable little cubbyhole under the staircase in the hall. Only one telephone, in a house this size! She didn't blame Mary for yelling. She was out of breath by the time she reached the phone, and her voice betrayed this.

"I do beg your pardon," said the voice at the other end of the wire. "I ought to have told Mary to have you ring me back. I keep forgetting how large that house is."

The voice was that of a man—baritone, educated,

properly contrite. An attractive voice.

"That's all right," Carla said. "I'm sorry I missed you this morning."

"My dear Miss Tregellas, why should you apologize? I stopped by on my way to the office, on the chance of catching you. I wanted to welcome you, and ask you to dine this evening. It's short notice, I know, but since you won't be here long . . ."

"That would be very nice," Carla said, wondering why everyone she met was so happy to see her, and so anxious to see her go. She was also illogically piqued at the bland assumption that she would have no other demands on her time. "I'm not sure. . . ."

"Oh, do come," the lawyer said persuasively. "I've asked some people I'd like you to meet—the local gentry, if I may use the term. They were all friends of Walter's, and they're most anxious to make you welcome. Please?"

"All right. Thank you."

"Wonderful. I'll pick you up at seven, then. Be as casual as you like; no one dresses for dinner any longer."

Carla was smiling when she hung up the phone. He sounded like a man who was accustomed to having his own way, but his manners were certainly charming.

She emerged from the cramped little room to see Mrs. Pendennis, just out of earshot, but clearly agog with curiosity. With an inner quiver of laughter, she said, with as much aplomb as Lady Caroline herself might have exhibited, "Oh, Mrs. Pendennis, I'm dining out this evening. Will you please tell cook?"

 FOUR

WHEN Carla came down the stairs at seven
o'clock, she heard voices in the drawing room. Mr. Fairman was early—an admirable trait, in a lawyer or an
escort. She wondered whether he was as attractive as his
voice, and reminded herself that the question was irrele-
vant. He was only entertaining her out of a sense of duty.
But when she saw the man who rose from the couch to
greet her, she forgot her manners and frankly stared.

He was incredibly good-looking—a younger Olivier,
tall and broad-shouldered, with rugged features and
heavy black brows.

In the first moment he seemed as struck by her appearance as she was by his. Carla hoped he was fascinated by
her charm and beauty; but she couldn't help remembering Mrs. Pendennis's openmouthed horror at the first
sight of her. She extended her hand.

"Mr. Fairman."

"Please call me Alan." He took her hand in both his. "Forgive my staring. Walter was the only Tregellas I knew well; I would never have believed his features could look so good."

Mrs. Pendennis, hovering, beamed her appreciation of the compliment.

"Won't you have another glass of sherry, Mr. Fairman?"

"Much as I hate to pass up Walter's wine, I think we had better be on our way, Mrs. Pendennis. If you don't mind, Miss Tregellas?"

"You had better call me Carla. I'm ready."

They left Mrs. Pendennis still beaming from the doorway. Carla felt like a girl going to her first dance, with Granny fondly watching. It was clear that Mr. Fairman was a Catch, in the old sense of that word.

He drove a sleek, new, red convertible, and as he handed Carla into the passenger seat he made another graceful comment, about its matching her dress. Once they had turned into the driveway he gave her a sudden irreverent grin, and remarked,

"Now we can relax. I hope you don't let Mrs. P. intimidate you. She is a devastating combination of nanny, governess, and Queen Victoria."

"I think she's sweet."

"She is, she is. And she is one of the last of a dying breed. Whether the world will be better or worse after they depart is another question."

"A little of both, I expect," Carla said. "There aren't many black-and-white moral issues, are there?"

"I'll be damned if I am going to discuss moral issues on a beautiful evening, with a beautiful girl," said her escort.

66

"Don't overdo it. Beautiful I am not. I'll buy charming, or fascinating—even lovely, after I've had a few drinks and have lost my critical faculties. But beautiful . . ."

"You probably have no critical faculties. How do you like your ancestral home?"

"I adore it."

"That proves my point."

Carla laughed. It was a beautiful evening; she was wearing a pretty dress, going to a party with a handsome man, in a fast car, with the breeze caressing her face. What more could a girl ask?

"I suppose we ought to talk about the house," she said reluctantly.

"Not tonight. How long are you planning to stay?"

"That's one of the things I want to discuss. I can't really make a decision until I know how much money there is."

Her companion's dramatic eyebrows lifted.

"But I thought my colleague in Boston made it clear—"

"Oh, I know I'll have to sell the house," Carla said. "And I had intended to stay only a few weeks. It was a crazy impulse, coming at all. But I was hoping—oh, are we here already?"

The house was a handsome modern imitation Georgian, set amid neatly tailored lawns. White trim glistened, windows sparkled, red brick glowed in the sunset light. Carla hated it.

"Oh, yes, we're neighbors. It's a five-minute walk across the fields. What do you think of the place?"

He leaned back in the seat, staring at the house with proprietorial pride.

"I can see why you don't like Tregellas House," Carla said. Her companion chuckled.

"That's a fairly tactful comment, for a Tregellas. I get the point."

Carla thought of apologizing, and decided against it. The family already had a presumably well-earned reputation for blunt candor; who was she to end the tradition? Alan took her arm in a firm grasp and led her to the front door.

Before he could ring or use his key, the door was opened by a girl. . . . After the first quick glance, Carla revised her appraisal. This was a woman, probably in her late twenties, though it was hard to judge her age. Her features were mature, but her shy smile and averted eyes made her seem young and awkward. She was wearing a limp cotton skirt and a blouse that would not have looked amiss on the Queen Mother; it had long, droopy sleeves and a bow under the chin. Her hair, a washed-out ash-blond, was drawn back and tied with a ribbon. Her only beauty was a complexion of the famed English peaches-and-cream softness. It was almost enough to compensate for the inappropriate costume and coiffure. The girl could have been a beauty if she had bothered to fix herself up.

With a fond smile that appeared to observe no flaw in appearance or manner, Alan introduced his sister.

"Elizabeth was so anxious to meet you she couldn't wait for the parlormaid to answer the door," he said.

Elizabeth flushed violently. Her fair skin was a handicap; it instantly betrayed the slightest emotional change.

"I'm sorry," she stammered. "I didn't mean—"

She gave her brother an agonized glance. Carla felt uncomfortable. Naturally a nonentity like this woman

68

would idolize a handsome older brother; but there was such a thing as dignity! She rushed—as she thought—to the rescue.

"I'm flattered! It was friendly of you to think of greeting me personally. We're not used to maids in the States, you know. Please call me Carla, and I'll call you—do you have a nickname, or do you prefer Elizabeth?"

Elizabeth was struck dumb by this admittedly effusive speech. She gaped unattractively until her brother pushed her gently out of the way and led Carla into the house.

"We've time for a quick one before the others arrive," he announced, smiling. "I planned it that way on purpose."

Since her ideas of English society dated from college courses in Dickens and Jane Austen, Carla was pleasantly surprised to find that the quick one did not consist solely of sherry. Alan mixed an excellent martini.

Elizabeth drank sherry. It had been years since Carla had met anyone who was so painfully shy. Yet she had a feeling that if Alan had not been there to direct the conversation, she might have established some rapport with Elizabeth. He was so scintillating that lesser personalities were overwhelmed. Not that she blamed him; it was Elizabeth's fault for not asserting herself.

Before they had time to do more than exchange the conventional questions and answers (How do you like Cornwall, Carla? I think it is a beautiful country, Elizabeth.), the bell rang, and the next guests were shown in. Obviously people didn't make a fetish of being late in this society. Ten minutes later all the guests had arrived, and Carla was trying to straighten them out in her mind.

Colonel and Mrs. Wingate were the first arrivals, and

the least interesting of the lot. As his title implied, the Colonel was a retired army officer, and his wife was a well-bred matron, given to good works and much preoccupied with the wickedness of the working classes. She had a slight, very correct, crush on the vicar.

Carla didn't really blame her. John Willis was slight and prematurely white-haired, with gentle blue eyes and an incandescent smile. He had a redeemingly human sense of humor; as they shook hands, and she murmured a greeting, he grinned broadly and remarked, "Go to the head of the class, Miss Tregellas."

"Carla—please. Why do you say that?"

"You didn't remark, 'My, you're the very picture of a sweet old English vicar.' I can't help looking like this, you know."

Before Carla could answer, they were joined by another guest, a tall, elderly woman with harsh features, who would have looked more at home in a military uniform than the portly little colonel.

"Nonsense, John," she barked. "You adore looking like a vicar. I suspect you bleach your hair in secret."

The vicar laughed, and the elderly woman, who had been introduced as Miss Truebody, fixed Carla with an openly curious stare.

"Not much of the family look in you, young woman—except for those smudgy gray eyes. Lucky for you. The Tregellases are not handsome people."

"Everybody keeps telling me I'm the spitting image of Cousin Walter," Carla said.

"Pay no attention," said Miss Truebody. "It's a nuisance, having too many ancestors. That's to say, we all have 'em; can't help it; better to ignore 'em."

At this point the last guest appeared, full of apologies for his tardiness.

"Damn fools will insist on rock climbing with no training, no proper gear. One of 'em was carried in just as I was dressing. Terribly sorry, Elizabeth—everyone. Ah, Carla, good to see you again so soon."

"You have met?" Alan asked, as the doctor shook hands with Carla. He did not sound pleased.

"Yes," Carla said. "I hope the poor man wasn't badly hurt, Simon."

"It was a girl. Broken leg, concussion—at the least. I sent her on to Truro for X rays. Colonel, can't we get more signs up along the cliff?"

"Doesn't matter. Damn fools ignore them anyway. Why waste money?"

Dinner was announced. They moved in a straggling group toward the dining room, the doctor foiling Alan's attempt to escort Carla. As they passed through the door, Carla happened to overhear a curious little exchange between her host and hostess.

"Didn't you ask him?" Elizabeth whispered.

"He's coming later," was the curt reply. "If he bothers to come at all. . . ."

It did not occur to Carla to wonder whom they referred to, but it did strike her as peculiar that the hostess should not know how many guests she was expected to feed.

The meal was not particularly memorable; and at first the conversation was equally prosaic. Carla answered the usual questions about her trip and her future plans.

"I really don't know how long I can stay," she explained. "Alan tells me I'm broke."

Mrs. Wingate looked shocked at this blunt reference to money matters, but Miss Truebody gave one of her brief, neighing laughs.

"You may not look like Walter, my girl, but you sound like him."

"Allowing for slight differences in idiom," the vicar murmured with a smile.

"He was always complaining about money," Miss Truebody went on reminiscently. "Many's the evening I've spent with him, trying to help him decide what to sell next. It's a mercy he went when he did. He liked to live well, and he couldn't have continued doing so much longer. But there must be something left, child. If there's money enough to keep on a cook and housemaid, I don't see why you should be an additional financial burden. You can't eat much, you're no bigger than a mouse."

"Thanks," Carla said gratefully. "You're the first person I've met who isn't trying to get me to go home as soon as possible."

This brought loud denials from everyone at the table, including Alan.

"I don't deserve that," he said plaintively. "Carla, please let's not discuss business now. Miss Truebody will tell us precisely what we're doing wrong, and what we ought to do next."

Miss Truebody grinned at him. "If you'd listen to me, my lad, you'd be the richest lawyer in Cornwall. I know a thing or two."

"I think you're a witch," Alan said, with a rather forced smile.

Miss Truebody smiled back at him, but the vicar appeared to find the exchange inappropriate.

"Speaking of witchcraft," he said smoothly, "I understand some of my parishioners are resorting to Arthur's Ring again."

"What's that?" Carla asked.

"One of the prehistoric pierced stones—tolmens, as they are properly called," the doctor answered. "Around here everything that isn't attributed to the pixies or the devil is named after King Arthur. People used to believe that passing a sick person through the hole in the stone would cure his disease. I wonder which of my patients has lost confidence in me."

"You take it very coolly, I must say," Mrs. Wingate exclaimed.

"I may as well, since I can't prevent it. Old superstitions never really die, you know. They don't even fade away; they linger in peoples' minds, and are revived when modern methods fail. As they often do, I regret to say."

"It is funny how superstitions hang on," Carla said. "We've got all kinds of weird cults in the States—satanism, séances, the works."

"Yes," the vicar agreed. "They are all forms of the irrational—survivals of magical practices as old as man himself. I do think this area is particularly susceptible. There are few regions more steeped in legend. Local festivals, such as the Furry Dance, which are being revived for the benefit of the tourist trade, commemorate remnants of dead religions—Roman, Druid, Celtic. One of my older parishioners swears he can hear the bells chime, on summer evenings, from the sunken churches of Lyonesse—" He broke off as Carla gave a soft exclamation. "Yes, my dear?"

"Nothing. I mean—was there really such a place as Lyonesse? It is a real honest-to-goodness folktale, not just

73

something Mrs. Pendennis invented?"

She had had several glasses of wine in addition to her cocktail, and she was feeling relaxed with these friendly people, or she might not have spoken so freely. The question was followed by a significant silence. The guests exchanged glances. Then Miss Truebody sniffed loudly.

"Damn the woman, is she still harping on that ridiculous story? Vicar, you must speak to her."

"My dear Miss Truebody, why should I? I've enough to keep me occupied with genuine sinners; an elderly lady's harmless delusions surely. . . " He stopped speaking and gave Carla a startled look. "Good heavens. It has just occurred to me that Mrs. Pendennis might believe. . . . She didn't by any chance imply—"

"Imply nothing. She told me I had better leave town before Midsummer Eve."

The vicar sucked in his breath. His frowning look, and the sober faces of the others, shook Carla's nerve. She would have felt better if they had laughed uproariously. She looked accusingly at Simon.

"You told me she had only confided in you. Apparently everyone knows about it. I'm going to feel like a fool."

"I'm afraid people in small villages are inclined to gossip," the vicar said ruefully. "I first learned of Mrs. Pendennis's—er—aberration a few weeks ago. Apparently she mentioned it to others as well. But you must realize, Carla, that the story of Lady Caroline's disappearance is well known. I believe it has even been printed in some of the local guidebooks. Every old family has such legends. They begin with a simple tragedy—

74

accidental death, elopement, suicide—and then the fictional trimmings are added."

"One can't help wondering, though," Elizabeth said unexpectedly. "What could have happened to her?"

"It's a morbid subject," Alan said disgustedly.

"Not at all," Miss Truebody said. "Anyone with a spark of imagination must wonder."

"But what's the point of speculating about something that happened two hundred years ago?" Alan demanded. "For all we know, the girl was in love with someone else, and decided to elope. Or she may have tumbled into a mine shaft, or a Pict house; the moors are riddled with ancient ruins. Not to mention the cliffs. . . . What the devil are you laughing about, Simon?"

"You," Simon said. "Scolding us for wasting our time on idle fancies, when you've obviously given the problem a great deal of thought yourself. Actually, what I find most interesting is the material that has accrued to the tragedy. The merman theme fascinates me. I'm something of a student of folklore, and I don't believe I've encountered this particular variant."

"But it is not uncommon," the vicar exclaimed. "We all know the stories of the mermaids who gave their hearts to mortals and were betrayed by them. Andersen's version is a modern retelling of an old theme, which was not, originally, a pretty tale for children. There are many stories of women wooed by half-human creatures of the sea—the seal men, who shed their skins when they come on land. Matthew Arnold's poem 'The Forsaken Merman'. . ."

"An aquatic demon lover," the doctor said.

"Really, what a ridiculous discussion," said Mrs. Wingate. She was seconded, unexpectedly, by Elizabeth.

"I don't think we ought to talk about it, if it bothers Carla," she murmured.

Carla appreciated the girl's thoughtfulness; the subject did disturb her much more than it ought. For that very reason, to conquer her distaste, she said firmly, "Not at all. It's very interesting."

"Yes, rather." Her host leaned back in his chair and smiled approvingly at her. "Too silly to take seriously, but rather fun. New to me, I must admit. What's this demon-lover business, John?"

"A common theme in folklore," the vicar replied. "Beginning with the mortal maidens beloved of the gods—Danae, Io, Europa. Under Christianity the old gods became demons. During the Middle Ages the female worshipers of Satan were physically embraced by their dark lord; we have descriptions of—" Seeing Mrs. Wingate's outraged look, he stopped abruptly. "I believe the theme is found outside Europe as well," he ended, rather feebly.

"Oh, certainly; Burma, China, Africa." The doctor, a scholar to the core, was happily oblivious of Mrs. Wingate's disgust. "Not that the lover is always a demon, in the sense of being evil. Arnold's poor merman is a proper Victorian; he seems more disturbed by the breaking up of the family than by a broken heart. But the idea that the Tregellas merman is the family bane is unique, I believe. Malevolent spirits haunt other old houses, but they come from hell, not from the depths of the sea."

The words cast a kind of spell over the company. It was broken by Miss Truebody, who exclaimed robustly, "What a pack of nonsense, Simon!"

"Hear, hear," said a voice from the doorway.

Carla recognized the voice. She turned, but not before

76

she had seen the face of Elizabeth Fairman flame into brief, surprising beauty.

"Michael," she said softly.

He lounged against the doorframe, pantherlike in his lean grace, and as out of place as a jungle animal in that staid group. He was dressed with deliberate sloppiness. There was a hole in the knee of his faded jeans, which fit his hips like plastic wrap; his shirt was open to the waist, and the long, predatory hands still showed the stains of garden earth. In the startled silence that followed his appearance he let his eyes wander insolently from one face to the next. With a surge of unwilling amusement Carla realized that his mobile, trained features were expressing his opinion of each guest, so subtly that only a close observer would have noticed. Miss Truebody got a faint quirk of the lips, Alan a lifted eyebrow, the Wingates a blank, idiot stare.

"Good evening all," he said, and smiled suddenly at Elizabeth.

Carla got only the outer edges of the smile; but she understood why Elizabeth looked dazzled.

"Do sit down," she gasped, waving her hands. "I'll ring . . . so glad you could come. . . ."

"Don't fuss, Liz," Michael said. "I just dropped in for a cup of coffee."

"We were about to move into the lounge," Alan said, with an expressive glance at his sister.

"Oh—oh, yes, of course. I'll ring. . . ."

Michael was seized upon by Miss Truebody and removed from the room amid a barrage of questions about the garden. The others followed. After the maid had served coffee and liqueurs, conversation died except for the voice of Miss Truebody, who was still talking about mulch. Michael glanced around the silent circle.

"We're boring the others, Miss Truebody," he said. "And I believe I interrupted a particularly thrilling discussion. Do go on with what you were talking about."

"It was not at all thrilling to me," said Mrs. Wingate. "I found it quite distasteful. And really, Vicar, I am surprised that you—"

"I'm only sorry that I am so ignorant," said the vicar, in his blandest tones. "Simon is the folklore expert. Actually, Simon, I have been wanting to ask you—something I read recently about survivals of ancient Near Eastern thought in the apocryphal literature. . . ."

So the subject of Michael's grandmother and her fancies was neatly turned; but Carla suspected Michael was not deceived. How much had he heard before he spoke and alerted them to his presence? Carla imagined he had heard quite a lot. Talk about demon lovers, she thought, studying his thin, dark charm, and Elizabeth Fairman's entranced face.

Michael spoke little, but his presence obviously cast a pall on the company. Before long the Wingates made their excuses, and Miss Truebody, offered a lift home, went with them. The doctor was the next to leave, after a few unsuccessfully suppressed yawns.

"I was rousted out at dawn this morning," he said apologetically. "One of the Redruth kids, some kind of virus. Thank you, Elizabeth, Alan. . . . Carla, I'll ring you soon, if I may."

Michael sat on—and on. It was obvious that Alan didn't want him to stay, equally obvious that he knew it and reveled in his host's annoyance. His manner toward Elizabeth would have been charming if Carla had not sensed artifice in every word and every gesture. He drew the other woman out with questions about her roses and her pets and her volunteer work at the hospital; and under his smile Elizabeth blossomed, oblivious of her brother's cold looks. Finally Michael rose to go.

"May I walk you home, ma'am?" he asked Carla.

It was the first time he had addressed her directly all evening.

"No, thanks," Carla said.

"I'll drive Miss Tregellas home," Alan said. "Good night, Pendennis."

Elizabeth half rose, as if to go with him to the door, but then sank back in her chair as her brother looked at her. Michael found his own way out; and Carla watched, in mingled pity and contempt, as the other woman faded into a pale ghost of her former laughing self.

"I think I'd better be going too," she said. "I hate to ask you to drive me, Alan. Perhaps if I hurry I can catch up with—"

"Don't be ridiculous!" Alan snapped. Then he smiled ruefully. "Sorry. That fellow rubs me the wrong way, I can't deny it. Naturally I'll drive you, Carla. But don't rush off. Let me get you a drink. Or more coffee—Elizabeth, will you ring for. . . . My dear, you do look tired! Why don't you go off to bed? Carla will understand, I'm sure."

"Of course," Carla said. Elizabeth rose, with an apologetic murmur. Her brother took her arm. She leaned heavily on it as they went out together.

Alan was back almost at once, looking grave, and when Carla again stated her intention of leaving he did not demur. They were in the car, turning onto the road, before he said abruptly,

"You must think me a disgusting mixture of bully and

overprotective big brother."

"I wouldn't put it quite that strongly," Carla said.

Alan laughed softly. "Do you always say precisely what you think?"

"I'm much more tactful than I used to be," Carla protested. "Look, Alan, you introduced the subject. You don't have to explain yourself to me, or—"

"But I'd like to. It's early yet, and it's a beautiful night —too beautiful to waste. May I show you one of my favorite views, and take advantage of your good nature —just for a few minutes?"

"Of course."

Carla's tone was not as gracious as her words. She was not really looking forward to a long, embarrassingly personal conversation. But when Alan turned off the road and stopped the car on a graveled point overlooking the sea, she decided the view was almost worth it.

The moon, nearing the full, cast a long, shimmering silver path across the dark water. The sky was spangled with stars, and the soft murmur of waves breaking on the rocks was as soothing as a song.

"Nothing out there but water, for almost three thousand miles," Alan said softly. "No wonder they thought this was the end of the world. Land's End. At sunset, when the clouds pile up into fantastic shapes like gilded towers and purple spires, it really does look like a heavenly city."

"I didn't know you were such a poet."

"I can't afford to be," was the bitter reply. "I wouldn't mind sitting here dreaming and thinking beautiful thoughts. That's what Simon does. Fine for him; but he doesn't have my responsibilities. Sometimes I envy him. But not often; Elizabeth is very dear to me. She's been ill. I think you can guess the nature of her illness."

"I wouldn't have guessed from her behavior; but you are implying . . . some kind of mental illness?"

"Yes."

"Well, for heaven's sake, why make such a thing of it? It's nothing to be ashamed of. Half the people I know are seeing psychiatrists."

"I'm not ashamed of it. But Elizabeth is. She's morbidly self-conscious—and terrified of a relapse."

"What was it?" Carla asked bluntly. "Depression, anxiety, something like that?"

"Something like that. You know how these damned psychiatrists are; you can't get a sensible answer out of them. She's done so well the last few months, and the doctor says it's good for her to entertain, take the responsibility for running the house. But I have to keep pushing her. I ran things myself for so long that it's hard for me to resign, and she isn't anxious to take over. It makes me look like a cad."

"Not at all. You know," Carla said, feeling her way with uncharacteristic caution, "it isn't always possible to be sweet and suave and calm, not when you love someone. Sick people are pathetic, but they can be exasperating, too."

"I knew you'd understand." He turned toward her, his eyes glowing as they reflected the moonlight. "You're a remarkable woman, Carla."

He took her in his arms.

Carla had time to admire the ease with which he maneuvered in the constricted confines of the front seat. It must have taken a lot of practice, she thought, as his lips found hers.

It was a pleasant, restrained kiss; but Carla had a feeling that he was holding himself back. He released her. Then he slid back under the wheel and stared up at the silvered sky.

"Was that a mistake?" he asked.

"That depends on what you had intended to accomplish."

"Ouch. I'd better take you home, until I can think of a reply to that one."

But his voice was cheerful and his smile more relaxed than it had been at the beginning of their talk.

"You'll think of something witty just as you're dropping off to sleep," Carla said. "That's when my best repartee occurs to me."

"Too true. What about lunch tomorrow? We can have our dull business chat first and then perhaps a spot of sightseeing, while the weather holds."

"I'd like that."

The old house was dark when they stopped in front of the steps, and Alan let out an exasperated exclamation.

"I wish Mrs. Pendennis weren't so confoundedly thrifty. I've told her again and again to leave lights on at night; she could easily fall and break something in the dark."

"Oh, I think it adds to the atmosphere," Carla said. "The place looks like something out of a Dracula movie, doesn't it?"

In spite of her words she rather wished Mrs. Pendennis had thrown caution to the winds and left a light burning. The dark trees behind the house cut off the moonlight and buried the building deep in shadows. The irregular roofline, turreted and chimneyed, made a grim outline against the stars. Something scuttled, squeaking, through the tall grass, and Carla let out a small involuntary echo of its cry.

Alan laughed, and gathered her into his arms again. This kiss was more assured and considerably more satisfactory.

"I must admit the Gothic aura has its advantages," he said, after an interval. "Carla, shall I wait till you get safely up to your room? Croon to me from the balcony, or let down your hair."

"Nonsense. Do you think the merman is lying in wait for me? He isn't due until Midsummer Eve."

"You aren't really worried about that, are you?"

"Of course not. Good night, Alan. Till tomorrow."

Mrs. Pendennis had left the door unlocked and, to Carla's relief, there was a feeble light at the back of the hall. With its help she negotiated the steps. Another dim bulb burned in the vast length of the upper hall; but only the fact that it was practically destitute of furniture saved her from a fall. She stubbed her toe agonizingly on the one table along its length. Moonlight forcing a limited path through a window beleaguered by branches enabled her to locate her own door. She flung it open— and recoiled, her breath catching in her throat, as a long dark shape, like a boneless tentacle, swept down toward her face.

Its mindless motion was quicker than her reflexive recoil; with a hideous sucking sound the thing struck her throat and smothered her face in damp cold folds that reeked sickeningly of brine.

 FIVE

CARLA clawed frantically at her mouth. She had had time for one brief scream before the substance gagged her. After she had pulled it away, there didn't seem to be much point to screaming again. She knew, even before her groping hand found the light switch, what it was.

The long tangled mass of it had been pulled apart by her fingers. Part of it still clung repulsively to her breast and shoulder, but one sizable section dangled, dripping, from her hand.

Seaweed.

Anger was beginning to replace her initial shock when someone materialized out of the darkness beside her. Carla spun around.

"Damn you, can't you walk, instead of gliding like a snake?"

"Temper, temper," Michael said. His nose wrinkled.

"I thought I heard you scream. Is that any way to speak to a rescuer? What's going on? The place stinks of—" Then his eyes widened, and he caught her wrists as she began to brush at the strands of seaweed draping her body. "Let me do that, you're smearing it. No, don't move; there's another batch of the stuff hanging from the lintel."

Carla let him steer her through the doorway, avoiding the seaweed, but she resisted when he tried to push her into a chair.

"I don't need to sit down, I'm not a helpless little old lady! I want to see how this trick was rigged."

"Simple. Someone draped a thick strand of the stuff over a nail. You walked right into it?"

"Yes." Carla shuddered involuntarily. Michael pulled the remaining weed free and dropped it onto the floor.

"Harmless, but mildly revolting," he admitted. "I might have let out a yelp myself."

"Nice of you to say so. Where did you come from so fast?"

"My room. And in case you think I am presuming, I assure you I would much rather sleep in the stable. I didn't think it wise for an old woman to be alone here at night, that's the only reason I moved in. In addition to her other infirmities, she's a bit deaf. I expect that's why she didn't hear you."

"She'll hear me clearly enough tomorrow morning."

"There's no reason to mention this to her."

"Oh, yes, there is."

"You don't think *she* did this?"

"She's the hottest suspect of all. Come on, don't be cute. This wasn't a harmless practical joke; you know what it was meant to suggest. Your grandmother may

85

have had the best of motives. She's nutty enough to believe she would be doing me a favor by scaring me away."

"Don't be ridiculous!"

"Well, who else would do such a thing? Unless you—"

"I'm a much more likely suspect," Michael said, in the smooth, flat tones of suppressed fury. "Can you see my grandmother climbing down the rocks to get this stuff and then balancing on a chair to drape it over your door? What do you take her for, some kind of eighty-year-old supergrannie?"

"I hadn't thought of that," Carla admitted, somewhat deflated.

"Anyhow, you've too much sense to believe that some aquatic admirer dropped in and left his calling card on the door," Michael said. "I expect you are more superstitious than you admit; most howling rationalists are, that's why they howl so loudly. But even you wouldn't fall for a clumsy trick like this. Hell, I could think up half a dozen tricks offhand that would have more style."

"I'll bet you could. It would make a super ballet, come to think of it. The maiden and the merman. What a starring vehicle for you!"

Michael's eyes narrowed to slits. For an unnerving moment, with shadows carving strange hollows in his face, he looked as inhuman as any creature of the sea or forest.

"Bitch," he said, and vanished as suddenly as he had appeared.

Carla took a long hot shower and scrubbed herself till her skin felt raw. But even after she had sought the comfort of the big canopied bed she seemed to sense the slimy touch of seaweed against her breast.

86

It had been a mean, malicious trick, but nothing more. Michael was right; no one could be naive enough to suppose that the incident would really frighten her—except, perhaps, Mrs. Pendennis. Carla couldn't help feeling a grudging respect for Michael's valiant defense of his grandmother, but although his objections had some weight, they did not rule out Mrs. Pendennis altogether. There might be places where the weed could be obtained without the strenuous climb down the cliffs, which was almost certainly beyond the elderly woman's powers. On the other hand, as Michael had been careful to point out, he was a pretty good suspect himself. Obviously he didn't care much for her, and he had had plenty of time to set up the trap before she got home.

In spite of his request she decided she would mention the occurrence to Mrs. Pendennis next day. Not accuse her; no, one could hardly do that. Just—mention it.

But when the moment came, she couldn't do it. Michael was at the breakfast table when she came down. His lowering glance and gruff good morning assured her he was ready to do battle if she introduced the subject. That wasn't what deterred her, though. It was the sight of Mrs. Pendennis's innocent blue eyes and sweet smile, as she inquired whether Carla had enjoyed herself the night before.

"Yes, thank you, very much," she muttered, and thought—Round one to the man in the blue jeans.

After breakfast Michael went to his gardening. He knew he had won. Carla excused herself to Mrs. Pendennis and returned to her room. The relationship between Michael and his grandmother baffled her. They hardly spoke to one another; Mrs. Pendennis was cool, almost hostile, when she did address her grandson. Perhaps,

Carla thought, she doesn't approve of his profession. A lot of ignorant people think male ballet dancers are queer, or effete, or just plain useless.

Well, it wasn't her problem. She wanted to leave early for her luncheon appointment in order to return the car to a rental agency in Truro; it was absurd to have it sitting in the garage eating up money she couldn't afford to spend. Mrs. Pendennis had assured her that the local bus stopped at the end of the driveway, and there was another car—Michael's, presumably. Though neither he nor his grannie had offered his services as chauffeur. . . .

Michael and his grannie were too much on her mind. Carla dismissed them with a shrug. She had an hour or two to kill before she left, and she meant to spend it exploring her room. She had been too busy to investigate all the nooks and crannies, and some of them looked interesting—the cupboards by the fireplace, for instance, and a door on an inner wall that she had never opened.

She tried the door first, expecting it to give access to a closet. Instead she saw a narrow landing, with a steep iron staircase leading down into darkness.

Not *Jane Eyre*, Carla thought—*The Mystery of the Spiral Staircase*. Nancy Drew, or some equally trite source. She stepped onto the landing, and then stepped back, as the worn planking creaked ominously. The stairs would have to wait. It would be foolish to descend them without a flashlight, particularly when they looked as if they might collapse at the slightest touch. If she fell it would be hours before anyone found her. And wouldn't it be jolly if she landed, at the bottom, on a heap of moldering bones wrapped in the tattered shreds of an eighteenth-century gown?

She shook her head. Lady Caroline couldn't be anywhere in the house; her agitated family must have searched it from top to bottom, and this wasn't a secret staircase; the door was plain to see. More to the point was the question of where the stairs led. Had they provided entry for a nocturnal visitor with a bag of dripping seaweed? Not that there was any need for such an unconventional route; the house had been wide open, and the sole occupant deaf and snoring.

The corner cupboards were empty. The shelves had been neatly lined with paper. Carla smiled, wondering what Mrs. Pendennis had expected her to put on them. Her traveling collection of china, perhaps? With a feeling of distinct anticlimax she turned to the bookcases. Her room was providing no thrills at all, despite its charm.

The books were a motley assortment; they reminded her of the ten-cent bins outside secondhand bookshops back home. There were a few old children's classics among them—gems like *Little Lord Fauntleroy* and *Greyfriars Bobby*—but the majority were fifty-year old bestsellers that no one had ever heard of after their brief success. She was about to turn away from the shelves when her eye fell upon a fat leather-bound volume lying on top of the books that filled the lowest shelf.

As her hand touched the worn leather, the room seemed to darken. In her ears sounded an ominous thunder, like waves beating on a rocky shore. Carla dropped to her knees, then slipped to a sitting position, her back against the bookshelves. She rubbed her eyes. Delayed jet lag? Something wrong with last night's fish? She hadn't felt so queer since the first year in college, when she had passed out on the bus after a week-long water-and-lettuce diet.

The dizziness passed, leaving no aftereffects. When Carla again reached for the book, it slipped easily into her hand. Bound in leather, with a stamped pattern of flowering vines on the cover, it was fastened with a gold clasp and lock.

Suddenly she knew what it was, knew as surely as if an identifying label had been glued to its spine. The lock was a tinselly affair; it had never been designed to resist hands as determined as Carla's. It gave way when she wrenched at it, and the book opened.

The leaves fell back readily, as if someone had constantly referred to one particular page, a page midway through the volume. The faded handwriting was delicate and uncertain, a young woman's writing. . . . Or was that only her imagination, an extrapolation of what she already suspected?

The writing looked blurred. She couldn't seem to focus her eyes. She turned to the first page and, with no sense of surprise, saw the words "My Diary," and a date, 1780. It was Caroline Tregellas's record of her last year on earth.

Carla scrambled to her feet, clutching the book in both hands, as if it might wriggle away from her. She wasn't thinking then of the unbelievable coincidence of finding it. She was gripped by a consuming curiosity.

But as she sat down in a chair by the window, she realized she would not find any astounding revelations as to Caroline's fate. The diary must have been read by her grieving family. If it had contained any pertinent information, they would have made it known. Or, if the information had been unacceptable—if, for instance, Caroline had been pregnant by the stable boy, and contemplating suicide—the diary would have been destroyed.

Yet someone had read it—often. Again she let the book open at random and found herself looking at the same page she had first seen. The date was June 22.

It was the last entry in the book, but not the last day of the girl's life. Midsummer Day was June 24. The twenty-third would be Midsummer Eve. Probably Caroline wrote in her diary every evening, just before she went to bed. She had never had a chance to inscribe the events of the twenty-third.

Carla turned back to the first page and read:

"In summer, when the sun beams down from an azure heaven, the sea surrounding this promontory has a smiling, innocent face. Golden gorse and purple heather nestle in the fissures of the caverned granite cliffs. . . ."

There were several pages of this sort of thing. Carla read on in growing exasperation. Were all eighteenth-century damsels as verbose and as coyly sentimental as Caroline? Probably. A girl of good family had few acceptable amusements. Needlework, music, an occasional ball. . . . There were plenty of servants to do the work; young ladies had lots of time on their hands.

After Caroline had exhausted her repertoire of adjectives on the beauties of nature, there was a paragraph of more mundane comment.

"Mrs. Poldane began work on my wedding clothes. There is a great deal to be done, since I have outgrown last summer's wardrobe. I am to have two ball gowns, one in the polonaise style, of red-and-white-striped satin, and a robe à la française, very elegant, with garlands of silk roses and leaves. . . ."

Carla tossed the book aside. Later she would read more of it. The domestic details were rather interesting; Caroline had had a normal, healthy feminine interest in fashion. But now it was time she got ready to leave for Truro.

It was not that easy to dismiss the book from her mind. As she drove along the leafy lanes, following Mrs. Pendennis's slightly involved directions, she found that instead of concentrating on her route, or admiring the scenery, she was seeing a mental picture of the bookshelves where she had found Caroline's diary. There was something wrong in that image, a jarring note. . . . Of course. The diary itself was the false note. It was out of place, not only physically, in its size and shape, but in its contents. No wonder her eye had been drawn to it. It had no business being where it was, among works of light fiction, impermanent and valueless. Like the portrait, it had been placed in her room deliberately, by a person or persons unknown.

She forced herself to concentrate on her driving, for the traffic was getting heavier, and she still had a tendency to drift to the right when her thoughts wandered. The route was easy to follow once she got onto the main east-west highway from Land's End to Plymouth, but she encountered further distractions as soon as the A30 neared the sea, at Penzance. It led through the center of town, past the Post Office and the domed Market House, then descended to skirt the bay. The sunny beaches were well populated; beyond, the fairy-tale spires of St. Michael's Mount dominated the horizon.

She was so busy gawking that she missed the turn and had to consult her map before she found the route again. This part of the drive was new to her, and it was so distracting that she was running dangerously late when she finally found herself on the rim of the bowllike hollow in which Truro lay, but the view was so pleasant that she pulled off the road and took a few minutes to stare. It was a cozy-looking town, with the spires of the cathedral rising in the center and a setting of rich green trees and plowed fields, lush with spring crops.

After she had given up the car, she had to ask directions to Alan's office. Fortunately it was not far away, but she was fifteen minutes late when she arrived.

"Not bad at all," Alan said, brushing away her apologies. "I assumed you'd lose yourself at least once, especially if you followed Mrs. P.'s directions. Have a chair and let's get the boring part over quickly."

His office, in a solid-looking old house near Lemon Street, had a quiet elegance that contrasted with the modernity of his private residence. Alan's business manner matched the office—quiet, confidential, efficient.

"Here's the situation in a nutshell," he said, spreading out a mass of papers across his desk. "Walter Tregellas left all of which he died possessed to the nearest relative who still bore the Tregellas name. That seems to be you. I won't bore you with genealogical details; suffice it to say that we checked thoroughly and found no one who was more nearly related. You needn't worry about a claimant popping up out of the blue," he added with a smile. "It wouldn't be worth his while. As residuary legatee, you inherit the house and its contents, and the ten-odd acres surrounding it. Nothing more. What you have, my dear girl, is a combination albatross and white elephant."

"What about taxes?" Carla inquired, squirming uneasily in the heavy carved armchair. It looked impressive, but it had too many protruding corners to be comfortable.

"The death duties are paid." Again Alan permitted himself a small, unprofessional smile. "It's almost as if Walter had calculated, to the day, how long he could live without leaving the estate in debt. At that, I had to sell the choicer objects in the house; that's why the place looks rather bare. But those were Walter's instructions."

"And the staff wages?"

"By the terms of the will I am empowered to sell whatever is necessary to pay them, for a period of approximately six months. We'll be fortunate if we can last that long, actually. But Walter felt, and I quite agree, that the house should not be left empty while it was in the process of being sold."

"Six months," Carla echoed. "What happens to Mrs. Pendennis after that?"

"Walter arranged for a small annuity. As for the six-month period, that's a maximum. I doubt that we can manage for more than three; and the sooner we sell, the better. If we can sell."

"I can't imagine who would buy the place," Carla muttered. "Impractical romantics aren't rare, but romantics with money. . . ."

"I'm sorry," Alan said. "It's a shame to see a place like that leave the family after so many years. I wish I could save it for you."

"No, that's silly. What on earth would I do with it? The annual expenses would cost more than I make in a year. But can't I stay on longer than I had planned, maybe till the end of the summer? Would it be that much more of a drain on what is left? I could eat out."

Alan didn't find this amusing. "I can't advise you, Carla."

"Why not?"

"Because I'm no longer impersonal." He looked at her and his wide dark eyes met hers with an almost physical shock. "I don't want you to go. . . . Oh, well, why not? June, July, August; it's only three months. I'll think of something."

"We could let Mary go," Carla suggested. "I can do her work; I have a feeling she doesn't do much anyway. And a cook is a ridiculous luxury. . . . Stop laughing; I'm serious. What's so funny?"

"You. Fighting the downfall of the house of Tregellas by doing the washing up. . . . No, darling, it's sweet of you to think of it, but leave the problem to me. We'll manage. I'll investigate, see if I can't find a buyer. And now, thank God, that's settled. Let's get out of here."

They lunched at a little inn near Falmouth, perched on a rocky ledge above the bay. Carla tried to discuss practical matters, but Alan refused to do so. Instead he told her stories about Cornwall. Some of them were so amusing, and his dialect was so effective, that she was helpless with laughter; others were grim enough to rate a shudder. They intrigued Carla even more than the doctor's ancient legends, for they were concerned with the more recent history of the area that was casting an increasingly potent spell over her imagination. Alan spoke of the mines, whose abandoned engine towers still stood stark above the hills, looking more like castle ruins than the practical devices they had been; he told tales of terrible disaster and foolhardy courage, and of the eventual failure of the great lodes of tin and copper, which had cast the entire duchy into a severe economic depression. He talked about the smugglers, running their duty-free cargoes of brandy and silks into rocky coves under the noses of the excise men, and of the wreckers, who had lured ships to destruction on the reefs, for the sake of the wealth they carried; about Turkish pirates and English rebels, and the last stand of the Plantagenets, in the shape of the young pretender Perkin Warbeck—or Richard IV, as his Cornish supporters proclaimed him.

"He claimed to be one of the Lost Princes in the Tower," Alan explained. "His story of how he escaped was never very convincing, but the Cornishmen didn't want logic, they wanted a leader for their rebellion against Henry the Seventh. Perkin was married to a pretty Scottish princess; he left her in the safety of Saint Michael's Mount while he marched out to war. He lost, of course. Romantic lost causes always do fail."

"And what happened to the poor princess?"

"Oh, Henry the Seventh eventually married her off to one of his friends—after he had beheaded her husband. You see, my dear, things weren't always so nice in the good old romantic days."

"I don't know why you keep accusing me of being a romantic. I am a very practical, hard-headed— Now you're laughing at me again."

"Not laughing, just smiling, with genuine appreciation. We'd best be off, or we won't have time for any sightseeing. I suppose you want to do the whole horrible bit—Saint Michael's Mount, the pirates of Penzance, quaint villages and artists' colonies. I'm game. But I warn you, I balk at shopping. You'll have to do that on your own."

"After that bleak conversation on finances, I won't dare buy a thing," Carla retorted.

96

As they stood on the veranda of the inn, Alan threw his head back and contemplated the sky.

"Unbelievable weather. Let's make the most of it while it lasts."

They did make the most of it—all afternoon, and all next day. When Carla protested about taking Alan from his work, he overrode her objections with a smile and the phrase she was learning to loathe— "Let me worry about that." But he was such a delightful companion that she was willing to overlook his lordly manners. A man who lived with a wishy-washy woman like Elizabeth couldn't help being a male chauvinist. The process of retraining would take a little time, that was all.

On the afternoon of the second day, she forced him into the promised visit to St. Michael's Mount.

"It's the absolute quintessence of dull tourism," he protested. "Everybody goes; you'll be surrounded by trippers, no atmosphere at all. And it's no Mont Saint-Michel, just a rather boring castle and some ruins. It looks much better from a distance."

Despite his dire predictions, Carla enjoyed every moment of the trip, though the little boat was indeed crammed with tourists and the castle did look more impressive from across the bay.

"I don't care what you say, there's something indestructibly romantic about a castle on an island in the sea," she insisted, on the return trip.

"I told you you were a romantic at heart. Let's find a pub. It's too early to dine."

"Alan, I cannot have lunch with you every day, and dinner with you every day, and tea with you—"

"Why not?"

"Because today I am having tea with the vicar," Carla

said, and grinned at his crestfallen expression.

"What about tomorrow?"

"Tomorrow Simon is taking me on a tour of the local antiquities."

"Aha. Do I scent a rival?"

Carla considered a number of replies, and found none of them suitable. His voice was light, but the question had implications that went beyond the words. In fact, she was considerably confused about Alan, and how he felt about her. Their physical relationship had not advanced beyond a few kisses, and although she was not in the habit of falling into bed with every attractive man she met, Alan's failure to follow up his initial advances piqued her a little. Even more important, she was uncertain of her feelings for him. A cooling-off period might not be a bad idea.

He took her silence for a rebuff, and was quiet most of the way home. As they drew up in front of the house, he turned to her with a smile and said cheerfully,

"Actually, I suppose I should spend a few hours working. The weekend is almost upon us; may I see you then?"

"Sure."

"I'll ring you." He leaned across her and opened the door. "Don't get drunk on the vicar's sherry. It's not as good as Walter's."

Carla went in feeling relieved. She liked Alan; she didn't want to be on bad terms with him, especially since he was her lawyer. Was that why he had turned cautious, because he didn't believe in mixing business and pleasure?

She showered quickly and stood brooding over her wardrobe, trying to select something appropriate for an ecclesiastical visit. The afternoon was warm and sticky; with a shrug, she finally selected a flowered sundress. She had nothing demure in her wardrobe, and anyway the vicar hadn't struck her as a particularly prudish man. Rummaging through the dresser drawer for a pair of earrings, she caught sight of the diary, lying where she had tossed it two days ago. Maybe tonight she would have time to read more of it. She had returned late the previous evening, after a tour of the pubs of Falmouth, and had been in no condition to concentrate on Caroline's stilted prose.

When she went downstairs she found Michael in the hall.

"Hurry up," he said. "You're late."

"What's it to you?"

"I also have been invited to tea." He flung open the door with a flourish and a low bow straight out of the formality of "Sleeping Beauty." "Haven't you observed the unusual elegance of my attire?"

"I observe that your shirt is buttoned," Carla said caustically. "And that there are no holes in your jeans. Do you really think the vicar is prepared for all that style?"

He fell in step beside her, thumbs hooked in his belt.

"Let's declare a truce, shall we?"

"I wasn't the one who started the fight," Carla said.

"If you'd stop making remarks about crazy old ladies, we'd get on better."

"I'm sorry about that. It was rude. She's very sweet, and I guess she can't help having a bee in her bonnet."

Michael's eyebrows shot up and he gave her a queer look; but all he said was, "Aren't we in a charitable mood today! I suppose it's the seductive influence of our local Don Juan."

"There you go again! Who's making rude remarks now?"

"Sorry. None of my business. Here, this way. We had better take the path, it's quicker."

"You really know your way around," Carla said, as he led her down a path between tall rhododendron, badly in need of trimming, and across a seemingly trackless field.

"I should. I grew up here."

"I didn't know that."

"A son of the soil, that's me. My mother was only six or seven when Gran came to work here, as a youngish widow. I was born in the house."

He cleared the fence at the bottom of the field in a single flowing leap, so effortlessly beautiful that Carla's breath caught. Then he turned to help her over the stile. She made no comment; it was obvious that he hadn't been showing off, he had just been doing what came naturally.

"I don't understand," she said. "If your mother was Mrs. Pendennis's child, then your name. . . ."

She gulped down the rest of the sentence, as the truth dawned on her. Michael nodded.

"Got it. Would you believe we might be related?"

"You aren't Walter's son!"

"I rather doubt it," Michael said coolly. "But naturally that's what the old biddies in the village have always believed. Even Gran denies knowing who my father was. Walter was damned good to me—supported me, educated me till I was able to take care of myself. I got to know him rather well in his last years, but he never admitted he was my father."

"It doesn't bother you?"

"Why should it?"

"Because people can be very stupid and very cruel," Carla said.

Michael shrugged, the muscles of his shoulders moving like oiled silk under his thin shirt.

"My lower school years were one prolonged fistfight," he admitted. "But I rather enjoyed fighting. After I had established my place in the pecking order, they stopped baiting me. Kids can be cruel, but they have a much more practical view of social relationships than adults do."

They had reached the top of the village street. Michael took her arm.

"Silly-looking shoes, those. You had better hang on to me."

Carla was grateful for his firm grip as they descended. She had worn a pair of high-heeled sandals, to do honor to the vicar, and they were certainly impractical for this steep, uneven slope. They had almost reached the bottom of the hill when the inevitable happened, despite her caution; one foot slid out from under her and her full weight swung from Michael's hand.

His fingers released their hold. Carla had a moment of heart-stopping panic, as the rough stones seemed to rush up at her face; then her right hand caught something solid, and she came to an ignominious stop against the wall of the next house.

Michael stood staring at her, his arms hanging limp. His face had gone white under its tan.

"I'm sorry. Are you all right?"

"Smudged," said Carla, scowling at the streak of whitewash on her skirt. Her heart was pounding, but she had no intention of betraying how badly she had been frightened.

"You could have cracked your skull," Michael said in a queer stifled voice.

"Probably just scraped my knees. Forget it." She reached out to take his arm again. He flinched back as if she had struck at him.

"You'd be better off without my so-called help," he muttered.

"Don't be so dramatic," Carla said crossly. "And this time concentrate on what you're supposed to be doing."

They made it to the bottom without further incident. Michael released his grasp with unflattering promptness.

The paved space at the bottom of the hill extended on the north into a small quay, where boats bobbed at anchor. Between the quay and a shelving curve of rock to the south was the public beach, less crowded than the big beaches of Penzance and Falmouth, but cheerfully littered with browning bodies, bright beach towels, and screaming children chasing one another. The small business area, clustered around the curving side of the plaza, was dominated by the square stone tower of the church.

"Early Perpendicular?" Carla asked, and won a sour smile from Michael.

"Have you been studying up on church architecture to impress John? It's rather a good church, I understand, if you care for such things. The hammer roof is supposed to be better than the one at Saint Ia's."

"Cornish saints have the most bizarre names," Carla said, picking her way across the rough paving stones.

"That's because we're a different race here," her companion said. "Even the vicar is an alien. He came here from Saint Ives two years ago, and his family have lived in Cornwall for only six hundred years."

Carla couldn't be sure whether he was joking or not. His face was perfectly grave.

The vicarage was on a ledge behind the church. John greeted them and ushered them into the parlor, and Carla let out a cry of pleasure. A wide window had been cut into the western wall, framing a magnificent view of the beach and the bay beyond. Clouds, piling up in the sky, were beginning to glow with the crimsons and gold of sunset.

"My predecessor did that," the vicar explained, following her glance. "I'd never have had the courage to meddle with an old house like this. But I enjoy it enormously. The view is never the same, but it is always awe-inspiring, especially when storm clouds gather."

"Thoroughly impractical," Michael said.

"Oh, quite. There are heavy shutters outside, but even so the draft in winter is frightful. It's worth it, however. Now do sit down; I'm sure you must be hungry."

Carla was not hungry. She had had a large lunch, and it was with a sinking heart that she saw the inevitable enormous heap of clotted cream. Her initial enjoyment of the comestible had obviously been reported to every housekeeper in town, and failure to eat it would be a personal slight.

They talked, somewhat stiffly at first, of general topics. Carla thought Michael was behaving quite well until she happened to glance at him and realized that he was doing a caricature of a country boy having tea with the vicar. His faintly anxious expression, as he sat awkwardly balancing a teacup on one knee and a plate of scones on the other, was too much for her; her description of the visit

103

to St. Michael's Mount ended in a spontaneous gurgle of amusement. The vicar, following her gaze, let out a robust laugh.

"Very good, Michael. But if we are boring you, you have only to change the subject."

"It's Carla's fault," Michael explained, removing the endangered cup to a table with a deft flick of the wrist. "She's intimidated by the cloth. You ought to hear the awed tones in which she says, 'The vicar.' And her a Methodist born and bred, I have no doubt."

"How did you know?" Carla asked in surprise.

"It was a reasonable guess," the vicar said with a smile. "John Wesley, the founder of Methodism, converted Cornwall in person and virtually single-handed. The Cornishmen had a wicked reputation in his day; they were smugglers and wreckers of ships, hard-drinking, brawling miners—or equally hard-drinking, brawling country squires. Wesley changed things for the better. There is no doubt that he was a man of great spiritual gifts."

"That's a generous appraisal of a rival," Carla said.

"One really can't look at it that way, can one? Any man who strives for the glory of God and the betterment of his fellow man is not my rival, but my brother in Christ."

Carla put her half-eaten scone back on her plate. The vicar's gentle, aesthetic face relaxed into a wide grin.

"Sorry. I didn't mean to sound pompous."

"You didn't. I'm all choked up," Carla said, returning his smile. Their eyes met in a warm communication of understanding.

"If you two are going to get maudlin, I'm leaving,"

said Michael rudely. "The Cornish are suckers for any new religion—Druids, Roman priests, God knows what all."

"Any country that is often overrun by invaders will see a succession of religions," John said comfortably. "I suppose it is rather tedious to modern young people like yourselves."

"It might have seemed tedious to me at one time," Carla admitted. "But being here, seeing things with my own eyes, and knowing that they are part of my heritage . . . I'm reveling in all of it."

"I'm so glad. Perhaps we ought to divide our forces and really show you Cornwall. I suppose Alan has been concentrating on the more modern bits."

He smiled, and Carla laughed aloud at this candid admission that her activities were well known to the community.

"Well, I did get him to Saint Michael's Mount, as I told you, but it took considerable pressure. He prefers smugglers and highwaymen. I loved the Smugglers' Museum, at Polperro. Tomorrow Simon is taking me on a prehistoric tour. Dolmens and tolmens and fairy rings."

"You couldn't find a better guide. Perhaps another day you might like a tour round the churches. That's my specialty."

"And what do you have to offer?" Carla asked, turning to Michael.

His face closed up like a trap.

"Tomatoes, lettuce, onions," he said, in a singsong like a street peddler. "I haven't time for frivolity. Anyway, I don't know anything about anything. As a guide I'd be useless."

A brief silence followed his statement, which sounded —and was probably meant to sound—unfriendly and critical.

"How is your grandmother?" the vicar asked suddenly.

"Never better."

"Physically, do you mean? I truly hope so. But I am concerned about her mental state. She seems to have succumbed to a most distressing delusion."

Carla looked at him admiringly. He had the ability of a truly compassionate person to bring up difficult subjects without the slightest suggestion of rudeness. Michael accepted the challenge less aggressively than she would have expected, almost as if he had been anticipating an attack and was relieved to have it out in the open.

"I don't understand why everyone is making such a fuss about it," he muttered. "It's no more unreasonable than consulting a fortune-teller, or running one's life according to the astrology columns. A lot of people do such things."

"Perhaps so." The vicar's voice had a new note of quiet authority. "But you must face the fact, Michael, that she is getting on in years. I'm not worried so much about the delusion itself; but as a portent of things to come—"

"Senility, you mean," Michael interrupted.

"That, of course. But that isn't my chief concern, not while you are there to look after her. What concerns me is the possibility—remote, I admit, but present—that she might be driven to act on her delusion."

Michael's head swung toward Carla. His eyes narrowed. The message in them was as clear to her as a verbal pronouncement. She remained silent, not because of the implicit threat, but. . . . She didn't know why.

Michael turned back to the vicar. "You can't mean to imply that that poor old woman might harm someone."

"Oh, dear me, no. We all know that Mrs. Pendennis is incapable of any antisocial act. Her loyalty to the family. . . . No, no. I only feared she might harm herself, or worry herself into a stroke. How seriously does she take this legend, do you suppose?"

Michael was stubbornly silent, his eyes on the floor. Carla was sympathetic; but she felt she had done enough by keeping quiet about the seaweed incident.

"She takes it very seriously," she said bluntly. "Either that, or she is putting on quite an act, which I don't believe. Look, maybe you two ought to discuss this sometime when I'm not around."

"But you are concerned," John said, in tones of surprise.

Carla started to say that naturally she was concerned about the old woman, when the real meaning of the vicar's comment struck her. He didn't mean interested; he meant involved. She felt as if he had flung a heavy coil of rope around her. When she had joked about playing lady of the manor, she had not realized what that role meant. It meant responsibility, and she didn't want it, any more than she wanted the unrealistic glamour the term had first suggested to her.

The vicar failed to notice her reaction. He took it for granted that she knew her duty and would do it.

"I really feel that we ought not ignore the situation," he said earnestly, winding another loop of rope around Carla's conscience with the casual pronoun.

"But what can we do?" she demanded, almost angrily.

107

"I can't help it if she thinks I'm Lady Caroline returned from a watery grave. Good heavens, I think it's a horrible idea."

"Ah, so that is how the fantasy began," John said. "She has mentioned the legend before, but I felt certain something had happened recently to set her off. Um—er—at the risk of sounding pedantic, may I inquire, Carla, whether you actually do resemble the lady?"

"How should I know? There is a portrait—I guess it's supposed to be a portrait of Caroline—but it looks like nobody in particular. It's all faded and dark."

"Of course. But I'm afraid that doesn't help. People see what they expect to see, Carla; when Mrs. Pendennis looks at that portrait she sees your features. What really bothers me is her insistence on a specific date. Unless you do leave before Midsummer Eve—"

"I have no intention of doing that," Carla said aggressively, and then caught herself in surprise. Until that precise moment she had had no idea what she planned to do. The words had come out spontaneously, as if spoken by another personality using her vocal cords.

"I'm glad you'll be staying," the vicar said pleasantly. "It would be a pity to cut your visit short. But I do feel we ought to endeavor to get Mrs. Pendennis's fancy out of her mind before that time."

"But how?" Carla asked again.

"My ideas are amorphous," John admitted. "One possibility might be to investigate the origin of the legend. If it can be proved to be a relatively modern invention —concocted, perhaps, by the brother of the deceased lady for purposes of his own—"

"There speaks the eternal optimist," Michael growled. "You can't combat fantasy with logic, John."

"At least the truth might reassure Carla," said the vicar, with a sudden shrewd look at that young woman. Taken aback, she shook her head violently.

"I don't need reassuring. What do you take me for?"

"It can't do any harm," John insisted. "I don't suppose you are really disturbed, but the situation is not a comfortable one for you. At worst we may discover some interesting bits of folklore. Have either of you any other ideas?"

"I'll keep an eye on her," Michael muttered.

"Yes, you must do that. And with your permission, I will consult Simon." Michael said nothing. His look, however, was darkly antagonistic, and the vicar continued firmly, "He already knows the situation, Michael, and your grandmother speaks more candidly to him than she does to me. Indeed, it was a conversation with him that aroused my concern. He takes this more seriously than I was inclined to do."

"Oh, hell, discuss it with the whole village," Michael snapped. "What difference does it make? Come along, Carla, it's getting late."

"Much as I would like to detain you, I think you had better go," the vicar agreed. Apparently he was accustomed to Michael's moods. "The weather is worsening."

Carla had been so absorbed in the conversation she had failed to notice the fading light. Now she realized that the clouds had settled and were beginning to drift in as low banks of fog.

The vicar took her hand as she made her farewells.

"Do have a look around the house," he urged. "Old manuscripts, family histories, diaries. . . . Is something wrong?"

"No. I'll look, John, and let you know what I find."

"Very good. Oh, by the way, Michael, I forgot to ask —did your friend find you? I met him on the highway this afternoon and gave him directions."

"Friend?" Michael, wrapped in some dark thought of his own, started. "Oh. Yes, he found me. Thanks. Come on, Carla."

The village, so quaint and pleasant in the sunlight, was quite another place under a cloudy sky. The gray stone had darkened, and the narrow windows looked withdrawn and hostile. The beach was almost deserted; only a few diehards lingered, and the dim light had taken the color from their gay bathing suits and towels.

Michael did not take her arm when they began the ascent. Carla wasn't afraid of falling on an upward path, but she stepped carefully.

Neither of them spoke at first. Carla had plenty to occupy her thoughts. She wished the vicar had not raised the subject of Mrs. Pendennis's delusions. She had almost forgotten them during the past carefree days, and she was inclined to subscribe to the ostrich theory. You could make things a lot worse by thinking about them too much. So maybe she was selfish; but it would never have occurred to her that there might be any harm in Mrs. Pendennis's wild ideas. A practical joke now and then, perhaps, but she could take that in her stride. Now that it had been suggested the housekeeper might come to harm as a result of her fancies, Carla's Methodist conscience would not allow her to ignore it.

Apparently Michael observed her abstraction but misinterpreted its cause. As they reached the top of the hill and turned into the lane, now filled with drifting wisps of white mist, he said,

"About that friend of mine. . . . I hope you don't mind if he stays on for a few days. He's sleeping in the stable —he has his own camping gear—and he can eat his meals in the village if you'd rather. . . ."

The ingratiating, awkward tone was quite unlike his usual voice. Carla found it disturbing.

"It's no concern of mine," she answered shortly. "You'd better ask your grandmother."

"She's not the lady of the house."

"Well, I don't care. So long as he doesn't set fire to the stables while he's under the influence."

"He doesn't drink . . . much."

"I wasn't thinking of liquor."

"I gathered as much. You believe he's one of my 'artistic' friends, and therefore prone to all sorts of perversions. At least you would consider them perversions."

They had left the path and were crossing the field; the fog had closed in, bringing damp, clammy air with it. It was not too thick as yet, but objects at a distance were shrouded in a pallid veiling.

"I do consider drugs somewhat perverse," Carla answered sharply. "Anything beyond an occasional joint, anyway. Your other habits are no business of mine."

Michael broke into an unexpected peal of laughter.

"He's not my boyfriend, if that's what you're thinking."

"That never entered my mind," Carla said truthfully. It wasn't always easy to be sure; she had been fooled before. But somehow she had no doubt whatsoever that Michael's habits were heterosexual.

They reached the stile over the fence. This time Michael climbed it in orthodox fashion. Carla followed;

after a moment's hesitation, Michael offered her a hand.

"I shouldn't have worn these stupid shoes," she said, tottering.

"They look good on you," Michael said. "You have nice legs, and the ankles of a true aristocrat, as Walter might have said."

"Why—thanks. What brought on this sudden burst of charm?"

"I have a favor to ask," Michael said coolly.

"Oh?"

"I want you to sell me your house."

"What?" Carla stumbled, in sheer surprise. Michael righted her effortlessly.

"I haven't much cash," he admitted. "But we could work it out. Monthly payments, or something of the sort. Well?"

"What on earth would you do with it?"

"Turn it into a hotel—one of those quaint country inns that charges exorbitant rates to naive American tourists." And as she continued to stare at him, he continued, "It would work out, I think. Worth trying, anyhow. Well, good Lord, what else could one do with the place?"

"I can't imagine. No one but an impractical idiot would want to buy it. No offense meant."

Michael's eyelids dropped, veiling his eyes. He had long lashes, thick and black.

"None taken. Think about it, anyhow."

"You had better talk to Alan. He's my lawyer."

"He doesn't like me," Michael said plaintively.

"He's a businessman; if it's a reasonable offer, he'll consider it. I couldn't agree to anything without consulting him. You might try to cheat me."

"So I might. You could influence his decision, though. I'd consider it a favor, Carla. Gran doesn't have many more years left. I'd like her to end her days in the place that has been home to her for most of her life."

Carla looked at him suspiciously. His expression was quite serious, but she had learned that Michael was not to be trusted. Surely he didn't expect her to buy that sentimental speech.

"I'll think about it," she said.

"Thanks. I'll see you later."

They had reached the front door. Michael walked off without another word, hands in his pockets, and the thickening mists closed around him with an eerie suggestion of vanishment.

II

Carla was glad to stay in that evening. The climate of her ancestral homeland was certainly nothing to brag about—hot and summery one moment, clammy and cold by the end of the same day. Actually it wasn't cold, it was only damp and depressing, with cottony fog pressing in against the house. When Mrs. Pendennis suggested she might like a little fire in her room, just for company, Carla was glad to accept.

Newly reminded of the housekeeper's foibles, she watched her unobtrusively during dinner. The results of her surveillance were not reassuring. It was pitiful to watch Mrs. Pendennis's struggle to maintain her self-control when the slightest sound made her start, and her eyes kept wandering to the fog-shrouded windows. Pallid wraiths of mist moved against the glass as if demanding entry, until finally Mrs. Pendennis ordered Mary to draw the curtains. Michael did not appear at all.

Carla excused herself as soon as dinner was over. Her room was a refuge—cozy and bright, with a small fire flickering on the hearth. She put on a loose robe and got ready for bed. It was ridiculously early, but she was looking forward to climbing into the big comfortable bed with a book. Before she did so, however, she opened the French windows. A long tendril of fog curled in, like an ectoplasmic arm. Carla ducked under it and went onto the balcony.

She might have stepped into another world, a world of ghostly shadows and strange muted sounds. She was in a narrow cell, walled in on three sides by white mist. No wonder the dwellers in this sea-beleaguered country invented aquatic myths, when the water that surrounded them invaded the land in so many forms. The sights and sounds of the normal world were blotted out or monstrously altered by the mist. The murmur of the surf, far below, might have been wailing voices, and an occasional gust of wind set the white fog churning, as if something invisible struggled to be free.

An eerie glow lit the sky like a dim aurora. After it had brightened and faded several times, Carla realized it must be a lighthouse, possibly the one at Land's End, warning ships off the reefs that still claimed lives every year. She pitied anyone who was foolish or desperate enough to be out on the water on such a night. With a shiver she retreated into the bright sanctuary of her room, bolted the French doors, and drew the curtains. Now she was prepared to face Caroline Tregellas's diary.

An hour later she was ready to consign the book and its writer to the particular part of hell reserved for bores and bigots, and she had decided that if she had to be someone's reincarnation, she would rather it were not Caroline's. Had the girl really been as stuffy and prissy as her diary made her sound? All she did was babble on about the beauties of nature and the dull books she had been reading and the dull people who came to take tea. Even her raptures about her fiancé were as stilted as if they had been copied verbatim from a book.

Impatiently Carla flipped through the pages until she reached the final entry. There was more poignancy in the blank leaves than in anything the girl had written. However dull she might have been, she did not expect, or deserve, to die young, with all the ripe promise of life unfulfilled.

And that, Carla thought, is a phrase Caroline might have written! She was about to toss the book aside when she saw a slim break in the even surface of the edge, a slight separation of the pages as if something had been placed between them.

It was a piece of paper, folded twice, so that it bulked large enough to separate the pages just that little bit. Like the paper of the diary, it was yellow with age; the roughened surface of the folds suggested that the message had been read and reread.

Carla was conscious of a curious quickening of her pulse as she delicately unfolded the paper, though she suspected it would only prove to be a poem, or love letter, from dear William.

It was poetry, but not a love poem. No, not even poetry—the lines were sheer doggerel.

Go to the western gate at set of sun
On Midsummer Eve, and wait for what will come.

Underneath, in quite a different hand from the harsh, spiky writing of the verse, were inscribed the words, "Deliver us from the terror that walks by night. It grows stronger each day, and God does not help."

The writing was so tremulous and distorted that it was impossible to identify it, but Carla felt sure Caroline had written the final words; they might have been prompted by genuine anguish, but they had the same self-consciously theatrical quality she associated with her ancestress's writing.

Her hair wasn't standing on end, and her spine felt quite warm—not a single trickle of icy terror there—yet the insert was a disquieting discovery. It suggested that Caroline had been afraid of something during the six months before her disappearance. The western gate was the one that looked over the sea. "Wait for what will come. . . ." There was a shuddery suggestion in that phrase. But if Caroline had written the comment, who had written the verse? The handwriting was quite unlike hers.

Carla put the book down and swung her legs out from under the covers. She was not at all nervous; not at all. But she had to visit the bathroom before she went to sleep, and she had a feeling that if she didn't do it right away, she wouldn't dare get out of bed till daylight. It cost her a distinct effort to swing her legs down toward the floor. She found herself remembering a ghost story she had once read about a girl whose ankle had been seized by something that came out from under the bed. Why was there horror in the very vagueness of a word or a phrase? "Something. . . ." "What will come. . . ."

The humdrum but useful fittings of the bathroom

wiped away her morbid thoughts. There was comfort, too, in the fact that the door had a bolt on the inside. She took her time bathing and brushing her teeth, and used all the creams and lotions she carried with her but seldom had the time or the vanity to use. When she had finished she unbolted the door and stepped out into the hall.

Uneasiness touched her then, as she looked at the door of her room. Surely she had left it open. Perhaps the wind had blown it shut. She looked right and left along the dark corridor. There was not the slightest hint of a breeze or draft.

So it had swung shut by itself, Carla told herself. Doors in old houses did that sometimes. She turned the knob and opened the door.

The room looked normal enough, except that the fog had begun to filter in; a gray haze hung shoulder high, shifting a little as the opening door moved the air currents. Carla took a few cautious steps into the room. She was beginning to feel distinctly peculiar, yet there was no obvious reason for the sudden increase in her breathing. The bedside lamp was still burning, the draperies hung still and unmoving. The fire had died down to coals; that was why the room seemed darker. . . .

She took a few more faltering steps; and then a sharp reverberant knock sounded from somewhere close at hand. Carla's cosmetic bag dropped from her nerveless fingers and she turned in the direction from which the sound had come. Her head was spinning and her knees had gone wobbly, but her senses were operating with abnormal acuteness. She heard the snap of dying embers in the fireplace, tasted-mint flavored toothpaste—and saw something impossible. On the wall beside her, moved from its original position, was the portrait, in its heavy carved frame. But the face was no longer dim and impassive. Its eyes were wide and its mouth was open in a silent scream of terror; and despite the distortion of fear, the features were, unmistakably, her own.

SIX

IN the first moments, waking was only a continuation of the nightmare she had been having, a dream of watery green depths in which she drifted with the mindless motion of the current. Her face was wet and her hair clung damply to her head; when she opened her mouth to shout a protest, water trickled down her throat and she choked.

She opened her eyes, saw Michael's face, magnified into grotesqueness by its proximity to her own, and squeezed her lids shut again.

"No, you don't," he grunted, and dragged her to her feet.

"Leave me alone."

"No. Sit up straight and pay attention."

He dropped her into a chair and pushed her upright when she started to sag. Carla choked again as hot coffee scorched her lips. Finally she regained enough strength to push his hand away and take a more intelligent interest in the proceedings.

The sky was gray with dawn light. It was still foggy outside. The French doors were wide open and the room was clammy with mist. Michael stood before her, hands on his hips, glaring.

"An occasional joint now and then," he quoted; and Carla recognized her own words. "If that's your idea of an occasional joint. . . . What are you using?"

"Using?" Carla pushed dripping hair from her eyes. "You didn't have to drown me, did you?"

"You were dead to the world. I thought you had sense enough to go to bed before you spaced yourself out. That floor is hard."

The meaning of his words finally penetrated Carla's brain. She sat upright.

"Spaced out! I didn't take anything. It was the portrait. . . ."

It hung where it had hung on the first night she arrived. A square of painted canvas, flat, dark with age. Carla shook her head.

"Do you want me to tell you what happened?" she asked. "Or have you already made up your mind not to believe me?"

"You were damned hard to awaken," Michael said slowly. "But I might accept a fainting spell, or something of the sort."

"I tell you I'm not taking any kind of drug. How can I convince you?" On a sudden impulse she pushed up the sleeve of her nightgown and displayed a smooth, blue-veined arm.

"Okay," Michael said, the corners of his mouth twitching. "I didn't think you were shooting heroin. Sleeping pills, tranquilizers—aren't they the American middle-class vice?"

"Go ahead and look through my things. I've never taken sleeping pills in my life."

"All right, I believe you. What happened?"

Carla told him, in bald, sparse words. She expected a skeptical sneer, or a jeering comment; but Michael's face remained impassive.

"Hallucination," he said, when she had finished.

"No."

"The point about a hallucination is that you think it's real."

"I tell you, someone moved that picture. It was on the other wall, near the door to the iron staircase."

"When?"

"I'm trying to remember." Carla rubbed her forehead. "I didn't notice it when I came up to my room; it might have been moved by then, although I don't think so."

"Then Mary might have moved it, sometime during the day."

"Why should she? There's another thing. Did you open the French doors?" Michael shook his head. Carla went on, "Neither did I. They were closed, and locked, when I went to the bathroom."

"You're not making sense," Michael said. "First you insist that what you saw was not a hallucination—that the portrait actually came to life and gibbered at you. Then you imply that someone was in your room last night. Make up your mind; is it ghosts or burglars?"

"You're the one who is refusing to consider the facts," Carla retorted. "I tell you, someone moved that picture! Maybe I did imagine what I saw. . . . I must have imagined that part, mustn't I? But someone moved it, and someone opened the doors to the balcony."

Michael started to speak and then closed his mouth, tilting his head to study Carla suspiciously.

"Well, say it," she exclaimed angrily. "Whatever you were thinking. Don't spare my feelings at this late date."

"I was just thinking what a neat, consistent ghost story it makes," Michael answered. "The watery lover, floating in on the fog. . . . The dead girl, trying to warn her successor. . . ."

"You don't really believe that."

Michael didn't answer for a moment.

"Tell me once more what happened. In detail."

"I don't see what—"

"Tell me."

Carla went over it all again. Michael cross-questioned her like a prosecuting attorney. If there was any particular direction to his questions, Carla failed to see it— except for the general air of skepticism that pervaded everything he said and did. He was brooding over the note she had found in the diary, turning it in his hands, when she finally lost patience and ordered him out. He went without argument, remarking, "Go back to bed. You look bloody awful."

Carla had to overcome an inclination to stay up, just to spite him. Telling herself this was childish, she snuggled down under the covers, realizing only then how chilled she was, in body and in mind. "I'll never get to sleep," she told herself.

She awoke two hours later to find the room flooded with cheerful light. The sun had burned off the fog, and the occurrence of the past night seemed like a weird dream.

Carla got dressed and out of the room as quickly as she

could, without looking at the portrait. The breakfast room was deserted, which was not surprising, considering the hour, so she went to the kitchen, where she found Mrs. Polreath and Mary at the table, drinking tea. Mary gave her a grin and a cheery good morning and continued to sit, her elbows on the table. Mrs. Polreath stood up.

"Mr. Michael said you'd been taken poorly in the night," she said. "I do hope you're better."

"I feel fine," Carla said shortly. She wondered how Michael had accounted for his knowledge of her nocturnal activities. From Mary's knowing smile she suspected the worst; but then Mary always looked that way. "No, thank you, Mrs. Polreath, I just want coffee."

"It won't take any time to cook eggs and bacon, Miss Tregellas," the cook offered.

"No, really. I'm going out in a little while. I've been overeating ever since I arrived; you all cook too well."

Seeing that her presence inhibited the other women, who had been in the midst of a pleasant gossip, she drank her coffee quickly, lingering only long enough to ask Mary if she had happened to move the portrait. Mary's smile faded.

"No, miss, I didn't. Why would I do such a thing?"

"It must have been Mrs. Pendennis, then," Carla said. "I suppose she thought it would look better on the other wall."

She went out, leaving the two women staring uneasily at one another.

The world looked newly washed and hung out to dry. Water dripped from the eaves and branches. The sun-sprayed leaves sparkled like emeralds as the breeze stirred them. Carla took a deep breath. It was difficult to remember the terrors of the night, impossible to think of a sensible explanation for them.

She started down the weed-grown path toward the kitchen garden. There were several points she wanted to raise with Michael. He was altogether too facile with explanations, and too available in times of crisis.

When she pushed through the gate into the garden, with its neat rows of greenery, she saw a bare brown back bent over the beans. It was a tanned, muscular back; but she knew it did not belong to Michael even before the man, alerted by the creaking gate, raised himself to a standing position.

His face was tanned as evenly as his back, which was unusual; most redheads do not tan easily, especially those who have hair of the rare, flaming Little Orphan Annie shade. The coppery-red locks framed a face of astonishing but ingenuous ugliness. His nose looked as if it had been broken, and badly set; his mouth appeared to be twice the normal length. A pair of big, thoughtful brown eyes regarded her speculatively. Then the mouth opened in a smile of dazzling brilliance.

"Well, hello. You must be Carla."

"Who are you?" Carla demanded.

"Timothy O'Hara. I'm a friend of Mike's." Then, when Carla did not reply, the smile faded into a look of pathetic anxiety. "He said he'd asked you if it was okay for me to stay here. I'm trying to earn my keep, but I must admit I don't know a plant from a weed."

"Michael did mention you. Are you really sleeping in the stable?"

"Sure. I'm on a walking tour of dear old England. That's a euphemism for hitchhiking, actually. I don't walk unless I have to. I have to more than I'd like, and I've slept in a lot worse places than your stable. I appreciate it. Hope you don't mind."

Despite her suspicions of Michael Pendennis and anything related to him, Carla could not help but warm to the amiable smile with which she was being regarded.

"No, I don't mind. But really, Mr. O'Hara—"

"Tim. Mr. O'Hara makes me feel like *Gone With the Wind.* "

"Well—Tim. It must be awfully damp in the stable. Does the roof leak?"

"A little."

"It seems silly for you to be in a sleeping bag in the stable when the house is so big. There's plenty of room."

"You wouldn't mind?" The big brown eyes widened till they looked like the eyes of a kindly cow. "That's great, Carla."

"I thought I'd save you the trouble of making up a sad story," Carla explained. "I suppose you were planning to cough a lot?"

Tim threw back his fiery head and shouted with laughter.

"Am I that obvious? No, don't tell me. Frankly, I'd give anything—except money, which I don't have—to sleep in a bed again. I've been on the road for ten days, and I am not the outdoor type."

"Then why are you on the road?"

"I wanted to see the world." Tim leaned picturesquely on a hoe and beamed at her. Carla realized that he was younger than she had thought—in his early twenties, probably. "I've got six younger siblings and a very tired set of parents; next fall I've got to settle down and help the old folks put the other kids through college. This is my last fling before settling down to a life of grinding toil."

"You're breaking my heart," Carla said. "How did you meet Michael?"

"He's a friend of a friend, actually. When you're seeing England on less than five dollars a day, you scrounge up all the contacts you possibly can. It costs me that much just to eat—and I don't mean in restaurants."

"You look healthy enough," Carla said unsympathetically.

"Enough for what? While we're on that subject, how about going into Penzance with me tonight—see some of the night life?"

"On five dollars?"

"I'm planning to browse among your vegetables for a few days, so I'm a little ahead. Of course we could go Dutch, if you insist."

His grin was hard to resist, but Carla hardened her heart.

"Save up your money, and then we'll see," she said, turning to go.

"Wait a sec. Did you really mean it, about moving into the house? Mike's grannie scares me speechless; mean, sweet old ladies always do. I don't want to face her unless you—"

"I'll talk to Mrs. Pendennis."

Carla was halfway back to the house before she realized that she had forgotten her original purpose for going to the garden, and that by some mysterious power, without even a direct request, the ingenuous Timothy O'Hara had not only conned her into inviting him to stay, but had turned her, like an obedient robot, to make the necessary arrangements.

Charm was a weak word for what Timothy O'Hara had. Subliminal hypnotism was more like it. Carla smiled to herself and turned away from the house. It was hard to resent Tim's machinations, but they were about as innocent as the lures meat-eating plants spread out in order to attract victims. She was not going to be one of the victims.

She found Michael in a remote part of the grounds. He was on his hands and knees digging, or so she surmised; his back was toward her, and for a few moments she stood watching the ripple of muscle across his shoulders with detached admiration. Really, she thought wryly, most women would sell their souls for a summer like this one: not one, not two, but four attractive men in close proximity—five, if you counted the vicar, and you certainly could count the vicar, if you liked the gentle aesthetic type. It was almost as if fate had presented her with a sampling of the best of the crop. Alan, handsome, sophisticated, masterful; Tim, deliciously homely, irresistibly friendly; Michael, dark and brooding, with a body like a Michelangelo sculpture; Simon, sweet and blond and dedicated. . . . It sounds like a soap opera, she thought irritably, and coughed.

Still on his hands and knees, Michael turned and smiled amiably. Carla was relieved to see him in a good mood, though she reminded herself that there was no reason why he shouldn't be.

"Isn't it late to plant vegetables?" she asked.

"This is pleasure, not business. Or you could call it intellectual curiosity." Michael sat back on his heels. "Come and have a look."

There had once been a flower garden in this secluded

corner, fenced in by evergreen hedges. They were now rank and uncontrolled, with large patches of dead wood that needed trimming, but they were still sturdy enough to cut off the sunlight and give the place a dank, shadowy atmosphere. Brambly branches scraped Carla's legs as she picked her way through the weeds. Here and there a bright spot of crimson or pink raised a brave head above the tangle—roses, defying nature and neglect.

Michael had cleared a space about six feet square. At first Carla could see only a jumble of loose pebbles or chips covering the area. Then a patch of pattern caught her eye—a pattern recognizable because it was a motif her mind had been preoccupied with—the sinuous curve of a scaly, finned body.

Careless of her clean slacks, she dropped to her knees next to Michael. He was holding a brush, and as Carla leaned forward he swept it delicately across another section of the crumbling paving, and swore under his breath as several fragments shifted.

"Damn Walter. All this in his backyard, and he let it fall apart while he was concentrating on wine and wenching."

"What is it?" Carla whispered.

"Oh, it's Roman, undoubtedly." Michael glanced at her, brushing a lock of damp hair away from his forehead; and then, as she continued to look blank, he said, "It's a mosaic pavement, stupid. Or rather the remains of one. Look here."

He picked up a watering can and dribbled water over a section of fragments. It was as if the picture sprang into existence out of the ground; the water cleaned off a layer of dirt and brightened the colors of the tiny stones. Carla shied back.

128

"An octopus."

"Right. Over here. . . ." His finger traced the broken design. "This looks like a Nereid or nymph riding on a dolphin."

"All sea creatures. . . ."

"So it seems," Michael said briskly. "I don't know whether it can be restored or not. Most of the bits of stone seem to be here; perhaps we can put them back, like a jigsaw puzzle."

"Why bother?"

Michael's eyelids drooped; his long, thick lashes veiled his eyes.

"Why not? It might be valuable. Roman remains are scarce in Cornwall. This was a backwater even in the second century."

"A nice tourist attraction for your hotel?" Carla had recovered her self-possession. Her voice was sharp, denying fantasy.

"Right again. The first thing is to build a shelter over this, before it deteriorates any further. I'll do that today. It won't cost you anything," he added, with a sidelong glance. "I can get some old lumber from the outbuildings. They will have to be torn down anyway."

"I wasn't worrying about that."

"Then what are you worrying about? I thought you agreed with John that we should investigate the legend. It's possible that this very pavement—which was in fairly good condition until recently—started the story. The sea theme, I mean."

"Oh, I hadn't thought about that. But I wanted to talk to you about John's suggestion."

"What's to talk about?" Michael returned to his work.

129

His long, lean fingers moved delicately in their finicky task.

"You didn't seem too enthusiastic about the idea at first."

"I've had time to think about it. It's probably a good idea. Harmless and mildly interesting at the worst; and it just might keep poor old Gran from having a stroke along about the twenty-third of June."

His tone was mild and reasonable, his reasoning excellent. Carla could not have explained why she didn't believe a word he was saying.

"I don't suppose you've had time to tell Alan Fairman about my offer," Michael went on, his head still bent over his work.

"No. I'll probably see him this weekend."

Michael started to hum. Carla recognized the tune; it was not a ballet theme, but one of the Rolling Stones' comparatively melodious offerings, and it was obviously intended to put an end to their conversation.

Time was getting on, anyway. After groveling in the garden she would have to bathe and change. She retreated, with a last hostile glance at Michael's apparently oblivious black head.

The encounter had delayed her, and Simon was waiting in the drawing room when she came back downstairs. He gave her jeans and cotton shirt an approving look.

"Good. We'll be covering some rather rough terrain today. If you're man enough. I mean—"

"I'm man enough," Carla said, laughing. "The English language really is chauvinist, isn't it?"

"We're trying," Simon said plaintively. "I promise not

to take your arm, or help you over any fences; and if you are attacked by a wild bull, you're on your own."

"Fair enough."

It turned out to be one of the most enjoyable afternoons she had ever spent, the sort that leaves a sharp, undying imprint on the memory. Simon took her first to Chysauster, a prehistoric village dating between 100 B.C. and 100 A.D.; and Carla, who had never had the slightest interest in archaeology, felt a curious thrill at the sight of the massive stone walls, some of them six feet high. The eight houses, ranged along either side of a wide street, were each built around a central courtyard. Carla ran her fingers along a row of rough stones, and turned to see Simon watching her.

"Having an attack of déjà vu?" he asked.

"I guess that's what it is. As if I had been here before."

"Scientists explain the feeling by claiming that you must have read about the place, or seen something resembling it."

"Do you believe that?"

"No; but then I'm hopelessly romantic. A great part of our brain is terra incognita, you know, its function unknown. What if that portion is packed with memories —not only our own forgotten experiences, but those of our ancestors?"

"Ancestral memory," Carla said thoughtfully.

Simon shrugged and reached for his cigarette case.

"It makes more sense than vague ideas of reincarnation. Walter traced your family genealogy back to the thirteenth century; God knows how much farther back it would go if records had been properly kept. Someone has to be descended from the people who lived in these houses. Why shouldn't you be one of them?"

"I thought I was descended from a Roman princess," Carla said, half jokingly.

"The Romans intermarried—and interbred, without benefit of clergy—with the local people they found here, as earlier conquerors had done. We're all mongrels, Carla; all of us have some grunting caveman or other for an ancestor." His blue eyes were dreamy, fixed on some invisible object beyond normal vision.

Suddenly he started and dropped his cigarette, which had burned down in his hand. Carla laughed, and Simon smiled ruefully as he blew on his scorched fingers.

"A proper fate for a dreamer—to have his fingers burned. Have you seen enough? Let's proceed to the next stop."

"Where are we going now?" Carla asked.

"Fifteen hundred years in time, and a good long walk," Simon said.

He wasn't joking about the walk. The path led from the little village of Madron, where they left the car, across fields and over fences, through meadows and streams, always climbing. Carla found the going hard, but did not say so; and Simon, true to his promise, did not insult her by offering a helping hand. He was irritatingly unshort of breath, though he was carrying the heavy picnic basket his housekeeper had filled for them.

Presently Carla saw looming up on the horizon a massive structure that looked like a great stone bench. The cromlech was only a few yards from the high road. The massive capstone, seventeen feet long, was supported by three stubby granite slabs. Carla studied it for a while and then said disparagingly,

"As cromlechs go, this isn't much. Why is it so low to the ground?"

"It collapsed in the nineteenth century," Simon explained, looking a little hurt at her criticism. "When they put the capstone back in place, they had to shorten the supports. I'm sorry you don't like it."

"It's really very nice," Carla said.

Simon laughed. "No, you were right the first time. I've seen better cromlechs." He struck a dramatic attitude, the picnic basket held at arm's length, and declaimed,

"What mighty dead lies here,
Lone on this moorland drear,
Where, from o'er Morvah's sullen-moaning seas,
O'er cairn-crowned heights rolls on the unceasing
        breeze
In mystic, wild career?
Haply here is the grave,
Of Briton warrior—"

"That's enough," Carla said. "I retract my rude remarks. It's the grave of a warrior brave, and I shouldn't have spoken frivolously."

"Might be one of your ancestors," Simon pointed out.

Skirting the monument, they struck off across the field. Now Simon took her arm.

"There are abandoned mine shafts all over the place," he said casually. "See the engine house on the hill over there? That was the Ding Dong mine, one of the oldest in the county. We can lunch there, or we can go on another half mile or so and share our sandwiches with the Nine Maidens."

"The poor girls you told me about, who were turned to stone for dancing on the Sabbath?"

"Yes. We may as well go on; there's nothing much to see at the mine except the engine house, and that's outside the scope of today's tour. Far too modern."

Carla was out of breath by the time they reached the monument of the maidens. Six of the original stones were still standing; three of the girls had subsided since the circle was named.

"I hope you're feeling peckish," Simon said, as he began to unpack the lunch. "Mrs. Chynoweth seems to have given us enough food for an army, and I daren't take any of it back for fear of hurting her feelings."

Carla wiped her perspiring brow and assured him that her appetite was in excellent condition. The weather was perfect, sunny and breezy. Keeping up with Simon's long legs and experienced hiker's stride had been hard work.

They lunched on Cornish pasties and beer, fruit and seedy cake. Simon left the remains of the feast, which was indeed ample for several people, atop one of the fallen stones, with appropriate words of offering. They walked off some of the food returning to the car, and then drove west to see Boscawen-Un, another Bronze Age stone circle. Simon seemed to be tireless; and although Carla was honestly interested, she began to flag after a few more antique monuments. It was with considerable relief that she heard Simon announce that they would stop in Mousehole for tea.

"It's not prehistoric, but it's frightfully, frightfully quaint," he explained.

The town was quaint, and Carla loved it. They had tea in a shop by the tiny harbor, and Carla was ashamed to find that she was quite able to eat her share of the tea cakes, warm from the oven and redolent of spices.

"I won't be able to fit into any of my clothes, if this goes on," she complained thickly, through a mouthful of cake.

"You could easily gain a few pounds," her companion said, looking her over. "Mind you, I've no complaints about the present contours, but as a doctor. . . ."

"Don't you think I look healthy?"

"Oh, quite. You don't have any—problems, do you?"

"You mean with Mrs. Pendennis and the family curse?" Carla looked at the last cake, struggled briefly with her conscience, and succumbed. Simon ran his fingers through his tousled hair and let out a long breath.

"I'm relieved you aren't brooding about it. I wasn't sure. . . ."

"Why the hell should I brood about it?" Carla demanded, unreasonably annoyed. "Is there something I don't know, or do you really believe I'm neurotic enough to get upset about a silly fairy tale?"

"My dear girl! I didn't mean to give you any such impression. Surely you realize it's Mrs. Pendennis I'm concerned about?"

"What do you think she's going to do?" Carla asked angrily. "Everyone keeps throwing out dire hints, but you're all so vague. . . . I'm sorry she's cracking up, but I don't see what I can do about it. I am not going to cut short the first vacation I've had in years because of a senile old woman. If she's liable to have a heart attack or something like that, she ought to be in a nursing home."

"I couldn't do that to her," Simon said quietly. "Even

if I had the authority, which I do not, it would be the equivalent of a death sentence to a woman of her pride."

Carla's eyes fell. "I'm sorry. I wouldn't do it either. But honestly, Simon—"

"You still don't understand," Simon said. "You've got it all backwards, Carla."

Then Carla did understand. The knowledge came as no surprise; it was as if it had been in her mind all along.

"You think she might hurt me? That is really wild, Simon. Don't tell me Lady Caroline had a sweet old housekeeper from whom Mrs. Pendennis just happens to be descended."

Simon laughed self-consciously.

"Your imagination is even better than mine. No; Mrs. Pendennis comes from Sussex, I believe. Her husband was the Cornishman. But damn it, Carla, you can't entirely dismiss the possibility that in an effort to save you from what she considers a very real and terrible danger, she might do something harmful."

"She'd have to be crazy to do a thing like that. You're the doctor; is she crazy?"

"I could be Sigmund Freud himself and still be unable to answer that one. She has delusions, certainly. Whether they could slip over into paranoia. . . ."

"Thanks a lot," Carla said. Simon reached across the table and took her hands.

"I'd rather anticipate the most farfetched improbability, and be prepared for it, than risk anything happening to you. I'd never forgive myself, Carla."

Carla's hands relaxed in his warm, hard clasp. His blue eyes were anxious. Such a lovely blue, the shade of cornflowers, of Kashmir sapphires, of Siamese cats' eyes.

"Nothing will happen," she said gently.

"Just be on your guard. She looks harmless and frail, but it doesn't take any strength to close and lock a door. There are rooms in that old ruin no one has entered for fifty years."

"Someone would find me. Michael and Tim are there—"

"Tim?"

"He's a friend of Michael. An American, in England on vacation."

"What's his last name?"

"O'Hara."

Simon shook his head.

"I don't know him. Michael has his own problems, Carla. Don't be so quick to accept people."

"Are you warning me against Michael now?"

"Oh, hell, I seem to be saying all the wrong things today." With a rueful grimace Simon released her hands. "I suppose I'm warning you against life. Don't trust anyone; isn't that the usual rule?"

"How about the vicar?" Carla asked.

Simon's face relaxed into a smile. "If you can't trust John, you can't trust anyone."

"What do you think of his suggestion that we investigate the legend?"

"It probably won't change Mrs. Pendennis, but it can't do any harm. Might even be interesting. Have you come up with anything as yet?"

"I haven't really looked," Carla admitted. "I haven't had time. Michael has been clearing that mosaic fragment in the garden."

"Really?" Simon's eyes lit up with interest. "I do remember hearing about it. Pretty badly damaged, is it?"

"It's a mess. Come by and see it."

"Not today." Simon looked at his watch. "I've got evening surgery, and I'm afraid we're running late. It's your fault. I've had a wonderful time."

"So have I. Thank you."

"We'll do it again soon. And next time I won't sit around making dire predictions."

At Carla's insistence he dropped her at the gate. After a bath and a discreet application of iodine to various cuts and scratches, she stood on the balcony and watched the sun sink toward the sea. She could not imagine ever tiring of that view. Really, it would be like tearing up roots to leave this place. Going back into the room, she made a childish, defiant face at the picture of Lady Caroline. Even if she had not wanted to stay on, the clumsy efforts to frighten her away would only have strengthened her determination. Just as well she hadn't mentioned the incidents to Simon; they would have confirmed his worst fears.

Mrs. Pendennis was conspicuously absent from the dinner table, but Michael and Tim were both there. The latter leaped up when Carla entered and pulled out her chair with a flourish. She thanked him with a smile and turned to Michael.

"Where's your grandmother?"

"Not feeling well. I made her go to bed." Carla started to rise, and he snapped, "Sit down. No need to play the gracious chatelaine; there's nothing wrong with her except that she's almost eighty."

Michael was himself again—rude and sarcastic. Carla wondered what had happened to set him off.

The ebullient Tim managed to keep a conversation going, while devouring enormous amounts of food. Michael was grimly taciturn, and Mary, who was serving,

138

was so busy smiling at the two young men she kept spilling things.

"I haven't eaten this well for weeks," Tim announced finally, scraping the last crumbs from his plate. "Not that I don't deserve it, after working like a stevedore all afternoon. My fingers are full of splinters."

"What were you doing?" Carla asked.

"I told you I meant to build a shelter over the mosaic," Michael answered. "Don't let Tim lead you astray. I did most of the work."

"Oh, yeah? Look at those splinters." Tim extended a muscular hand and tried, without success, to look limp with fatigue.

"I expect you'll want to go to bed early, then." Carla pushed her chair back.

"Hey, I thought we were going out on the town," Tim exclaimed.

"After your hard day?"

"Nothing restores a man like a little frivolity. Does wonders for women, too. Get your purse, or whatever else you need, and let's go."

"But I don't—"

"Sure you do."

"You may as well give in," Michael said. "Don't you know Tim is irresistible to women? It's his incredible ugliness that disarms them; they feel sorry for him, and before they know what's happening. . . ."

"Please." Tim held up his hand. "Don't betray my technique, I spent years developing it. Come on, Carla."

They drove through the twilight toward Penzance in Michael's old car, with Tim telling jokes and singing snatches of rude songs. Michael hadn't exaggerated a great deal in his description of Tim's appeal. His enormous vitality swept others along with him. The condition of his bruised, blistered hands testified to the work he had done that day, but one would never have guessed it from his behavior as they toured pub after pub, sampling different varieties of beer, playing darts—Tim lost every game, amid shouts of gargantuan laughter—dancing, singing, and exchanging stories and jokes. Not until the last pub closed its doors did Tim consent to turn homeward, after exchanging vows of undying friendship with their drinking companions.

"Do you want me to drive?" Carla asked.

Tim gave her a hurt look. "You don't think I'm drunk, do you? My God, woman, I'll never get drunk in this country; they close the bars too early. These licensing hours are a bad joke, I tell you. You're sure there isn't anyplace in town where we could get another drink?"

He had already been assured of this dismal truth by all the other habitués of the pub, but Carla confirmed the fact and they started home. After a few moments Carla relaxed; he drove quite competently, and it was obvious he hadn't been exaggerating his ability to hold liquor.

A high, clear moon cast silvery light over the turreted outline of the house. After he had stopped the car, Tim sat looking at it appreciatively.

"It's straight out of a Hitchcock movie," he said. "You know, with the proper PR man to handle it, this place could make a fortune as a hotel. It's absolutely rotten with atmosphere."

"Michael told you what he wants to do?"

"Sure. We're going to be partners."

"Oh, are you? What about your poor but honest parents and your six siblings at home?"

Tim turned from his rapt contemplation of the house to look at her. His face was in shadow, but his eyes glittered.

"It doesn't matter how I make the money, darling, so long as I contribute. I think there's some beer in the fridge; how about a nightcap?"

Carla refused this affable invitation rather coolly and started up the stairs, while Tim went toward the kitchen, whistling softly under his breath. As she approached her door, another door farther down the corridor opened, and she saw Michael standing there.

"Back so soon?"

"The pubs closed," Carla said. Michael laughed.

"That's right, they do close, don't they? Well . . . good night."

He was still standing there, watching her, when Carla closed her door behind her.

Feeling a little foolish, she walked around the room, looking behind the bed-curtains and into the wardrobe. The French doors were closed. Defiantly she threw them open and glanced onto the balcony. Nothing stirred except moonlight-spangled shadows.

She went back into the room and continued her tour of inspection, staring defiantly into the blank painted face of Lady Caroline as she passed. Then she reached the inner door that led to the staircase, and came to a halt.

There was a bolt on the door—a new one. Polished brass shone in the lamplight.

It had to be Michael who had put it on. He had probably done the job while she and Tim were out, for she hadn't noticed it earlier. There was no bolt on the inside of her bedroom door, however. Carla considered this fact with conflicting emotions. She got into bed, taking Caroline's diary with her, but before opening it she sat staring up at the dim folds of the canopy, thinking disturbing thoughts.

Tim was a liar. He had had a quick answer to her question, but she felt sure he didn't have six brothers and sisters back home, and she was just as doubtful of his claim to be a casual tourist. He and Michael were up to something. If it was only an innocent business deal, why weren't they candid about it? They were already making plans, even before she had accepted their offer.

Michael had put a bolt on the door leading to the staircase, but not on the one opening onto the corridor. A suspicious woman might wonder whether he was trying to forbid entry to someone else while leaving it open to himself. In fact, a suspicious woman might wonder about a lot of things. The attempts to frighten her, the near-accident on the steep village street . . . and now Tim, an ally of uncertain antecedents. But then other people seemed to want her to leave Cornwall. Simon's gruesome hints about poor old Mrs. Pendennis, Alan's complaints about money, or the lack of it. . . .

Could the house have a value she didn't suspect? Wild visions of buried treasure and veins of valuable ore ran through Carla's mind. She dismissed them with an exasperated shrug of bare shoulders. The old tin and copper mines were played out. As for buried treasure, that was too fantastic to consider. The house and the family were as old as Adam, according to Simon, but the Tregellases had apparently spent their money as fast as they had acquired it—sometimes faster. Old and aristocratic they might be, but they had never possessed kingly wealth.

Michael's idea of a hotel might be feasible, but she

142

doubted that it would ever be a gold mine to its owner. It would take months of hard work and a considerable investment to get the house into condition—more hard work and a lot of luck before it would start making money. The land might be worth something to a developer, but again, not enough to justify such a complicated plot as she envisioned.

No. There was no reason why anyone would want to get rid of her in order to lay hands on her inheritance. Perhaps the well-intended concern of other people had made her overly sensitive. After all, nothing had happened that couldn't be explained away. Even the seaweed incident had been harmless, a silly practical joke. Well, if someone wanted the house, he could have it. She would sell to the first person who made a reasonable offer. The new owner could take possession at the end of the summer, and she would return to her humdrum, boring life. . . .

Carla swore under her breath and opened the diary. No more fantasies, no more vain desires. She had promised herself she would give up the house without regret.

She forced herself to concentrate on the faded writing. As she read on, and the late-night silence of the old house deepened, she found her interest growing. Behind the sterile details of everyday life she began to sense something—a mood, a mass of emotions that could not be wholly concealed by the long-dead girl's careful prose. An occasional flash of humor, or outburst of honest sentiment gave her an increasing sense of kinship with Caroline Tregellas.

Oddly enough, Caroline's references to her fiancé did not convey such sentiment. Her delight over a basket of furry kittens, her pleasure in the first primroses of spring seemed more genuine than her love. Of course proper young ladies were not supposed to admit sexual passions; yet Carla had an idea that the provincial society of that pre-Victorian period had not been particularly puritanical. People had personal hangups, though, in any era. Perhaps Lady Caroline was afraid of marriage. Over and over she reiterated Lord William's attractions —his handsome blue eyes, his shining fair hair, his tall, well-knit body. . . . Did she protest too much, or was she simply too conventional to express her longing outright?

But of course she wouldn't, Carla thought suddenly. Her diary wasn't private, not really; children and young, unmarried women had no privacy, few rights of any kind. Children could be beaten and tortured and savagely humiliated. There was no appeal from a parent's decision. Even a married woman was at the mercy of her husband; he could handle her property, or her person, as he liked. The lock on Caroline's pretty diary was a meaningless token. She would have been a fool to write her real thoughts in it.

Obscurely troubled, Carla raised her eyes from a paragraph describing a visitor's new morning dress to the portrait of her kinswoman. Was it only her imagination, or were the features beginning to be obscured by a moving mist? She didn't wait to see. With a convulsive sideways movement she turned out the light and lay huddled in the dark until finally she fell asleep.

 SEVEN

ALAN called next morning. Mrs. Pendennis
came to tell her, as she was lingering over her coffee.

"I hope you're feeling better," Carla said.

"Better? I feel quite well, my dear, thank you." Mrs.
Pendennis smiled at her. Carla's answering smile was
diluted by bewilderment. The old lady had never looked
better. Her cheeks were prettily flushed, her shining
white hair was impeccably groomed. Had Michael lied
about his grandmother's indisposition? And if so, why
had he lied?

She was still pondering this question when she
squeezed into the cubbyhole under the stairs where the
telephone lived; Alan had to repeat her name twice before she answered.

"Oh, hello, Alan. I'm sorry; I was thinking of something else."

"I rang to see if there was any chance of seeing you this

weekend." Alan's voice was unusually tentative, and Carla felt a small, unworthy prick of satisfaction.

"I am rather busy," she said sweetly. "What did you have in mind?"

"Dinner tonight?"

After the initial lie it would never have done to accept his first invitation.

"I'm afraid not," Carla said.

There was a pause, as if he expected her to explain her plans. Carla remained silent, smiling to herself.

"What about tomorrow, then?" Alan asked. "I thought we might go sailing."

Carla hesitated, and Alan went on, "I'm sorry to have waited so long to ask you. I guess I'm too late."

He sounded so downcast that Carla relented.

"No, that's not the problem; I'm not busy, and I'd love to do something. But to be perfectly honest, I'm not a good sailor. Unless it's absolutely dead calm, terrible things happen to me."

"Oh, well, then, why don't we wait and see what the weather is like? We might bathe, if you think it's too windy for sailing."

"That would be nice."

"I'll ring you about ten, then, and we'll decide."

"Fine. Oh, Alan, before you hang up, I want to ask you something—or rather, tell you something. Michael wants to buy the house."

Even before Alan spoke, something in the quality of the silence that echoed along the line warned Carla of what he was about to say.

"Absolutely out of the question."

"Why?" As always, his masterful tone roused all Carla's stubbornness.

"For one thing, I doubt he has any money. These artistic types don't save."

"He suggested we could arrange monthly payments."

"What with?"

"Alan, don't you think we might at least investigate his financial situation? If he does have the money—"

"I can match any offer he could make, Carla. If necessary, I'll buy the place myself."

"I see," Carla said slowly. "That's the real reason, isn't it—you don't want Michael for a neighbor. Why not?"

"I'd rather not discuss it over the phone."

"We don't have to discuss it at all," Carla said. "It's up to me, isn't it, to make the final decision?"

"Of course." She distinctly heard a long slow breath, as if he were counting to ten. When he spoke again his voice had lost its harsh note. "I'm sorry if I was short with you. I think you'll understand when I explain. I'll tell you all about it tomorrow. All right?"

"I suppose it will have to be all right."

"Please, Carla, don't—"

"I'll talk to you tomorrow," Carla said, and hung up the phone.

Guilt set in as soon as she had done so, and she walked slowly toward the front door, wondering what had provoked her into such a childish display of temper. Alan was arrogant, but he was trying; she ought to be more patient with him. His lawyer's caution in questioning Michael's finances was perfectly reasonable, and he might have excellent reasons for not trusting the other man. Heaven knew she had her own doubts about Michael.

Standing on the doorstep, she spread her arms wide and took a deep breath of air—nice, clean country air—

147

her air. Her doorstep, her house. The early sunshine was being obscured by gathering clouds, and Carla studied them with guilty satisfaction. If it rained next day, she would have a good excuse not to go sailing.

She had lied to Alan about her plans. For one thing, with a man that sure of himself, it would never do to be too available. But she was also disinclined to go out. The more often she was reminded of the necessity to give it up, the more she liked her house. It was strange that her moments of discomfort, even of fear, did not really affect her mounting passion for the old place. She wanted to explore it in greater detail, sit dreaming on her balcony as she watched sunset and moonrise, excavate Roman remains in her garden. And perhaps some night, when Lady Caroline tried to break through the veil, she would be ready to listen. . . .

Surprised at herself, she dismissed this train of thought. She must have buried tendencies toward romanticism after all. Too much time spent with Simon, perhaps.

Which reminded her that she had intended to invite Simon and the vicar for tea. It was short notice, but they might come that day if she suggested the need for a conference.

Still she lingered, reluctant to go inside. The shift of shadow and sunlight across the overgrown lawn had its charm. She was becoming so enamored of the house that even the weeds looked good to her. As she stood there, a large gray tabby cat came trotting around the corner of the house.

He came to an abrupt halt when he caught sight of her, rather like a man who encounters an unexpected obstacle on his way to a pressing business appointment. Carla had no doubt of the animal's sex; it had to be a male, and a functional male at that.

"The kitchen cat, as I live and breathe," Carla said. "Excuse me; I don't believe I know your name."

The cat continued to stare at her. It was a handsome creature, despite one scarred ear. The scar was old; she had a feeling that few other cats would willingly tangle with this one, now that he had his full growth. He was very large, almost three feet from his whiskers to the end of his twitching tail, and very little of his size was fat. His eyes were a pale, clear green, like seawater, and they regarded her unwinkingly, violating all the folktales she had ever read about the superior psychological strength of human versus animal stares.

She sat down on the steps. "I don't suppose you would consider sitting on my lap," she remarked. "You don't look like a lap cat."

The cat's tail, which had been parallel to the ground, lifted. It sauntered toward her, and then, to Carla's surprise, it climbed the steps and sat down next to her. Idiotically flattered, she stroked the sleek back.

They were still sitting there, the cat's rumbling purr forming the perfect background for Carla's mindless content, when Michael came in sight. As soon as it saw him, the cat's purr changed to a low rumble. Its ears went back.

"It doesn't like you," Carla said, pleased. She rubbed the cat behind the ears. It purred briefly. "What's its name?"

"He doesn't have one." Michael emphasized the male pronoun. He sat down on the lowest step and glowered at the cat, which glowered back at him.

"I'm going to call him Arthur," Carla said.

"Not too appropriate. Arthur was chaste and God-fearing."

Carla looked down at the cat. It was still leaning affectionately against her, but something in the set of its spiky ears, as it contemplated Michael, suggested trouble to come.

"I know," she exclaimed. "I'll call him King Carter. Alan told me about him; he was the most famous smuggler in Cornish history. He fortified his own private bay and fought off the king's customs men with cannon when they came after him."

"I know who he was. Call the damned cat anything you want."

"Don't you like cats?"

"I don't like this one." As if he had understood the insult, King Carter let out a low growl, and Michael got hastily to his feet. "I'm looking for Tim. Have you seen him?"

"Not this morning."

"Did you enjoy last evening?"

"Yes, thank you. I had a very pleasant time."

"How nice." Michael shifted uneasily from one foot to the other. "Er—have you spoken with Fairman yet?"

"I'm going to see him tomorrow," Carla said. She could see no point in reporting Alan's hostile reaction to Michael's offer. The decision of what to do with the house was up to her, and she needed more information before reaching a decision.

"Oh. Well, let me know."

"Right."

"Right," Michael repeated. He hesitated for a moment and then turned and walked away. King Carter rose to his considerable height, stretched thoroughly, and started down the steps after him.

Abandoned by all, Carla went in to make her telephone calls. The vicar accepted her invitation with alacrity.

"I've found something rather interesting," he said. "No, I can't tell you now; you must allow me to prolong the suspense, it's my little weakness. Not an important discovery, I'm afraid, just curious."

Carla was unable to reach Simon, who was in his surgery, but his housekeeper took the message and promised the doctor would let her know.

She spent the rest of the morning out of doors, avoiding Tim and Michael, for she was in no mood for social intercommunication. A snatch of Irish ballad, wafted over the wall of the kitchen garden, warned her that Tim was at work—reluctantly, she surmised, for the ballad was a very melancholy one.

Presumably Michael was with him in the garden; at least she saw no signs of him when she approached the place where he had been working on the mosaic. Overnight, a substantial-looking hut had sprung up. She hadn't realized when he spoke of a shelter that he had anything that complex in mind; but of course it wouldn't do simply to roof over the mosaic; it needed protection from windblown rain as well. The hut was rough and unpainted, but well built. Once again Carla wondered why a dancer of Michael's undoubted talent would waste his time doing manual labor.

She was mildly vexed to see that the door of the shed was padlocked and that the key was nowhere to be found. No doubt Michael was taking precautions against vandalism, but it irked her to be locked out of anything on her own property.

She wandered far afield, finding occasional sad traces of what had once been well-tended pleasure grounds—a marble bench, stained and broken, amid a rank growth of rhododendron, a fallen arbor, mounded over with tangled roses. Her sneakers and the bottoms of her jeans were soaking with damp by the time she reached the western gate and stood leaning on the wall looking out over the sea.

"Go to the western gate at set of sun. . . ."

It was rotten verse. "Come" and "sun" didn't even rhyme. But then folk sayings don't have to rhyme, Carla thought.

The breeze on the exposed headland was crisp. It blew the hair back from her forehead and whipped the ends of her scarf across her face. It was a day of alternate shadow and sunlight, and Carla admired the shifting shades of color across the water. It looked like a giant tourmaline, all iridescent blues and greens. She wondered if she would ever gain enough courage to descend the steep path to the little bay. It would be lovely to swim there, and to lie naked on the shining white sands with the warm sun on her body.

She won an approving smile from Mrs. Pendennis when she came down to lunch washed and brushed and on time. She and the housekeeper ate alone. As Carla surveyed the dainty linen mats and delicate china, she didn't wonder that Michael and Tim preferred to lunch elsewhere. They were probably munching thick sandwiches and drinking beer out of the bottles, letting the crumbs fall on the ground and wiping their mouths on their sleeves, in perfect masculine comfort.

Mrs. Pendennis was in excellent spirits. She didn't mention either of the subjects that upset her—her grandson or the legend—and Carla avoided them too. Simon had called while Carla was out, saying he would be delighted to come to tea. Mrs. Pendennis, obviously pleased at the prospect of entertaining, was giving Carla a detailed list of what she planned to serve when the latter was suddenly struck by a disconcerting thought.

"Will you be joining us, Mrs. Pendennis?" she asked.

Mrs. Pendennis looked shocked. "No, my dear, thank you. That would not be quite the thing."

Carla was relieved, though she tried not to show it. It would not have been possible to discuss Mrs. Pendennis's emotional problems in her presence. It was going to be awkward enough anyway, with the old lady in the house. Carla could picture the three of them with their heads together over the tea table—the vicar's silvery locks, Simon's golden hair, and her prosaic brown— whispering and glancing over their shoulders like gossiping charwomen.

Spurred on by John's hints of revelations, she intended to spend the afternoon searching for an exciting contribution of her own. Under Mrs. Pendennis's guidance she had seen less than half of the main floors of the house, and nothing of the attics or the cellars. The very idea of attics intrigued her—back home they had never had anything more extensive than a crawl space under the roof—so after lunch she climbed the narrow stairs at the end of the corridor, opened a creaking door, and stood daunted and dumbstruck at the vista before her.

The sunlight was dimmed by grime-encrusted windows. Dust motes, disturbed by the opening of the door, swam thickly in the feeble rays. The vast space, big as a barn, was absolutely crammed with junk. Chests, boxes, old furniture, piles of magazines and sheet music, heaps of rags, rough wooden shelves piled with books banished from the library. . . .

Carla's first thought was that the place was an absolute firetrap, and that it was a wonder the house hadn't gone up in flames years ago. Her second thought was purely mercenary. She knew very little about antiques, but surely there must be something of value among all those objects. They were hers, such as they were; hadn't Alan said "the house and its contents"? And this was only one of the attics. Vast as it was, it covered less than half of the house.

With only a few hours at her disposal, it was obviously a hopeless task to look for clues in that mammoth chaos, but as Carla retreated she promised herself a thorough search in the near future. Even if there was nothing valuable to be found, she might discover mementos she would want to keep.

The library was the obvious place to start looking for family records, and after getting lost twice she finally found the room in question. She had glanced into it briefly on her first tour, but Mrs. Pendennis had not allowed her to linger. Standing in the doorway, looking at a shabby but pleasant room, Carla wondered why. Had this been Walter's favorite retreat, and thus full of sentimental memories to his old housekeeper? She suspected that it had. Squares of lighter flooring showed where rugs had once lain—rugs valuable enough to be sold, evidently, in Walter's declining years. The worn green velvet draperies reminded her of Scarlett O'Hara, for these were also moss green with heavy gold tassels, but they would never make a dress. They were threadbare. There were several cracking leather armchairs, a sofa whose velvet covering suggested mousy inhabitants, a desk, and a heavy table. And shelf upon shelf of books.

Carla sighed and began scanning the shelves.

Her impatience grew as she read the titles, the great majority of them unfamiliar to her. Most were cheaply bound in faded cloth—the popular nonfiction and novels of eighty years. A shelf of crumbling paperbacks betrayed Cousin Walter's fondness for spy thrillers. Carla was fairly sure the room held nothing of value. In his last years Walter would not have neglected this accessible source of cash. Anyway, the Tregellases did not appear to have been collectors of rare books.

Eventually she had to go down to tea with empty hands, after changing her clothes and washing off the dust of her labors. Simon was already in the drawing room, talking to Mrs. Pendennis, who excused herself as soon as Carla appeared. The vicar arrived almost immediately. He was wearing casual clothes—an open-necked shirt and tweed jacket—instead of his collar. He looked younger and less remote out of costume, and the warm smile he gave Carla reminded her that, High Church or Low, British clergy were not bound to celibacy.

"You've no idea what a treat this is," Simon said, running his fingers through his ruffled hair. "Another of those damned hikers took a tumble off the cliffs near the village. Broken ribs, fractured skull. . . . And when I finally got home from the hospital, Mrs. Chynoweth had decided to turn out the parlor, as she quaintly puts it. Ah —Mrs. Pendennis, that tea tray looks splendid. And so do you, if I may say so."

The housekeeper had entered the room so quietly

Carla did not see her until Simon spoke. In Carla's opinion she didn't look splendid; the change that had taken place since lunchtime was rather startling. Even her voice had altered; it was a low, barely intelligible mumble when she spoke.

"Thank you, Doctor. I trust everything is satisfactory. Please ring for Mary, Miss Tregellas, should you require more hot water. I trust—that is to say—there is no hurry about dinner; it will be a cold meal and can be served at any time; you won't hurry with your tea, I hope."

Carla stared at her in surprise. The vicar said in a determinedly cheerful voice, "No, indeed, Mrs. Pendennis. I plan to stay here until I'm asked to leave, and I'm sure Miss Tregellas won't do that for a good long time."

Mrs. Pendennis's face brightened. "I'm so glad, Vicar. Then, if you will excuse me. . . ."

When she had gone the three conspirators—for so Carla was beginning to think of them—exchanged glances. John got up and tiptoed to the door. He opened it a crack and peered out; then he gave a nod of satisfaction and returned to his seat.

"She's gone upstairs—to rest in her room, I should think. We can speak freely."

"I should say there was need of free speaking," Simon said, accepting the cup Carla handed him. "Lord, but the poor old soul has deteriorated in the past week. Good work, John, catching her meaning; I couldn't imagine what she was driving at."

The vicar's fine-boned face was grave.

"She wanted to be sure Carla would have someone looking after her as twilight approaches. Thank you, Carla—no sugar, just lemon, please. . . . That's illogical, you know. Lady Caroline's lover couldn't keep her from her fated rendezvous, so why should we be more reliable guardians?"

"Logic!" Simon waved it away with a flourish of the hand that held a watercress sandwich. "There is no such thing in her system. . . . Hold on. Are you intimating that she is pretending to be concerned about the legend in order to cover up a more practical fear?"

"The possibility had occurred to me," said John. Carla was finding it easier to think of him by name instead of by title now. "But I can't really believe it. What danger could there be?" He turned to Carla with his grave, charming smile. "It isn't as if you had a vast estate and a number of unprincipled relations waiting to inherit, is it? And I assure you we've no unhinged village villains who harbor a deep-seated grudge against the family."

So he, too, had considered wild possibilities. Carla appreciated his candor; the fact that she was not the only one to entertain fantastic theories made her feel less foolish.

"Besides," John continued, accepting a slice of cake from the plate she offered, "if she knew of a real danger she would warn Carla."

"Unless the danger involved a conflict of loyalties," Simon muttered.

Carla shook her head. "If you're thinking of Michael, I doubt that there would be a conflict. She's no doting grannie. It really surprises me, especially in view of the effort he's put forth to help her remain here. Does she resent his illegitimacy?"

"Ah, so you know." John gave her a keen look.

"Michael made no secret of it. Why should he? I guess

157

I ought to tell you, though, that he has offered to buy the house. Does that give him a motive for playing funny tricks on me?"

Her voice was heavy with sarcasm, and Simon, at whom it had been directed, looked startled.

"No, of course not. I wasn't implying that Michael—"

"Just a moment." It was the vicar speaking; his voice had an authoritative note. "A motive for what, Carla? This is the first I've heard of funny tricks, as you put it; I gather, from your tone, that they were not really amusing. What has happened?"

Carla knew then that unconsciously she had been wanting to tell someone. She recounted her adventures, with one exception—her near-fall on the village street. That, she told herself, was an accident, pure and simple. There was no need to mention it.

John's face lengthened as she went on, and Simon emitted little grunts of distress.

"This is frightful," he exclaimed, when she had finished. "There is a degree of malice—"

"It's a bit more complicated than that," John broke in. "The second episode—the one involving the portrait— disturbs me a great deal. Carla, forgive me—but you don't strike me as the suggestible type. Had you eaten or —er—drunk anything that would produce hallucinations?"

The same suggestion from Michael had infuriated Carla. Now she simply shook her head.

"I don't blame you for wondering. You don't have to believe me, but honestly, I hadn't taken anything—not even a glass of wine."

"I don't like this at all." John tugged at his lip. "Carla, don't you think—"

"If you're going to add your voice to the chorus that is singing 'Carla, go home,' you're wasting your breath," Carla said. "In fact, I might stay on over the winter."

"What?" Simon almost dropped his teacup.

"I don't see why I can't," Carla insisted. "I was up in the attic this afternoon. The place is full of old things. I'll bet I can sell some of them. And there's Walter's wine. I'll sell the fifty-year-old claret, and drink Manischevitz—or water. I can get along without a cook or maid. Maybe I can even arrange to sell the house and not give possession till spring. I have saved some money—not much, but enough to—"

"You love the place that much?" Simon asked incredulously.

"Yes, I do. Isn't this the time of life when people should indulge their crazy impulses—before responsibilities to other people limit choice? I've never done anything like that. I was a square, studious adolescent, and I'll be middle-aged and practical soon enough."

As she spoke she wondered fleetingly what old Mr. Fawcett, her Boston lawyer, would think of this decision. He had been a little disappointed by her down-to-earth attitude at the beginning of their interview. If he could hear her now, he would probably wonder what had happened to change her in such a short time. Her friends at home would wonder too; but these new friends had not known her pre-Cornwall personality. From their expressions she could tell that they were surprised—but not as much as she was at herself.

Finally John said, with a smile tugging at the corners of his mouth, "It's an impractical, foolish idea, Carla. . . . I'm in complete sympathy with it."

"Really?" Her voice sounded like that of an excited

child, and John's smile emerged into the open.

"I only wish all youthful follies were as harmless as this. If you find yourself getting in over your head financially, you can always call a halt."

"Harmless, do you say?" Simon banged his teacup down into the saucer. The others looked at him in surprise. He went on, his voice coarsened by a touch of accent Carla had not heard before. "It's a daft, stupid idea and I'm amazed that you encourage it, John. The girl has been attacked twice—"

"That's putting it rather strongly," the vicar interrupted. "I quite agree that if Carla is to stay on, something will have to be done about Mrs. Pendennis; but something will have to be done in any case. You don't suppose her mental problems will be cured by Carla's departure, do you? No, no. They will simply take another form."

"Are you suggesting that Mrs. Pendennis carried out these tricks?" Simon demanded.

"The first one, yes. The second. . . ."

"Was Carla's own imagination getting out of hand," said Carla, eating scones and clotted cream with grim determination. She was really getting very tired of clotted cream.

"Was a combination of fatigue, nervous tension, delayed reaction from the journey," said the vicar. "What else could it have been?"

Simon growled wordlessly. He split a scone and spread it with jam.

"Have some clotted cream," said Carla.

"What? No, thanks, can't stand the stuff. I suppose your theory is the only possible one at that, John. But I don't like it. The seaweed trick was harmless enough in

160

itself, but an accumulation of such incidents can build up, prey on the nerves—"

"Don't be silly," Carla said. "In case you haven't noticed, Simon, I am not one of those nervous, fluttery little women. If I catch our trickster at work, I'll stop the tricks for good, believe me. Maybe John has a point, about proving the legend is false. I mean, if I'm still alive and kicking after Midsummer Eve, poor old Mrs. P. will have to admit she was wrong. Like those solemn idiots who climb on top of a mountain singing hymns and waiting for the world to end. . . . When it doesn't, they have to creep quietly back down and pretend nothing ever happened."

"I think that is an excellent parallel," said John approvingly. He glanced at Simon, who was devouring watercress sandwiches and scowling as he chewed. "Unless Simon has any further objections, I suggest we proceed with our research."

"I have one objection," Carla said. "I mean, the whole story is such an obvious fabrication; how can you disprove a fairy tale?"

"It must have a substructure of truth," John argued. "The girl did disappear. . . ."

"Did she? I haven't seen any genuine evidence of that yet. All I've heard are secondhand embroidered versions of the story. So much of it is obviously pure fiction—like the girl's title. Her father was a country squire, not a lord or a knight; how does she get to be 'Lady Caroline'?"

John's jaw dropped.

"An outsider sees things the rest of us miss," he said with a smile. "You're quite right, Carla; the title is pure fabrication—an added romantic touch. But I don't see that it matters."

"Then there's the time lapse," Carla went on. "Why two hundred years? Why not every century? It's an odd interval, isn't it?"

"Now that is a point," the vicar murmured, stroking his jaw. "Obviously what we must do is seek out the original written version of the story—composed, as I understand it, by the lady's younger brother. I have heard a great deal about that manuscript, but I have never seen it. We certainly ought to make sure Mrs. Pendennis has reported it accurately. Where can it be, do you think?"

"I went through the library today, in a cursory fashion, without finding it," Caroline said. "I suppose I could ask Mrs. Pendennis, but I'm afraid of upsetting her."

"It would be better if someone else asked," John agreed. "Simon, you are the obvious person; she has great confidence in you."

"Very well," Simon said without enthusiasm.

"You said you had made a discovery, John," Carla said. "Haven't you kept up the suspense long enough?"

"It isn't much, really. But it occurred to me to look at the family monuments in the church. Some of them are as old as the structure itself—fourteenth century." Carla choked on a crumb and the vicar smiled sympathetically. "It is rather overwhelming, isn't it? Haven't you seen your family genealogy? It must be around somewhere; Walter worked on it for years. Simon, you might ask Mrs. Pendennis about that also."

"Go on," Carla said impatiently.

As if determined to tantalize her, the vicar proceeded methodically, "Naturally, the church has been restored and rebuilt a number of times. One of the least-altered sections, as you might suppose, is the crypt. That is

162

where I discovered the memorial brass I wish to bring to your attention." He reached into his pocket, brought out a folded paper, and proceeded to unfold it with a deliberation that made Carla want to shout with frustration. "Here we are. The brass is in surprisingly good condition, considering its age, although it is somewhat corroded by the salt air. . . ." He glanced up, saw Carla's face, and grinned. "I took a rubbing," he said, and handed her the paper.

The corrosion he had mentioned had primarily affected the edges of the square tablet. The running ornamental border was hard to make out, though the sinuous curves were unpleasantly suggestive. The center of the tablet, bearing the inscription, was equally unintelligible to Carla, except for the name. It was recognizable even in its Latin form.

"I never could do Roman numerals," she muttered. "Much less Latin text."

"It's an 'In Memoriam,' fourteenth-century version," the vicar explained. " 'Pray for the repose of the soul of Margaret de Tregellas, in the year of our Lord 1380. The pardon for the saying of five pater nosters and five aves and a credo is twenty thousand years and twenty days of Purgatory.' "

"Pardon?" Carla repeated blankly.

"Don't you remember your Chaucer? The Pardoner was a well-known figure in the Middle Ages. The church sold these documents for money; it was one of the things Luther complained of most bitterly in his denunciation of the papacy." Then, as Carla continued to look bewildered, he went on patiently, "The family of the dead man or woman bought the pardon from the church. They could then promise, as this woman's family did, that if a passerby would say a certain number of prayers for the repose of her soul, the said passerby would be let off so many years of Purgatory."

"Ridiculous," Carla exclaimed.

"That's the Methodist in you speaking," Simon said, smiling for the first time in a long while.

"The point is that this is a large pardon," the vicar said. "It must have cost the family a great deal of money. There's another curious feature about this inscription. It gives a date, but does not mention the word 'died.'"

Simon took the paper from Carla's hand.

"I think I see what you're driving at," he murmured. "And I don't think I like it."

"Thirteen eighty," Carla repeated. "That was six hundred years ago. Are you saying that Margaret was one of the doomed damsels?"

"It doesn't say that she died," Simon said, scowling over the crabbed Latin. "Or that she is buried nearby.
. . . There is no *'hic jacet'*—that means 'here lies,'" he added, glancing at Carla. "One usually finds that phrase, or a word such as *'obiit.'*"

"Pardons of that size were only given to the worst of sinners," the vicar said. "What could she have done to warrant such extravagance?"

Simon flung the paper down on the table.

"You're a great help, John, I must say. What are you trying to do, prove the legend or disprove it? Show this to Mrs. P., and she will have a nice fit of hysterics."

"That was not my idea at all," John protested, in distress. "The origin of this story may well lie in a long-past disappearance or mysterious death."

"Very possibly. But all you've proved so far is that the story may go back as far as the fourteenth century. The

164

very absence of detail makes the implication more frightening. And we'll never be able to go back any farther; Walter couldn't get past the fourteenth century himself."

The vicar looked so crestfallen that Carla felt sorry for him. She wasn't too happy about his discovery either, but she forced herself to smile and shake her head.

"I wonder what happened to the sixteenth-century sacrifice," she remarked.

"An excellent point," the vicar said, brightening. "Do you know, Carla, I suspect that the two-hundred-year interval may have resulted from the fact that Squire Thomas—or whoever it was that put the legend into its present form—could not find examples of mysterious deaths every century. In other words, it is an artificial device, resulting from an absence of evidence."

"The genealogy might help," Carla said.

"I'll ask about that right now," Simon said, rising. "I'd like to have a look at Mrs. Pendennis before I go anyway. May I go on up, Carla?"

"Yes, of course. Do you want me to come with you?"

"There's no need. I know where her room is."

He ambled out, reminding Carla of a large blonde bear. His hunched shoulders suggested discouragement.

He was gone for almost half an hour. The vicar tactfully abandoned the subject of sacrifices and sea monsters and talked entertainingly about the antiquities of his beloved church. Carla was embarrassed to admit that she had agreed to go on a strictly secular expedition next day.

"I won't have time to go to church," she apologized. "But next Sunday—"

"You mustn't wait until then to see the church. The

family monuments are quite interesting, and we have a few rather fine pieces of carving that survived the restorers of the nineteenth century."

Finally Simon came back, his shoulders even more bowed and his face grave.

"I gave her a sedative," he said. "The poor old girl is in quite a state. Has she been like this all day?"

"No, not at all. She was bright as a button this morning."

"It's the witching hour of twilight that sets her off, then."

"That's what the poem said," Carla exclaimed. "The one I found in Caroline's diary."

"Diary?" Simon glared at her. "Do we have to drag every bit of information out of you, young woman? What's this about a diary?"

Carla told them.

"I didn't mention it because it's no help," she said. "I've covered a lot of it, including the days just before her disappearance, and there isn't a clue. Just the poem."

" 'Go to the western gate at set of sun,' " the vicar repeated, " 'On Midsummer Eve, and wait for what will come.' Dreadful doggerel, yet there is something about it. . . . Three main elements—the western gate, twilight, Midsummer Eve. Why is Mrs. Pendennis so alarmed just now? It's still almost two weeks until June twenty-third."

"I don't know, but she is certainly upset," Simon said gloomily. "I think she'll sleep now. I took the liberty of locking her door. Don't want her wandering about while she's semicomatose. Carla, you won't leave her alone tonight, will you?"

"I'll be here all evening."

"I'm going to have a word with Michael," John said uneasily. "Where do you suppose he is?"

"He wasn't upstairs," Simon said. "I looked."

"I'll look for him outside," the vicar said. He got to his feet. "Don't bother to come with us, Carla; we'll tell Michael his grandmother is unwell, and then be on our way. You aren't worried, are you?"

"No," Carla said, not quite truthfully, thinking that she would be much less worried if people would stop suggesting that she might be.

The men took their departure. Carla watched them saunter down the path. She could hear Mary in the drawing room, clearing away the remains of tea, but she did not go back in.

Later, from her balcony, she saw Simon's car drive away, with the vicar's bicycle perched on top like some prehistoric insect. Presumably they had found Michael, but she saw no sign of him, then or later, when she went down for the aforementioned cold meal. She had little appetite for it. The dining room was a dark room at any time of day, and the rain that had been half threatening all day now seemed imminent. The wind was rising— nothing like the vehement blasts of her first night, but strong enough to make the branches of the trees toss like wildly waving arms.

Mary, who served her, seemed uncharacteristically silent, but from her occasional comments Carla deduced that she was in a hurry, not because of the rain, but because she had a date that night. Of course, it was Saturday. Any girl who didn't have a date on Saturday night was a social failure. Carla comforted herself with the reminder that she could have gone out with Alan if she had been so minded. Lucky she hadn't accepted the invitation; it would never do to leave Mrs. Pendennis alone in the house, drugged and helpless. She had no idea where Michael was.

After the cook and maid had left, the house seemed very silent. She tiptoed upstairs and listened at Mrs. Pendennis's door. The reassuring sound of heavy breathing, almost heavy enough to be called snoring, reached her ears. In mounting irritation she wondered what had become of Michael and Tim. If they had planned to go out that evening, they might have had the courtesy to mention it to her.

Alone in the empty old house with Mrs. Pendennis, she felt a mounting sense of claustrophobia. If she could only be sure that Michael was somewhere around she could settle down to a quiet evening of reading, or of sorting through her numerous possessions. But not in the attic, not at night. The least unnerving thing she would encounter there would be mice. The library would certainly repay further investigation, however. She remembered suddenly that Simon had not mentioned the documents he had meant to ask Mrs. Pendennis about. She would have to call him and ask if he had found out anything.

Making sure the door was unlatched, she went outside, in search of the elusive Michael. The wind took her breath away at first, but she enjoyed its bracing, gusty freshness. The sky toward the east was black with clouds; but in the west the sun had splashed garish fantasy towers against the reddened horizon. As she watched, the wind blew purple battlements to shreds and formed new shapes: towering minarets of gold-streaked cobalt, soaring spires of scarlet and lavender.

Calling Michael's name, she went toward the garden.

The wind snatched her voice away and no one answered. Reaching the comparative shelter of the courtyard, she called again. This time there was a reply, though not in a human voice. The wailing howl startled her terribly, until she realized what it was; she let out a sound that was half laugh and half gasp as a sinuous furry shape leaped down from the stable roof and bumped against her ankles.

"King Carter! You had better come in. This is no fit night for man or beast, not even a Casanova like you."

But when she bent to pick him up the cat bounded away, his fur bristling. He did not seem to be angry, only excited. She had read somewhere that animals were affected by storms; it had something to do with the electricity in the air. Still, the cat's company was better than none. If she could persuade King to join her in the library and sit purring like a respectable cat, the house wouldn't seem so empty.

She followed King, who seemed determined to engage her in a game of tag. Keeping just out of arm's reach, he led her through the garden and out into the meadow. Ahead were the wall and the western gate, silhouetted blackly against the spectacular sunset.

It was stubbornness as much as any other motive that led Carla toward the spot the poem warned against. Not that there was anything to worry about, she told herself; even if one took the insane legend seriously, which she certainly did not, the danger hour was two weeks away. The extent of the horizon broadened as she approached the wall and the roar of surf below became a small thunder. The wind tugged at her skirt and tangled her lashes. There was a queer exhilaration in the sight and feel of nature building up to an explosion; and although she reminded herself that she must not be long absent from the house, she lingered, leaning on the gate and watching the windblown architecture of sunset. The cat perched on the wall not far away; hunched and motionless, it too stared at the brilliant west.

It would be easy, Carla thought, for a primitive imagination to see ethereal cities in the cloud shapes. Strange how the idea of sunken continents kept appearing in different cultures—Atlantis, the lost continent of Mu, the submerged towers of Ys and Lyonesse. . . . Lost in her fancies, Carla stood dreaming until a long arm of cloud reached out and grasped the sun. Darkness descended like a veil, and King Carter emitted a low moaning sound that made the hairs on Carla's neck stand up.

She reached out for the cat, who was now only a dark shape in the dusk, and felt the roughened hair along his backbone. He was growling, a low, continuous rumble, like a miniature echo of the greater growling of nature —the wind in the trees, the pound of the surf. When Carla scooped the cat into her arms, he continued to growl. He was as rigid as a statue and his head turned as she picked him up. He was staring out to sea.

Carla was quite ready to retreat, at top speed. She was not ashamed of being afraid, even though she knew her panic was irrational. But it was too late. The figure loomed up before her as if it had emerged from the ground, or from the sea. A last ray of dying sun ran along the outlines of its sleek, rounded head and lean body and long outstretched arms, as if outlining the shape in oily gold. The cat let out an almost human shriek, and Carla released it, echoing its cry, as long wet arms wound around her and pressed her close to a cold, damp body.

 EIGHT

"WHAT the hell is the matter with you?"
It was Michael's voice. A resistant, inner core of common sense recognized it, and Carla went limp in his arms. His body was warm now. She clung to him as she would have clutched at any solid, human object.

"Your nails need cutting," Michael remarked critically.

"What are you doing here?"

"I've been swimming, of course." Michael removed her clinging hands and pushed her away. "All you have to do is say no, girl; you needn't claw me to shreds. How am I going to explain those scratches to Vicky?"

"Who is Vicky?"

"You don't know her. Hey . . . you are in a state, aren't you? What's wrong? Has Gran—"

"No, she's all right. At least she was a few minutes ago. I was looking for you. What do you mean wandering off like that? I'm all alone here . . . and then you come up out of the water like some slimy thing. . . ."

Her voice broke. Michael understood, as he always did; but if she had expected sympathy she was disappointed.

"Oh, for God's sake! If you really believe all that rot about amorous mermen, why did you come down here? We'd better get back to the house."

His arm around her, he half pushed, half led her along the path. There was nothing fond about this embrace; his impatience was palpable in every muscle of his body.

"I can walk," Carla snapped, trying to free herself. "Let me go. I want to find King. He's around here somewhere."

"What do you want him for?"

"I want some friendly company. Here, King—kitty, kitty. Wait, I think I heard him."

"That was me, groaning," Michael said. He stopped. Standing on one leg, he lifted his foot and nursed it in his hands. "I just mashed my toe against a rock."

"It's your own fault, going around barefoot."

His feet weren't the only part of his body that was bare. The sun had come out for one last appearance before it sank for the night. In its ghastly crimson light Michael's wet body, attired only in skimpy trunks, shone like that of a devil from one of the hotter parts of hell. His dark hair clung to his skull. He would have looked magnificently threatening—a young Lucifer—if he had not been standing on one leg. Carla let out a choked laugh.

"Thanks for the sympathy." Wincing, Michael put his foot down. "Stand around here all night, if you like. I'm going back to Gran. You'd no business leaving her alone."

Before Carla had time to answer this unfair criticism, he left, limping affectedly.

Carla looked over her shoulder. The sun was gone except for a few streaks of crimson, bright as neon, crossing a purple-blue sky.

"Kitty, kitty," she pleaded.

A rustle in the underbrush heralded the arrival of King. Lean and slinking, he looked as uncanny as a mythological monster, but he allowed Carla to pick him up. She started along the path, and was alerted to Michael's proximity even before she saw him by the cat's stiffening body and low growl.

"Go on ahead," she said. "I think you must have kicked this cat or something. He hates you."

"I was waiting to be sure you found your way back," Michael said coldly. "If that's how you feel, you can fall on your—face, for all I care."

He went on at a rapid trot.

"There must be something wrong with a man that a cat doesn't trust," Carla said; but Michael was out of earshot.

She put King down as soon as they were inside and he streaked off in the direction of the kitchen. Carla went up the stairs, turning on lights as she proceeded. Mrs. Pendennis's door was open. As she approached it, Michael came out.

"How is she?" Carla asked.

"Dead to the world. Who knocked her out?"

"Simon. He said she was upset."

"Simon is. . . . Never mind. Go about your business,

whatever that may be. I'll watch over Gran."

"Where is Tim?"

"Gone to Penzance. Pub crawling is his idea of seeing merrie old England."

Michael stalked off toward his own room. Even in bare feet and half naked he stalked like a Gothic villain.

Carla went back downstairs. After some confusion she managed to put through her call. Simon's calm baritone reassured her as to Mrs. Pendennis's condition, and then grunted with disgust when she told him why she had telephoned.

"Sorry. I was somewhat distracted. Yes, I did ask Mrs. P. about the manuscripts. She says they are in the library in a cupboard under the east windows. The cupboard is locked, but the key is hanging on a nail in the butler's pantry."

"Good. I'll have a look at the material this evening."

"It's not a good night for reading ghost stories," Simon warned. "Is Michael there?"

"Yes, he's upstairs with Mrs. Pendennis. You're wrong, Simon. It's a perfect night for ghost stories. And I don't need a man in the house to feel comfortable, thank you."

"Female chauvinist," Simon said. She could tell by his voice that he was smiling. "I'll be at home all evening. Just put a light in your window if you want me."

"You're kidding."

"No. I can see your window from here. At least I can see a light, if there is one. Many is the midnight I have pondered, dreaming. . . ."

"Don't misquote Poe at me, not tonight. Can you really?"

"Yes, I can, really. Would you like me to come round?

174

We can investigate together."

It was an enticing suggestion, but Carla conquered her impulse to agree.

"You'd get caught in the storm. Thanks, Simon, but I'm fine." Then, before she could weaken, she said good-bye and hung up.

The butler's pantry, adjacent to the kitchen, was as big as the dining room of most American houses. Carla looked sadly at the empty shelves, which had once held the family silver and china. The keys were a reminder of the affluence of the old days—a whole bunch of them, all different sizes and shapes, on a heavy silver ring. When she lifted them from the hook they rang like far-off church bells. Like the sunken churches of Lyonesse, she thought.

She took the entire ring with her into the library, anticipating a frustrating period of experimentation, but the lock of the cabinet under the window was so small that only a few of the collection were even possible. She found the right key on the fourth try. It turned sweetly in the lock, and she saw two low shelves heaped with papers.

Sitting crosslegged on the floor, she took them out. All were family papers. A cursory examination told her that she had found the raw materials from which Cousin Walter had constructed his genealogy. This document was not a large sheet of paper, as she had expected, but a manuscript book handsomely bound in leather and filled, page after page, with neat old-fashioned writing.

Carla put it to one side and glanced through the other papers. Finally she found a folder labeled in the same neat writing she had recognized as that of her cousin. "Manuscript and commentary of Thomas Tregellas," the label read. Resisting the impulse to look inside, Carla put it with the genealogy and restored the other papers to the shelf.

After relocking the cupboard she got to her feet with the selected documents in her hand. The rain had started, and the wind was beginning to rise to a conventional Cornish gale. The library looked comfortable and pleasant in the lamplight; still, she decided she would be happier in her own room. She could always hide behind the bed-curtains if she got nervous.

After she had put the keys back, she wandered into the kitchen with a vague idea of making tea or coffee—something hot and full of caffeine, in case Walter's literary style was as dull as Caroline's. One look at the stove convinced her she was a long way from solving its mysteries. A bottle of amber beverage in the refrigerator looked interesting. Carla sampled it cautiously, and then took a long swig. It tasted of apples and of alcohol—delicious! Perhaps it was the famous cider of Devon and Cornwall. She had read about it, but had never been served it; did Walter, a connoisseur of fine old wines, scorn the local product? This might be a private hoard of the cook. However, Carla decided not to worry about minor moral issues. A few glasses of the beverage and she wouldn't worry about ghosts. If she saw any, she could blame them on the cider.

She looked in vain for King. Most cats of her acquaintance headed for the kitchen like an express train when they heard a refrigerator door open, but King was not like the plump neutered pets she had known. He was straight out of Kipling. He walked by his lone wild, switching his tail.

In spite of her scornful remarks to and about Michael,

she was glad to see that his door was ajar. It was going to be another wild night. The draperies covering the French doors were swaying, as they always did in a westerly wind. Carla stood watching them for a moment. They looked for all the world as if a silent struggle were going on behind them—arms flailing, legs thrashing. She put her papers down on the bedside table, crossed the room, and flung the draperies back. She would rather see the rain streaking the windows and hear the whistling whine the wind made coming through various cracks than watch those draperies billow.

Rain or no rain, the room looked cozy once she was in bed with a full glass in her hand and Walter's genealogy open on her lap. She was not quite ready to tackle Thomas's tale yet; anyway, it made more sense to get the background firmly in mind first.

After a while she forgot the wailing wind and the lash of rain. It was not only the euphoria of the potent cider that cheered her; Walter's prose had the same dry, exhilarating tang. She wished she had known him. He had a lovely sense of humor; though candidly proud of the ancient lineage he was tracing, he was cynically amused by his ancestors' weaknesses, and by the folly of his own pride.

His arrangement of the complex material was surprisingly easy to follow. One page listed names and dates, offspring and marriages, for a single generation; a star beside one name indicated the line Walter intended to follow on the next page. In between were long commentaries and descriptions, and as many scandalous stories as Walter had been able to dig up. Undoubtedly the neat manuscript was the final copy of long years of research.

It began with the present century and worked backward.

As people will, Carla searched for her own name, but failed to find it. Walter mentioned her great-grandfather, and explained that he had emigrated, but his was one of the many sidelines his descendant had not had the time or the inclination to follow through. Walter's version of why young William had left the home of his fathers was libelous in the extreme, involving a number of village maidens with names that seemed vaguely familiar to Carla. If Walter was to be trusted, she was distantly related to everyone within a fifty-mile radius. However, although Walter's data on family relationships appeared to be reliable, she suspected that his sense of humor had affected some of the background material.

Carla began to skip, but even so it was late before she reached the eighteenth century. She took another sip of cider and flipped through the pages till she reached the one she wanted.

The bare facts looked harmless enough. Lady Caroline's father had been Squire George Tregellas, born in 1730. His wife had been a Polreath—Arabella, born 1744. Arabella had begun breeding, as the eighteenth-century quaintly expressed it, almost as soon as she walked in the front door of Tregellas House. Caroline, her eldest daughter, was born in 1762. Several sons followed, all stillborn or deceased in infancy. Then came a quiescent period of almost ten years. (Had Squire George been away on business, Carla wondered?) The surviving heir, Thomas, was born in 1774. He had been only six years old when his sister walked out into the twilight. Two other stillborn children completed the register. Caroline's mother had died a year after her daughter's disappearance, which Walter had signalized by a question mark after the crucial date: "Caroline, b. 1762, d. 1780(?)."

A fierce blast of wind rattled the French windows as Carla turned to the commentary on this page of the genealogy.

For a moment she stared, bewildered. There was no commentary. The next page was another list of names— the names of the generation that had preceded Caroline's.

Carla stared accusingly at the bottle on her bedside table. It had gone down several inches, no doubt about that; but she hadn't drunk enough to cloud her wits. She still felt perfectly wide awake.

A brief survey told her the truth. Half a dozen pages had been ripped out of the book. Ripped, not cut; the ragged edges were plain to see, easy to count. Seven pages—including, no doubt, the story of Lady Caroline's disappearance.

Carla ran her finger along the ragged edges, as if by wishing she could conjure the missing section back into reality.

Why would anyone bother? The story was known, not only to her, but to everyone in the neighborhood. Mrs. Pendennis was the obvious suspect, she had had the book in her charge for months. But Carla rejected this idea almost at once. Mrs. Pendennis had been only too eager to relate the story to her. Unless. . . .

Unless Walter had discovered something that contradicted the version she had been told.

Conjecture was fruitless, of course. And yet, so infectious and so personal was Walter's writing that Carla felt she knew how his mind had worked. Naturally he would be curious about the family ghost story, and would try to investigate it. As she already knew from his cynical

179

comments, he had a logical mind, impatient of fantasy. What if he had discovered the truth about Caroline's disappearance? Once again Carla seemed to sense the presence of a hostile human agent—the same person who had been trying to frighten her with dire suggestions of the supernatural.

If the fatalities occurred every two hundred years, that would put the previous disappearance back to 1580. Carla thumbed through the pages until she reached the sixteenth-century entry.

The information was infuriatingly ambiguous. One daughter of the house, Elizabeth by name—after the Virgin Queen, no doubt—had died in 1578, at the tender age of sixteen. Walter's commentary didn't even mention her, except as one of "several children who did not live long enough to marry." The Squire Henry of that day was very prolific: sixteen children in all. So Elizabeth would not have been missed much.

The information on the fourteenth-century lady was even more sparse. Walter had copied the brass the vicar had found; his commentary speculated, with ribald humor, on the nature of the offense that had won the girl such an extraordinary pardon. His suggestions included witchcraft, heresy, and seducing a monk, but offered nothing particularly useful.

Carla tossed the genealogy aside. Her eyelids were getting heavy, but her curiosity was at fever pitch. Perhaps Thomas's manuscript would supply the information missing from Walter's account.

The manuscript consisted of a dozen large pages tied together with a black ribbon. It was not easy to read. The ink had faded, and the handwriting was both tremulous and affected. Carla skipped through the first pages,

180

which seemed to consist mainly of abstruse references to ancient myths, until she reached the meaty part.

The story was the same one she had heard from Mrs. Pendennis, including many of the florid literary descriptions. The housekeeper must have read the account many times to remember it so accurately. Thomas had missed his calling. He should have written thrillers. His purple prose sounded vaguely familiar to Carla; then she realized that he had probably lived long enough to revel in the Gothic horrors of "Monk" Lewis and Mrs. Radcliffe. Writers of that ilk had obviously affected not only his style, but the content of his tale.

Carla poured herself another glass of cider. She was about to return to the manuscript when she was electrified by a sound where there should be none. She had become accustomed to the rattle of the French doors. This sound did not come from that direction, but from the door on the inner wall. It was now secured by the new bolt; but as Carla stared at it she could have sworn the panel moved slightly, as if a heavy weight had pressed against it.

Carla got out of bed. Tiptoeing, she crossed the room and carefully opened the door that led into the corridor. Michael's door was ajar; light spilled out from within. Carla moved quietly; indeed, she had a pleasant sensation of floating weightlessly, like a fairy. She had reached Michael's door before he was aware of her appr—

It was the first time she had seen his roo— dennis had not included it on the tou— sive, being furnished with the — bare necessities she had seen out— the movies)—a peeling iron beds— and a chest of drawers. But Mi—

cluded a few items not normally found in a bedroom. A long mirror on one wall gave her a momentarily dizzying view of a duplicate Michael, busily engaged in weird contortions. He had put up a bar—or was it a barre?—on the opposite wall, and was performing a series of exercises. His costume, tights and sweat shirt, was faded to a nasty gray, and his face was taut with strain.

He saw her, reflected in the mirror, and whirled around. For a moment his eyes blazed with anger. Then the anger faded and he came toward her, moving with long quick strides, but noiselessly; he was barefoot.

"What is it?"

"There's somebody at the door. The inner one, where you put the bolt."

She had his serious attention for a moment. Then he caught sight of the glass of cider, which she had forgotten to put down, and his features froze in a look of contempt.

"You're drunk," he snapped, snatching the glass.

Carla's hand flew up to cover his mouth.

"Sssh. I may, or I may not, be slightly under the influence," she said, with dignity. "Nobody ever told me about cider. I would be the last to deny that I am not entirely—hic!—myself."

The hiccup surprised her as much as it did Michael. She moved her hand from his mouth to hers and struggled to control her breath, conscious of the fact that she was not presenting a very convincing case. "However," she continued, from behind her hand, "I am not drunk. There is something behind the door. Or rather, to be perfectly accurate, there was something there; I can hardly suppose that he, she, or it has remained there while we engage in this long, fruitless discussion about my—"

"Shut up," Michael said in a peculiar voice. "I warn you, Carla, stop talking, or I am going to do something I will regret. We'll investigate your improbable visitor. No. On second thought, you had better stay here."

"I have no intention," Carla began firmly. She found herself talking to empty air. Michael had pushed past her into the hall.

She followed. Really, he was very rude. She was walking quite well—no staggers, no swaying. He was rude to imply that she had had too much to drink. A little cider, for the stomach's sake. . . .

However, there did seem to be something wrong with her vision. She ran smack into Michael, banging her nose painfully against his shoulder blade as he stood in her doorway. Her yelp of pain was muffled against his shirt. He turned with the quick economy of motion she had so often admired and swept her into the circle of his arm as she staggered back.

"You were right," he whispered. "You're drunk, but you're right. Sit down before you fall down. I'll see who is there."

He lowered her to the floor and advanced purposefully toward the door. The bolt squeaked when he drew it back, but he moved so quickly that he had the door open before the sound had died into silence.

From where she sat Carla could see past him into the space behind the door. The sight shocked her into relative sobriety. For one breathless moment she thought she was seeing the ghost of Lady Caroline; the pallid, elongated face that stared at her, its eyes dilated to colorless shapes, its dank hair darkened by dripping water looked less than alive. Then she recognized the face, and the additional shock sobered her completely.

"Elizabeth," she gasped. "Elizabeth Fairman. What on earth—"

Elizabeth paid no attention to her.

"Michael," she said hoarsely. "I knew I would find you, I prayed. . . . Oh, Michael, help me."

Whatever Michael had been expecting, it was not Elizabeth. Carla could see only his back, but it was as rigid as rock. Elizabeth reached out for him and then, at last, he moved.

"It's all right, Elizabeth. You're all right now. Can you tell me what's wrong?"

She leaned into the support of his arm as he led her to a chair. Her face twitched horribly, as if some mechanism under the skin were moving muscles she could not control.

"Give her some cider," Carla suggested. "She's in shock."

"Cider be damned. I wouldn't give her so much as an aspirin." Michael spoke without looking at her. He was intent on Elizabeth, who held his hands in a tight grasp.

"I'd better call Alan," Carla said.

"Don't tell Alan," Elizabeth cried. "He'll be so disappointed. He trusted me. He thought. . . . Please, don't tell him."

Michael turned his head. His eyes met Carla's.

"Michael, I have to," she said. "You see that, don't you?"

She didn't wait for an answer. Really, she had no choice in the matter.

After the usual struggle with the unfamiliar telephone system she got through to Alan. She told him in a few blunt words; kindness was impossible in a case like this, one might as well get the bad news out and over with.

He was silent for a long, painful moment.

"I'll be there in five minutes," he said finally. "Wait for me."

Carla waited downstairs by the front door. He was there in less than five minutes, though it seemed longer than that to her. He must have driven like a crazy man, she thought, as she hastened to let him in.

"Where is she?" was his first question.

"Upstairs. Alan—" She put her hand on his arm as he pushed past her. "Michael is with her. I know you don't like him and I'm beginning to guess why; but he's been fine with her tonight. Don't make a scene."

"In front of her? What do you take me for?"

There was no scene. Elizabeth rose from her chair as soon as her brother appeared, and stumbled into his out-stretched arms. Alan led her out, pausing only long enough to say quietly, "Thank you, Carla. I'll ring you tomorrow."

Carla didn't go downstairs with them. She turned back to Michael, who was kneeling beside the chair in which Elizabeth had been sitting. His bowed head and lean body gave him the classic look of a character out of a Greek tragedy; but when she spoke his name he looked up at her with an irritated frown.

"Don't bother me. I'm thinking."

"Think someplace else. I've had it. I—" Carla waved her arms, momentarily without words. "I'm dead tired, and depressed and discouraged. That poor girl. . . . I want to go to bed."

Sitting back on his heels, Michael gave her a long, measuring look.

"Ancient tragedies don't seem so important, do they?" he said.

"How did you know I was reading about—"

"I recognized old Walter's genealogy." Michael nodded at the book, which was lying on the bed. "You wouldn't believe me, would you, if I said that this is all part of a single puzzle? Elizabeth, your weird family history—all of it?"

"I probably wouldn't. What are you driving at?"

"I don't know." Michael rose to his feet without his usual grace: a weary faun, an aging myth. "I've got some ideas I don't even believe myself. . . . Bolt that door before you go to bed."

"Why did you put the bolt on? Did Elizabeth—"

"No, Elizabeth did not come to visit me via that door. But everyone hereabouts knows of it; Walter used it in his younger days for purposes I needn't explain, and so did his father before him. The stair goes down to a gate by the kitchen. Across the fields, in the summer moonlight, the village nymphs gamboled. . . . Oh, go to bed. And give me that cider."

Carla followed his advice. Her head was spinning, but she didn't blame it on the cider. It had been a confusing evening.

 NINE

CARLA came down late next morning, but apparently the rest of the household was also running behind schedule. The smell of coffee led her faltering steps toward the kitchen, where she found Michael efficiently occupied at the stove. Tim was sitting at the table. He rolled one bleary eye in her direction and mumbled something that was apparently intended to be a greeting. Carla growled back at him and slumped into a chair.

"Eggs and bacon?" Michael inquired, waving a spatula.

"Oh, God, no," Carla muttered, and buried her aching head in her hands.

"Funny, that's what Tim said." Michael put a glass in front of her. "I mixed up a brew of this for him; you may as well have what's left. Go on, drink it; it will cure you or end your pain."

The liquid was a revolting brownish red. Carla

pinched her nose together with her fingers and chug-a-lugged the contents of the glass. For a horrible moment matters hung in suspense; then her stomach subsided and she was astonished to find that she did feel a little better.

"Dry toast and coffee," Michael said, supplying these items. "That'll larn you not to tipple in private."

Carla decided not to pursue the subject.

"How is Mrs. Pendennis?"

"Bright as a new penny." Michael flipped an egg and swore as hot fat splashed his hand. "Today is the staff's day off, but Gran wouldn't turn her hand to menial labor. With you two both disgustingly hung over, that makes me chef elect."

"Did you cook eggs for her?" Carla asked unbelievingly.

"Good God, no. She made herself tea and toast at dawn and is now upstairs getting ready for church. I had unlocked her door," he added. "I don't want her to feel she's being imprisoned."

"It wouldn't be smart to make her suspicious."

"It happens to be a particular nightmare of aging people," Michael said in the deceptively gentle voice she had heard before. "They fear senility. Being relegated to a public institution is worse than death to most of them. When you finish you might ring up about Elizabeth. I tried, earlier; but Fairman hung up on me."

Carla glanced meaningfully at Tim. He appeared too groggy to hear, much less understand, what they were saying, but all the same. . . . Michael saw the look, and snorted.

"Tim knows all about the situation. With half a dozen loonies wandering the premises, I can't watch them all.

188

I've recruited him as assistant keeper."

He slapped a plate of food down on the table and began eating.

"Michael, we can't go on like this. Something will have to be done about Mrs. Pendennis."

"Something is being done." Michael pushed his plate back and stood up. "Excuse me. I am about to drive dear old Gran to church. How proper can one get?"

After he had gone, Tim lifted his drooping head. He and Carla exchanged glances of profound mutual sympathy.

"Why don't you split?" she asked.

"Masochism," Tim mumbled. "Being raked over the coals by Mike is a little like sticking pins in yourself."

"You need a nice walk in the nice fresh air," Carla remarked, glancing at the window. The weather had cleared. It was a beautiful sunny day.

"So do you."

They contemplated one another in silence. Then Tim put his head down on the table and Carla went upstairs to lie down.

Michael's horrible drink did seem to help. After a while she felt strong enough to rise and face the day. She had been dimly aware of a bell ringing somewhere in the depths of the house, but she hadn't had the energy to pursue it to its source. Now she realized that it might have been Alan. Perhaps he had called to tell her he wouldn't be able to keep their date. She had better call him back. Anyway, common decency demanded that she inquire about Elizabeth.

Alan had called, but not to break the date.

"No, really," he said, when she expressed concern over the weariness that was apparent even in his voice,

"I'd like to get out, if you can bear with me. I suppose you don't feel like sailing? It's a glorious day, but rather breezy."

Carla suppressed a shudder.

"I don't think I had better, Alan. What about a swim?"

"Just what I need. May we use your little beach? I'm not in the mood for a lot of other people right now."

"That's a good idea. Can you leave Elizabeth?"

"Yes, certainly. She's much better this morning, and Simon has agreed to stay with her. I'll be with you in about an hour, if that is okay."

Carla was ready when he arrived. She was wearing a new bathing suit, with a matching wrap; the breeze was still cool, though the sun promised a warm afternoon. Alan's dim eyes brightened at the sight of her. He was also dressed for swimming, but carried shirt and trousers over his arm.

"I thought we might pop off somewhere for dinner afterwards," he said. "Isn't this the cook's day out?"

Carla agreed, feeling that he was entitled to some sympathy and consideration. In what she hoped was a friendly, undemanding silence, she followed him through the gardens toward the western gate.

It would probably be a long time before the name, and the sight of the structure, failed to send a shiver up her spine. Yet it looked innocent enough in the morning light, and the path down the cliff turned out to be less formidable than she had feared.

Alan preceded her, reaching back to give her a hand now and then, but there were plenty of rocks and weeds to cling to. The granite formed a natural staircase, which in some sections had clearly been improved by the hand of man. There was even a wooden railing in one spot; but when Carla reached for it, Alan snapped out a warning.

"That hasn't been repaired for years. Better not trust to it."

Carla had no leisure for gazing at the view as she descended. When she reached the bottom of the cliff she let out a cry of pleasure.

The sand glittered like snow in the sunlight. The surf rolling gently in looked like the train of a blue velvet robe edged with filmy lace. Between sheltering arms of rock the small bay basked in warmth, protected from all but a direct west wind.

The only object that marred the idyllic beauty of the spot was man-made—a tumbled heap of wood at the extreme end of the southern point.

"The remains of the old boathouse," Alan explained, when she asked about it. "It's gone the way of everything else on the estate. Avoid that part of the beach, there are rusty nails by the bucketful."

The water felt cold at first, but once she was well in, it was just what her jaded muscles needed that morning. She paddled happily, and Alan's head popped up beside her, sleek as a seal's.

"It's divine," she sputtered. "The water is so warm."

"All a matter of currents. Just don't come here alone. You're perfectly safe within the arms of the bay, but there's a tide out there that would drag you clear to the Scillies."

"I know, Simon already warned me." Carla turned on her back and splashed.

She was not really a strong swimmer, and was soon ready to go in. Stretched out on a towel, chin on her folded arms, she watched the flash of Alan's muscular arms as he swam back and forth as if doing a required number of laps. It was a healthy way to work off anxiety; when he finally waded up onto the beach, she saw that he was smiling.

"Now we can talk," he announced, sitting down beside her. "It won't be easy to concentrate on what I'm saying, though; mind if I spread a towel over that gorgeous body?"

"No, I need the sun. You'll just have to control yourself."

"You are a bit pale."

"I'm going to come down every day," Carla said dreamily. "Not alone; I can probably get Tim to come with me. Or Michael." She saw Alan's face change, and sat up, forgetting her suntan. "We might as well get it out, Alan. Why do you dislike him so much?"

"Surely you can guess. You've seen the way Elizabeth looks at him; the way she ran to him last night, when she was. . . . I can't help blaming him for her breakdown."

"I doubt that a psychiatrist would agree."

"Oh, they babble about childhood experiences and all that rot; I can't make sense of what they tell me. The fact remains that she was all right until he. . . . She had an abortion."

The last sentence came out like an explosion. Alan's face was averted; his fingers moved stiffly, sorting a handful of miniature shells.

"That's not exactly shocking, these days," Carla said, fumbling for the right comment. Alan had not struck her as a prude, but perhaps a man felt different about his sister. . . .

"I'm not the one who is shocked," he protested. "I know Elizabeth; I know that if she . . . yielded to a man, it would be because she was pressured and persuaded.

192

She's always been shy and unsure of herself. That's why the episode hit her so hard. She doesn't even remember it, Carla. That's why she turns to Michael. She thinks of him as her lover, not her seducer—her betrayer."

Carla was taken aback, not by what he was saying, but by the terms in which she expressed it. He sounded like an Old Testament Fundamentalist, or a Victorian father. It was so alien to the Alan she knew that she could hardly believe what she was hearing.

"Michael denies the whole thing," Alan went on. "He's perfectly safe in doing so. It's her word against his, and who would believe a crazy, mixed-up girl? But I believe her. I know she isn't . . . promiscuous."

"Of course not. Any woman who falls in love can be weak."

Good God, she thought, it's contagious; I'm talking the same sort of rubbish he is.

Alan went on in the same vein for some time, while Carla murmured sympathetically. The murmurs were not entirely sincere. She felt sorry for anyone who was so genuinely distressed, but she couldn't quite empathize with Elizabeth's illness, not if it was really caused by what modern society regarded as a minor misdemeanor. She was relieved when Alan finally said,

"Well, that's enough of that. I can't tell you how much I appreciate your sympathy, my dear. Shall we go in again?"

"We have to settle one more thing," Carla said. "The house. I promised Michael I would ask."

Alan sighed. "I thought we had settled that. Rather than see him have the house, I'll buy it myself. Honestly, Carla, he probably couldn't raise enough money to make a deposit on a bicycle. Even if I weren't personally biased, I would advise against dealing with him. I hadn't meant to mention it, since negotiations are still in the preliminary stages, but I may have a buyer. I think I can get a fairly decent price."

"I've decided to stay on over the winter," Carla said, and then started as he turned a face of blank horror upon her.

"Are you insane?"

"I've got it all figured out," Carla protested. "I'm going to fire Mary and the cook; I don't need them. The remaining contents of the house will have to be sold anyway, and I'll bet I can find enough antiques to tide us over through the winter. Alan, I'm really excited about it. I'm sure I can do it. If not, I'll just hand over the keys and move out. I have my return ticket. If I can't get my old job back, I'll work in a dime store or super-market."

"I don't know what to say," Alan muttered. "Give me a moment to recover from the shock."

"Why is it such a shock? It's a slightly impractical idea, maybe, but after all, Alan, I'm not incompetent. I've been looking after myself for years. If this fails, it won't ruin my life."

"I suppose you're right. I can't get over my conventional attitudes so easily, I guess." He smiled at her. "Give me a day or two to think it over. Perhaps I can work something out."

Without waiting for an answer he ran out and plunged into the surf. Carla followed more slowly. Lawyers were notoriously cautious people; Alan probably felt it was his duty to steer her into sensible decisions. But she was getting a little tired of his exaggerated reactions to her suggestions.

By tacit consent the subject of Michael was not raised again that day. They swam, and lazed in the sun, and swam again, and later in the afternoon Alan took her to an inn in a remote village, where they had several drinks and an excellent dinner. It was not, however, a very successful day. Alan was remote and distracted, and Carla thought he must be anxious to get back to his sister.

"Please let me know if there is anything I can do for her," she said conventionally, when Alan dropped her off; and then, to her disgust, she felt a deep flush rising over her face as he looked meaningfully at her. There was something she could do. She could sell the house, thereby forcing Michael to leave the area.

She was about to open the front door when King came out of the underbrush and leaned against her leg. Still ruffled by Alan's behavior, Carla bent to stroke him. He had a horrid, rasping purr, as if he were suffering from laryngitis. Now that she thought about it, she had never heard him meow. Perhaps the sound was not in his repertoire.

Carrying the cat, she entered the house. Michael appeared from the direction of the kitchen, so promptly that she suspected he had been watching for her.

"Well?" he demanded. "Did you talk to Fairman?"

"Yes, I did." Carla hesitated. She knew what Michael's reaction was going to be, and she was in no mood to endure another outburst of masculine ire. "How is Mrs. Pendennis?"

"She's in the village, dining with a friend. I'm going to fetch her soon. What did he say?"

"He said he'd buy the house himself before he'd let you have it."

"Oh, did he? I don't suppose he mentioned that he's no more affluent than I am. He must be up to his neck in debt for his car, and that ghastly house."

"He also said he has a potential buyer."

"Did he bother explaining why he's so damned antagonistic to me?" She hesitated, and Michael went on, "I suppose he invented some frightful tale of vicious behavior on my part. You might do me the justice to tell me what he's accusing me of, so I can defend myself."

"I don't see what you could say," Carla retorted. As always, his antagonism aroused the worst in her. "It's not surprising that a man should resent his sister's lover."

"Is that what he told you?" To her surprise Michael began to laugh. "And you believed him. You haven't a great opinion of my taste, do you? I'm fond of the poor little thing, but I assure you—"

"He said you would deny it."

She saw his face darken and the veins on his neck begin to swell, and braced herself for a roar of outrage. Instead Michael closed his mouth, rolled his eyes, and breathed deeply.

"All right, forget it for now," he said in a mild voice. "Are you making any progress with your query into the family curse? Don't think I am just being inquisitive; I'm asking because of Gran."

"Is she getting worse, do you think? I've been avoiding her, since the sight of me seems to set her off."

Michael nodded reluctantly.

"I can see her deteriorating. I swear, I don't know what's happened to her. She looks fragile and twittery, but believe me, she is a tough old woman without much imagination."

"Why the Hades don't you get her into the hospital for tests? I mean, it's ridiculous the way everybody sits around wringing their hands over poor dear Mrs. Pendennis, and nobody is doing anything to find out what's wrong with her. It could be a simple physical condition, and you're just letting her rot away while you mutter and mumble and shake your head."

"You're a cold-blooded wench," Michael said, staring.

"I'm the only one who has proposed anything sensible," Carla snapped. "My God, you men are exasperating! You're all playing games—even John, he's fascinated by his antiquarian research. If Mrs. Pendennis is suffering from a clot on the brain, we can talk to her from now till doomsday without making an impression."

"You may have a point."

"Then do something! I'd take her to the hospital myself, but I have no authority to make her go."

"I doubt that she'd go with me either," Michael said. He added, with difficulty, "She doesn't exactly trust me."

"I noticed that. I wonder why. Oh, for heaven's sake, go and pick her up, if that's where you were going. I'll keep out of her way this evening."

"What are you going to do?"

"First I am going to dig in the garden. I feel the need of physical activity. Then I plan to spend the evening reading family papers in my room. Tomorrow I am going to explore the attic. Is that specific enough for you?" Michael nodded, as if mesmerized, and Carla finished, "I'm so glad you approve. Good-bye."

After changing to old slacks and sneakers, she came back downstairs. Michael had vanished. At least I got through to him, Carla thought, with satisfaction. I've been dying to tell him off for days. And all the rest of them, too; they sit around emoting, and speculating and theorizing. . . . Men!

Having worked herself into this mood, she was not displeased to find Tim morosely tying up tomato plants. She had a few things to say to him too.

The beaming smile that spread over his face at the sight of her softened her a little. "Are you feeling better?" she asked.

"I may live. Much as I hate to admit it, Mike is right about healthy outdoor exercise. It's shaken some of the fumes out of my brain. Did you come to help? Angel!"

"I don't know much about gardens."

"Me either." Tim leaned on one of the stakes he had been using and looked vague. "He said something about spraying the tomatoes. What do you spray tomatoes with? What do you spray tomatoes *for?*"

"They get worms, I think."

They exchanged blank looks, and then both burst out laughing.

"Poor Mike," Tim said, recovering himself. "We're lousy assistants, aren't we? Sit down and let's chat."

"No, I came to work. I don't think I'll take a chance with the vegetables, but I can cut some of the dead wood out of the roses. Have you got any garden tools?"

"Whole shedful," Tim said, waving a limp hand.

Carla found a pair of clippers and got to work. After cutting the overgrown grass from around the bases of the plants, she began trimming the old dead stalks. That was safe enough, even for a nonexpert. From over the wall came a plaintive crooning. Tim had a pleasant tenor voice, and he went through a long repertoire of saccharine Irish love songs. Carla grinned as she listened, but did not yield. Finally she straightened up, sucking a scratched finger, and surveyed her work with pride. It really did look better. She had only cleared a small part of the rose garden, but the part she had done looked fine, at least to her inexperienced eyes. She returned to her work with renewed energy.

After a time she realized that the tenor crooning had stopped. She straightened her aching back and looked around. Atop the wall, not far from her, was a weird apparition: Tim's face, apparently balanced on top of the wall.

"How did you get up there?" she asked.

"I'm hanging by my hands," Tim replied, in stifled tones. "Aren't you ready to stop work? I'm exhausted. Anyhow, it's getting dark."

"I guess I might as well. Ouch. I've got a million thorns stuck in me."

At her request, Tim checked to make sure Mrs. Pendennis was out of the way before she went in. When he came back, Michael was with him.

"I persuaded her to lie down," he reported. "She's got some damned little white pills that Simon gave her...."

"So what's wrong with that? Simon is a doctor; I'm glad one of you male creatures is doing something practical."

"Oh, very practical," Michael said. "When people get in your way, just dope them till they're dizzy. I told her I'd take her some soup in a while, but she was looking pretty groggy."

"I could do with a little snack myself," Tim said, just in time to avert a brisk exchange between Carla and Michael. Carla shrugged.

"You can make me a sandwich while you're at it," she

said pointedly. "I saw the remains of a roast in the fridge."

The three of them got the meal together, such as it was: sandwiches of rare roast beef and thick homemade bread, a can of Campbell's soup, and beer. Michael took soup up to his grandmother and returned to report that she was ready to sleep. He sat down at the table and looked disapprovingly at Carla's hands.

"Don't you have sense enough to wear gloves when you work around roses?"

"I couldn't find a pair that fits me."

Despite her protests, Michael insisted on operating. She was squirming by the time he had extracted the last thorn and painted the hole with iodine. When they had finished eating, Tim and Michael tossed to see who would do the dishes. Carla had pointed out that not only were her hands too sore to put in soapy water, but that she was the owner of the house. Tim lost. He did the job as badly as he possibly could, but neither of his companions offered to take over.

The jokes and friendly insults and the casual food had created an atmosphere so relaxed that Carla found herself lingering, instead of returning to her reading. It was a glorious night, and she was in no mood for Squire Thomas's wild stories. But nobody offered to take her for a walk in the moonlight, so eventually she got up from the table.

"I'll be in the library for a while," she said.

Tim caught his friend's eye and gave a wide yawn.

"I'm for bed, with a good book. I still haven't recovered from last night."

Michael volunteered nothing.

"Are you going swimming again?" Carla asked.

"Probably not. It's rather late. Why do you ask?"

"So I won't have hysterics when I see a dripping figure approaching the house," Carla said. "Actually, you're pretty stupid to go down there alone."

Michael refused to respond to this insult, and they separated.

With moonlight silvering the window and a soft breeze stirring the leaves outside, the library was a delightful room. Carla unlocked the cupboard and began sorting through the papers.

As she had expected, the cupboard held many of the raw materials out of which Walter had constructed his family history. The old letters and account books were interesting, but Carla did not linger over them. She was looking for the eighteenth-century material.

Finally she was forced to admit defeat. Either Walter had kept that part of his working papers elsewhere, or the unknown who had removed the pages from the genealogy had made a clean sweep of the source material as well. She found nothing that bore on the family mystery.

The fruitless search had taken an inordinately long time. The papers were jumbled indiscriminately into boxes and envelopes, with very little attempt at organization. Many were undated, so she had to skim through the body of the text before she could determine when they were composed. Glancing at her watch, she was surprised to see how late it was. The silence was profound; even the mice seemed to have gone to sleep.

Carla closed and locked the windows. The library was in the front of the house; there was nothing to be seen on the lawn except dark masses of overgrown shrubbery and, at the end of the driveway, an occasional flash of headlights from a passing car.

She went upstairs and climbed into bed with Squire Thomas's manuscript. She opened it at the beginning—the part she had skipped over the first time she had tried to read it.

Thomas had been a scholar of sorts—the sort who piles up reference after reference to prove, not a point, but his own intellectual superiority. His pages were crowded with quotations in half a dozen languages, including Latin and Hebrew. Fortunately there was enough English for Carla to follow his argument.

In pagan Europe, Thomas reported, it was common to sacrifice a victim to a river god on Midsummer Day. Water gods in Africa, Burma, and China preferred virgin brides, but the European spirits were not so particular. There was a definite connection between water and fertility, however. Syrian maidens and Scottish lassies sometimes became pregnant while they were swimming as a result of the embrace of an invisible water spirit. And very convenient that belief must have been for careless young ladies, Carla thought cynically.

There were many legends about mermaids, but not so many about their male counterparts. However, other water spirits demonstrated decidedly male characteristics. The Great Sillkie was a Celtic spirit. A man while on the land, he reverted to his seal form in the water; and in either shape he was apparently a seductive lover. His story had been immortalized in one of the Child ballads; Carla now remembered having heard Joan Baez sing it.

So the legend wasn't quite as bizarre as she had believed. It had precedents. However, the Tregellas version was unique in one aspect—the reincarnation theme.

Where on earth, she wondered, had Thomas dug that up? In his day the idea had not been as familiar as it was in modern times, when half-baked misinterpretations of Oriental philosophies were known even to casual readers. Of course, Thomas was trying to find an excuse for his sister's behavior, and he was obviously acquainted with Eastern religious thought. . . . He was also obviously crazy, Carla thought sourly.

Thomas made a great point of the recurrence of water creatures in the family heraldry. He claimed that the curious knocker on the front door was of great age. It represented a mythical aquatic monster—not a fish. The Roman paving had been fairly intact in his day, and it too bore representations of strange creatures, half human, half fish. Yet as far as Carla could tell, Thomas's proof of the amorous merman's existence was based on an ancient parchment which he claimed to have found among moldering family papers in the attic. Apparently he had found his Roman princess in the same apocryphal source; he talked about her as if he had been introduced to her at a tea party, and Carla got a ridiculous mental picture of a lady dressed like Cleopatra as played by Elizabeth Taylor, who behaved like a nice young upper-class girl—except for her one unfortunate error of falling in love with a demon.

Yet Thomas's description of the merman had a certain evocative power. "He is fashioned, they say, with the sinuous slenderness of all sea beings; yet he is abnormally strong and powerful. There are gills in his neck; these he must have, to live underwater, but when on land, they close, and there is little to distinguish him, in outline, from a man. His hair is dark and sleek, like a seal's fur. It grows down upon his brow. He goes limping, it is said, for he is not accustomed to walking upon land."

A nice touch, that last one, Carla thought. Of course his feet would hurt, the poor thing. Somehow this part of the description came closer to genuine horror than anything else in the manuscript. It was so logical.

"So," Thomas concluded, "the soul of the doomed princess returns in the daughters of this accursed house, who prefer damnation to the mercies of Christ Jesus. Always it is the female who succumbs to temptation, and so it will be until the end of time."

Carla's reaction to this sentiment was a regrettable obscenity. Thomas was a worthy descendant of that fink, Adam, who had bleated, "The woman tempted me," when he was caught cheating. If Thomas was a chip off the old block, it was no wonder Lady Caroline had fled from her family to the damp embraces of a merman—especially one who looked like Thomas's description.

She let the manuscript fall onto her lap and looked at the portrait.

It was barely distinguishable. Only the gleam of the gilt frame could be seen in the shadows. Yet Carla had a feeling of something stirring, something beyond the normal boundaries of the senses.

A month ago she would have laughed mockingly if someone had suggested that she would be vulnerable to any suggestion of otherworldly interference with her ordered life. A month ago. . . . But she was not the same person she had been before her visit to the Boston lawyer. The change was as unbelievable to her as it would have been to her former friends. The photograph of the old house had acted like a magnet, drawing her to it across three thousand miles of ocean, and its pull had intensified with every passing day. Now she was caught in the web of the past that still lived on within the ancient walls.

It could all be explained rationally, no doubt. A psychologist would find hidden frustrations and childhood neuroses, and would accuse her of dwelling in the past as a means of escaping the present. Carla's fingers beat an irritated tattoo on the cover of the manuscript. She couldn't accept such facile diagnoses. On the other hand, she was no more ready to believe in the supernatural.

Abruptly she threw back the blanket and got out of bed. The portrait was getting on her nerves. She had always been a firm believer in facing her weaknesses, but there was such a thing as going too far. The portrait was a nuisance; so get rid of it. Out of sight, out of mind.

"No hard feelings, Caroline," she said aloud, and took the frame in her hands.

There was no reaction from Caroline. The picture came neatly off the wall, and it fit nicely inside one of the cupboards.

Neurotic or not, Carla felt better once it was out of sight. She got back into bed—at least her leg muscles were getting exercised, even if nothing else was—and peered inquisitively into the folder from which she had taken Thomas's manuscript. Where was the famous parchment he kept referring to as if it were Holy Writ? It wasn't in the folder, and she didn't remember anything that ancient among the papers in the library.

The next-to-last page of Thomas's masterpiece gave the answer. The parchment had been in such bad condition that he had destroyed it, after copying the readable portions.

Carla's lip curled. Whom did Thomas think he was fooling? Himself, of course; maybe he was so far gone that he had imagined the moldering parchment and its contents. The quotations had a striking similarity to his own literary style.

They began abruptly, in the middle of a sentence.

". . . are of a race accursed, from the sin of their first ancestress, who gave herself to a soulless creature of the deep. It is said that he has the inhuman beauty demons can assume if there is need; the dwellings of his people are sunken deep beyond the west, a strange city of coral spires and towers of mother-of-pearl. Though their blood is cold, they have human lusts, and so, from time to time they emerge to grasp. . . ."

At this interesting point in the narrative Carla's reading was interrupted. The wavering shriek seemed to come from her open window; but she knew it had not originated outside the house. Mrs. Pendennis's window was not far from her own. Like her own, it would be open for air on such a lovely night.

Her skin was prickling with a horror that Walter's calculated prose had not been able to induce. It took considerable courage for her to get out of bed and open her door.

The corridor was lighted; she thanked God, sincerely, for that small blessing. Where the hell was Michael? Hadn't he heard the scream? He was as close to it as she was. Surely his windows would be open, on such a mild night.

She couldn't wait any longer. The echoes of the cry still lacerated her nerves. She walked down the hall and knocked softly on Mrs. Pendennis's door.

There was no answer—no sound at all from within.

Carla tried the knob. The door was unlocked. It swung back under the pressure of her hand.

Mrs. Pendennis was lying on the floor. The bed-clothes, half on the bed, half wrapped around her, suggested a wild, but abortive, attempt at flight. The old woman's eyes were wide open, and for a moment Carla's heart stopped. Then she heard the harsh rattle of the housekeeper's breathing.

Half-remembered articles on first aid flooded her mind. A doctor—that was the first thing. She turned, in time to run full-tilt into Michael.

His chest was heaving in and out like a bellows. When he tried to speak, his words came out broken by gasps.

"What happened? Who—"

Then he caught sight of his grandmother. Pushing Carla out of his way, he bent over her prostrate body.

"She's had a stroke, I think. Stay here. Don't move her."

He had no sooner disappeared than Tim wandered in, yawning and rubbing his eyes.

"I thought I heard something," he mumbled.

"Yes, you heard something. A lot of help you are." Carla stepped to one side. Tim's eyes focused.

"Wow. Is she dead?"

"No. Don't touch her."

"Not me." Tim sat down in the nearest chair. "Poor old girl. Looks like a stroke."

He was the calmest of them all, and in better shape to notice trivial details. His nose wrinkled, and he sniffed like a dog.

"Funny smell in here."

Now that he mentioned it, Carla smelled it too. Fading but unmistakable, the smell of sea water—brine. Unwillingly, drawn by an impulse she could not account for, she went to the window.

There was no balcony outside Mrs. Pendennis's window, only a sheer drop to the ground two stories below. Yet on the window ledge, shining slimily in the lamplight, was a wide, wet trail like that left by a giant snail. It went over the ledge and down, and disappeared.

 TEN

DAWN was brightening the sky before Michael returned from the hospital. He found Tim and Carla in the kitchen. Neither had been able to sleep, and Carla had spent the night making pot after pot of coffee. She filled a cup for Michael as he slumped wearily into a chair.

"Could you eat some breakfast?" she asked. "Or do you want to go straight to bed?"

Michael was unmoved by her kindly concern.

"I'm not going to bed."

"How's Mrs. P.?" Tim asked.

"Still unconscious. Nobody is willing to make any predictions as yet, but the doctor said her heart is surprisingly good for her age."

"I wonder when she'll be able to talk." Carla put bacon in a pan. Michael's temper was bad enough when he wasn't hungry. Perhaps food would wipe the scowl off his face.

"If, not when," Michael said shortly.

"She saw something," Carla muttered.

"You can't be sure of that. There must be pain, in these cases—or time enough to be terrified of what is happening to your body."

Carla glanced meaningfully at Tim.

"You tell him," Tim said. "I can't bring myself to do it."

"And you an Irishman," Carla jeered.

"What are you talking about?" Michael demanded.

Carla told him about the smell of salt and the strange sticky trail on the windowsill. She had insisted that Tim look at it too. Not only did she want a witness, she wanted to be sure her own senses weren't tricking her.

"Come now," Michael said skeptically. "Are you implying that your demon lover is so simple he can't find the right room? You make him sound like a character in one of those French farces—in and out of bedrooms."

"Something was in that room," Carla insisted. "If you don't like the demon lover, then it was something alive and human. Mrs. Pendennis saw it, and it frightened her into a stroke. Michael—at the risk of sounding like Agatha Christie, do you think we could spread the word that she's dying—that she'll never be able to speak?"

Michael considered the suggestion with no sign of the contempt she had expected. Finally he shook his head.

"Not unless you can persuade Simon Polreath to tell the same story."

"He was there?"

"Of course. He's her doctor; they rang him as soon as we arrived at the hospital and he came rushing over.

Dedicated chap," Michael added, with no change of expression.

Carla had been cooking while she talked. Now she scooped eggs and bacon onto a plate and gave it to Michael. He contemplated the greasy ensemble without enthusiasm.

"I'm not sure I understand what is going on," Tim said. "Are you two seriously suggesting that an elderly lady's life may be threatened by a killer because she caught him in the act of . . . of what, for God's sake? This is crazy."

"It does sound crazy," Carla admitted. "Tim, do you want some eggs?"

Tim eyed Michael's plate. "No, thanks."

"I know I'm a rotten cook," Carla snapped. "But you had better get used to my culinary skills, or lack thereof, if you plan to stay on. I'm about to fire Mrs. Polreath."

"Good idea." Michael took a bite, shuddered visibly, and said, "Carla, would it hurt your feelings very much if I—"

"Not at all." Carla sat down at the table. "Go ahead, throw it out. If you're going to cook, you can do a couple of eggs for me."

Michael shot the contents of his plate into the trash and began breaking eggs.

"Let's spell it out for Tim," he said. "Carla is beginning to suspect, as I have suspected for some time now, that someone is trying to persuade her to leave Cornwall posthaste, if not sooner."

"But it's all so halfhearted," Carla complained. "I'm still not convinced, Michael; if someone really wanted to get rid of me, surely he would have done something scarier."

"You happen to have a fairly high fright threshold," Michael said, and then negated the compliment by adding, "and you're horribly stubborn. However, your hypothetical villain has been handicapped. He doesn't want us to call the police."

"How do you know that?"

"It's obvious, isn't it? You are vulnerable—anyone is—to a really determined attempt on your life. If someone wanted to injure you, he could do it easily enough. He hasn't. He's been careful to do nothing that would justify a complaint to the authorities."

"Wait a minute," Tim said. "You're arguing backwards. Isn't it equally possible that nothing serious has happened to Carla because your unknown doesn't want to hurt her? Or even that there is no unknown criminal—that all the tricks have been silly, somewhat malicious jokes? That adenoidal Mary might be dumb enough to do them, prompted by someone who has a fancied injury against the family."

"You admit, then, that someone was in Mrs. Pendennis's room tonight?" Carla asked.

Tim's eyes fell. "I have to, or go back to the banshees and Irish baloney I discarded when I was a kid."

"All right," Michael said. "Then we must concede the possibility of danger to my grandmother. She was trying to get out of bed when she passed out. Maybe she felt the attack coming on and was attempting to reach help. But maybe she saw something she shouldn't have seen."

"Maybe, maybe," Carla muttered. "Maybe I'm being too fanciful. There are too many holes in your theory, Michael. For one thing, the villain knows quite well where my room is; if he's after me, why didn't he go straight there? But the biggest objection to a plot is that of motive. I've thought and thought about it, and I can't come up with a sensible reason why anyone should be so anxious to get rid of me."

"Buried treasure," Tim suggested, entering into the spirit of the thing. "Are you sure old Walter didn't bury a miser's loot somewhere on the grounds? Thanks, Mike, that looks good."

Michael distributed the results of his cooking, and Carla, who did not suffer from false pride, ate with relish. She needed the energy, for she was planning a busy day.

"No buried treasure," Michael answered. "Walter wouldn't have sold the family antiques to keep going if he had had any reserves. There's no tradition, not even a hint, of anything of the kind."

"There has to be a reason," Carla insisted. "Or else we're all imagining things. Which is possible. This house seems to inspire fantasy."

"But you still want to stay," Michael said. It was not a question.

"I have every intention of staying. And I'm going to start working on it today. When do Mary and Mrs. Polreath come in?"

"Eight."

"I'll tell them both we don't need them anymore. Then I'm going up to the attic. I don't know much about antiques, but anything old is worth money these days. American tourists will buy any sort of junk; they think they're getting bargains over here. I noticed a couple of antique shops in Truro. I'll take the bus in tomorrow, and talk to some dealers."

"Such energy," Tim exclaimed.

Carla turned on him.

"As for you, Tim O'Hara, I don't believe more than about half of what you told me. I don't know what you and Michael are up to, but I know you're up to something. That's all right with me. You're welcome to stay, but you'll have to earn your keep, and I don't mean standing around leaning wanly on a shovel. The grounds are a disgrace. Use that scythe I saw hanging in the garden shed and whack down a few weeds."

"Yes, ma'am," Tim murmured, his eyes wide.

"I haven't made up my mind about your offer yet," Carla continued, turning to Michael. "But I'll tell you one thing: I am not going to be driven out of my house by anybody or anything, especially a childish old fairy story. I'm going to stay here until I'm tired of the place, or I run out of money, and then I'll decide what to do with the house. In the meantime, let me make it perfectly clear that I do not trust you—or Alan, or his sister, or your grandmother, or Tim, or—"

"How about John?" Michael interrupted. His face was quite expressionless as he listened to the tirade.

"I don't trust him either. But I don't mistrust him quite as much as I do you. I mean, what the Hades do you want with this house? You've got a brilliant career ahead of you. You'd be insane to bury yourself here, in a life of drudgery—"

"Hey, Carla," Tim exclaimed. "Don't you—"

"Shut up," Michael said.

"Yes, do," Carla said. She was fully wound up and in no mood to be interrupted for any reason. "I don't care what Michael's reasons are so long as they don't inconvenience me. I may sell him the house and I may not. It depends to some extent on what he does between now and whenever I decide to sell. So bear that in mind. I'll be back down to deal with the cook after I get dressed. And," she added, as a parting shot, "since Michael doesn't care for my cooking, he can earn his keep by taking over the job. Lunch at one, please."

She stalked out of the room, her head high and her skirts billowing, without waiting for a reply. But as the door closed behind her she heard something that sounded suspiciously like Michael laughing.

When she came back downstairs, wearing old clothes and a scarf over her head, she found the kitchen empty except for Mrs. Polreath, who was staring in dismay at the heap of dirty dishes.

"I'm sorry about the mess," Carla said. "We had a bad night."

"Yes, miss, I was sorry to hear it. How is Mrs. Pendennis getting on?"

"Not well, I'm afraid. She may not regain consciousness."

"Oh, dear, that's a pity. But then she is not young; and she had a good life."

Carla doubted this, but was not prepared to debate it.

"Where is Mary?" she asked.

The cook's face betrayed embarrassment. She turned away and began running water into the dishpan.

"I'm so sorry, Miss Tregellas, but Mary won't be coming in today. She—she has a better position, you see, in a shop in town. I told her how wrong she was not to give notice, but you know how these girls are."

"Yes." Carla studied the cook's averted face. "I understand. Do you, by any chance, have a better offer yourself, Mrs. Polreath?"

From the startled jerk of the other woman's shoulders, Carla knew she had hit the mark.

"That's all right," she said. "In fact, I was going to tell you that I can't afford to keep you on. I'll miss your marvelous cooking, but I'm sure you know what the situation is. I'm a working girl myself. I haven't any money either."

"Yes, miss, I understand." Mrs. Polreath turned. Guilt and relief struggled in her face. "Then you'll be leaving soon, miss? I wouldn't want to think of you all alone in this big house—"

"I'll be fine," Carla said. "What could possibly happen to me? Believe me, Mrs. Polreath, this place is a lot safer than Boston. If you want to leave right now—"

"No, miss, I'll finish my day, so long as I'm here. But I still don't feel—"

"Nonsense. It's not your problem. What about your wages?"

"Mr. Fairman takes care of that. If you're sure—"

"Quite sure. I only wish I could thank you properly for your good work. I'm going up to the attic now, if you want me for anything."

Once she had left the room, Carla's bright smile relaxed into a frown. She had not been looking forward to depriving a woman of what might be badly needed wages; it was a relief to know that Mrs. Polreath had already decided to leave. But her reasons for leaving were obviously as false as Mary's excuse of a better job. Mary had always been afraid of the house. Now she and the practical, less superstitious cook had decided that Mrs. Pendennis's attack was the last straw. Carla wondered what wild version of that event had reached the village, via the invisible grapevine that informs small towns. It wouldn't have to be much wilder than what had actually occurred.

Her mouth set in a tight line. She had not changed her mind. Nobody was going to drive her out of her house.

She attacked the attic with magnificent energy. It turned out to be great fun; her acquisitive instincts were much more developed than she had realized. Remembering the vogue for secondhand clothes, Carla saw silver, if not gold, in the trunks of old-fashioned garments. She shook out dress after dress, admiring the crumpled silks and brocades, the neat hand stitching and delicate embroidery. People didn't make clothes like these anymore. Old as they were, the fabrics and techniques were marvelous. Some of the dresses dated back to the late nineteenth century, if she was any judge of styles.

Heaving and puffing, she shoved the trunks aside and glanced at the books. No point in wasting her time there, she would have to ask a reputable dealer to look them over. She wouldn't recognize a first edition unless she had a checklist.

The furniture was something else that would require an expert's appraisal. An old brass bedstead tempted her; she had admired a less elaborate specimen in a shop back home and had found the price far beyond her means. Maybe she could keep a few pieces—ship them back home eventually, if the cost wasn't too great.

She was trying to decide what to tackle next when she heard a hail from below. She went to the top of the stairs.

"It's the telephone, miss," Mrs. Polreath reported. "Mr. Fairman. I wonder, would you fancy a cup of coffee and a bite of food? You've been up there for ever so long."

"Thanks," Carla said gratefully. "I'll be right down."

She picked up a box that seemed to contain old letters. She could look through them while she drank her coffee.

217

Alan didn't even say hello. His voice was sharp with alarm.

"I've just heard about Mrs. Pendennis. Are you all right?"

"Of course."

"I've heard some rather wild stories."

"I'll bet you have. For heaven's sake, Alan, the poor woman had a stroke. We've been more or less expecting it, haven't we? It isn't catching."

"Then—it was natural? Nothing happened to cause it?"

"I wouldn't exactly say that. . . . No, Alan, I don't want to go into it now. I'm busy. Did you call just to ask after my health? How is Elizabeth, by the way?"

"Splendid. I did have a business matter to discuss."

From his voice she knew he was annoyed at her brusqueness, but she was not in the mood to cater to wounded vanity.

"Yes?" she said briskly.

"First, that wretched Mary has informed me she won't be back. She came in this morning to demand her wages."

"Yes, I know. Mrs. Polreath is quitting too."

"Good Lord. I'll see what I can do to find replacements."

"Don't bother. I told you I couldn't afford household help. Anyhow, with the rumors that seem to be circulating, I doubt that you could persuade anyone to come. We don't have a very nice reputation hereabouts."

"Carla, you can't stay there alone."

"Yes, I can. What else did you want to ask me?"
Alan sighed.

"You are the most stubborn. . . . Well, perhaps this will

solve all our problems. I've had an offer for the house."

"Really? Who from?"

"A firm of builders. They want the land, not the house, of course. But they have made an excellent offer."

He named a figure. It meant nothing to Carla; she could translate pounds into dollars, but comparative values were still a mystery to her.

Alan misunderstood her silence.

"I assure you, Carla, it's a great deal more than I had hoped to get."

"Then you advise me to accept it?"

"I certainly do."

"I'll consider it," Carla said. "But I'm not ready to sell yet."

"You weren't serious about staying on? This offer won't stand indefinitely; they want immediate possession so that they can begin work while the weather holds."

"Then tell them no."

"Carla—"

"I'm going into Truro tomorrow," Carla said. "Suppose we talk about it then. But you can tell them that I've no intention of moving out before the end of the summer. Maybe not then."

Silence. Carla smiled rather grimly to herself and pushed her damp hair back from her forehead. She could picture what Alan's face looked like, and she was glad she wasn't there to see it.

"All right," he said after a moment. "Shall we have lunch tomorrow? I'll ply you with liquor and try to make you see sense."

"Okay. I'll be in your office about twelve."

She had meant to ask him about antique dealers, but

decided against it; he had behaved better than she had expected, but it was clear that she wasn't going to get any cooperation out of him. Strange, how he had put her off with regard to his sister. It was impossible that a girl who had been in Elizabeth's state two days earlier should be "splendid" now.

She squirmed out of the cubbyhole to find Mrs. Polreath waiting with a tray. The smell of fresh coffee blended enticingly with the aroma of freshly baked cinnamon bread.

"Will you sit in the dining room, miss, or where?" the cook asked.

"I'll be in my room for a while," Carla said, taking the tray and surveying its contents admiringly. She hadn't realized how hungry she was. "Thanks, Mrs. Polreath. This looks delicious."

"Thank you, Miss Tregellas. Luncheon at one?"

"Fine."

Carla splashed water on her grubby face and hands before sitting down to her elevenses. She ate two rolls, dripping with butter, before she turned to the letters.

To keep or not to keep? It seemed a pity to throw them away; they were all fifty years old, or more. One bundle had come from a lieutenant in the First World War; they were addressed "Darling Marian," and the black ribbon that bound them suggested to Carla that the boy had been killed in action. The last letter was dated June 14, 1917.

Carla was about to dump the whole lot into the wastebasket when purely mercenary considerations held her hand. Letters from famous people might be worth money. She was no expert on the minor celebrities of British letters or politics. Modern biographers cursed the families of people like Emily Dickinson for destroying personal papers; she didn't want to deprive some university of the privilege of paying her good money for some famous man's love letters. The stamps might even be worth something.

Cheered by the prospect of money, however remote, she washed her sticky hands and returned to the attic. It was getting hot up there under the rafters. Even the flies' buzzing sounded lethargic.

She had wondered how to get into the other attics— for others there must be, the one she had been exploring covered only one wing of the house. Her explorations that morning had exposed the top of what appeared to be a door, hitherto concealed behind trunks and boxes. Fortified by food, she now applied herself to clearing access to it.

She was dripping with perspiration by the time she had done so. The door had obviously not been opened for decades. It was draped with cobwebs spotted with the mummified bodies of hundreds of spidery dinners.

Nothing on earth, not even the certain knowledge that the treasure of the Incas lay beyond the door, would have induced Carla to touch it with her bare hands. Looking around, she saw an old mop and seized it, wondering why on earth anyone would bother to preserve such a thing. Perhaps it was left over from a long-past spring cleaning.

The spiderwebs tore away in filthy tatters as she swiped at them, displaying an even more formidable obstacle—a thick board nailed across the door. Carla braced her feet, seized one end of the plank, and pulled. There was a screech of rusted nails and a yielding sensation, but the board stayed in place.

The skeleton of an ancient umbrella proved too frail to do the job. It bent in two at her first attempt. She had better luck with a pair of fire tongs, but she was gasping for breath before the plank finally came loose. To find, after that effort, that the door was locked, was the final frustration. Carla kicked wildly at the door, à la James Bond, and was as gratified as she was surprised when the rusted lock snapped.

The room within was twilight-dark. There were windows, but they were encrusted with fifty years' worth of dirt. The mop extended before her, to ward off cobwebs, bats, and other perils, Carla ventured tentatively into the room. She expected mice, but heard no sound; perhaps they had already been frightened into their holes by the crash of her entrance.

Under the dirt of years the room was surprisingly neat, though it was filled with objects, every inch of it. Apparently it had simply been closed up when it became too full to hold anything more.

Carla hesitated, debating with herself as to whether to have lunch and a rest before continuing. She needed a flashlight. Yet her acquisitive instincts spurred her on to make at least a preliminary investigation. The earliest objects in the first attic seemed to date back to around the turn of the century, give or take twenty years. If the material here was older, it might be even more valuable. She attacked the nearest container, a large barrel to the right of the door.

The top had not been nailed down. It lifted easily when she took it in her hands. The interior was filled with straw which smelled horribly of mice and mildew. Carla poked at it. Something rustled.

"They are more frightened of me than I am of them," she told herself.

This was probably true, but it failed to convince her, and the first touch of the rotted straw made her recoil in disgust. Momentarily dissuaded, but not defeated, she retreated.

After a long hot shower and a change of clothes she went downstairs in search of the things she would need later. Delightful smells from the kitchen turned her steps in that direction. The cook started nervously when she came in.

"I'm sorry I'm a bit late with luncheon," she apologized. "It will be ready soon, miss; would you take a glass of sherry first?"

"There's no hurry about lunch; I was looking for some things," Carla explained. "Do you have an old pair of rubber gloves? And a flashlight?"

Both these items were available. Carla appropriated them and a handful of rags, for dusting. The garden shed contributed a hammer and a pair of pliers.

Lunch was a slightly uncomfortable meal. Mrs. Polreath, driven by her Methodist conscience, had produced food of such astounding quantity and quality that even Tim's mammoth appetite could not do it justice.

"She feels guilty about leaving," Carla explained, as Michael eyed the heaped-up platters in astonishment. "My mother used to do that—cook, I mean—when she had done something she regretted afterwards."

"Lovely idea," Tim said, piling his plate.

"You've never mentioned your parents," Michael said. "Are they still living?"

"My father died two years ago. Mother's in one of

those retirement villages in the Southwest. She loves it. She plays golf and bridge every day, and goes to macrame classes, and drives a little golf cart. Michael, I'm sorry, I forgot to ask. Any word from the hospital?"

"I hadn't expected any. I'm going in this afternoon."

"While I," said Tim, "scythe. What is the proper verb form?"

"There isn't one," said Carla. "Doesn't one 'wield a scythe?' "

"I don't think that is a good description of what I have been doing," Tim admitted. "To wield an object implies some degree of skill. If I cut my leg off, do you pay workmen's compensation?"

"Work seems to agree with you," Carla said heartlessly. "You're in a very good mood."

In fact, there was something a little forced about his banter. Carla thought he might be babbling in order to cover up Michael's silence, for the latter spoke hardly at all, and excused himself before the dessert. Mrs. Polreath looked disappointedly at his empty chair when she carried this dish in—a mammoth trifle, covered with whipped cream and oozing jam at every seam.

"I made Mr. Michael's favorite dessert. Wasn't he hungry?"

"I'll eat his share," Tim said hopefully.

"Put it in the fridge, Mrs. Polreath," Carla said. "I'm sure he'll enjoy it later. He's going in to see his grandmother, and I expect he's a little preoccupied."

After lunch, Tim suggested a swim.

"Of course we must rest for an hour or so first," he remarked guilelessly. "It wouldn't do to swim on a full stomach."

"You can work off the full stomach with the scythe,"

Carla said. "I'm going back to the attic."

"How about later?"

"We'll see. If you are tired of scything, you might have a look at the rail along the path down to the beach. It's very rickety, I am told. If it can't be repaired, it might be safer to remove it."

"Yes, ma'am." Tim came to attention, his hand at his forehead.

"I'm leaving now," Michael said from the doorway. "See you later."

As she climbed the stairs, carrying her equipment, Carla thought longingly of Tim's suggestion. It would be much more pleasant to lounge on the beach than grub in a hot, dusty attic. After she had put in a few more hours' work, she would let Tim off for the day, and enlist him as lifeguard. That job would be much more to his taste than what he had been doing.

Only will power—and greed—forced her into the dark, dirty room she had opened that morning. Its temperature must have been over a hundred degrees. Standing in the doorway, she shone the flashlight around. The room was so full it was hard to distinguish any single item, but a marble-topped washstand and a tall carved wardrobe looked interesting. Most of the articles were in bags, boxes, trunks, or barrels. Some of the smaller boxes could be dragged out into the greater spaciousness of the outer attic, but heavy barrels, like the one she had opened, would be more easily investigated in situ.

Even with the rubber gloves on it took nerve to plunge her hand into the moldy straw packing. Ignoring agitated rustles from the depths of the barrel, she fumbled cautiously. Her fingers closed over a solid object and she lifted it out.

It was a cup of heavy earthenware, with designs in blue on a white background. Carla turned it over. The marks on the bottom meant nothing to her, but a vague memory stirred; she had seen reproductions of similar china in a department store. She delved again, bringing out another cup and a small plate with similar patterns. One cup was chipped, but the other pieces were in good condition. Carla put them aside, and tried another barrel.

Two hours later she had dragged many of the smaller boxes out into the larger attic, and had disinterred more dishes, a mass of disintegrating fabric whose original function was no longer discernible, a collection of children's toys, and other miscellaneous objects. She might have gone on indefinitely, ignoring a fierce headache born of heat and bad air, if Tim had not called up to her.

"Here I am," she shouted, and heard his heavy footsteps mount the stairs.

"What the hell are you doing?" he demanded, looking around the room. "You look like a chimney sweep."

"I'm having a wonderful time," Carla gasped. "Look at this cup."

"Hideous."

"It was somebody's everyday dishes," Carla said. "The good china wasn't packed away, it was used—sold—broken. But some neat housekeeper put this away when it was no longer stylish. It's old. I'll bet it's worth money."

"That thing?" Tim looked at it with more respect, but shook his head doubtfully. "It looks like Woolworth's worst to me. Why don't you quit for the day? It's as hot as a pizza oven up here."

"As long as you're here, you can drag out some of the heavy boxes for me. I want—"

226

"Oh, no. You'll have a heart attack if you stay up here much longer. I'll haul the stuff out for you tomorrow if you insist, but you've done enough for one day."

"Just one more trunk," Carla said.

"Okay. But if you aren't downstairs in ten minutes, I'll come back up and drag you down."

Much as she hated to stop, Carla had to admit he was right. She was getting light-headed. But the trunk she wanted to investigate looked particularly intriguing. Leather, brassbound, it had once been a handsome and expensive piece of luggage, and she had just about broken her back dragging it out. She was relieved to find that it was not locked. The lid creaked and clung, but it lifted when she pushed.

The contents had been wrapped in a heavy oiled paper, now brittle with age. Under the paper was a mass of fabric, crumpled and yellow. With the utmost delicacy Carla lifted it out.

It was a wedding dress. She knew that, as certainly as she knew whose dress it had been, although the style and fabric had nothing particularly bridal about them. The white satin had turned a dark cream, and the silver embroidery was black with tarnish. The lace that trimmed the low neck and elbow sleeves had kept its color better than the satin, but it, too, was yellowed. The skirts hung limp without the petticoats or hoops that would have filled them out.

Carla got unsteadily to her feet. Vertigo seized her and she swayed dizzily, trying to keep her balance. Her eyes stung with the salt of her own perspiration. "I'm tired," she thought confusedly. "Tired and hot and cramped; that's all."

With the dress over her arm, she went slowly down

the stairs, clinging to the wall as she descended. Her knees still had a strange tendency to give way under her, and she told herself that they must be stiff from kneeling and squatting on a hard floor. She hung the dress in her wardrobe, careless of the sag of the fragile old fabric, and headed for the bathroom.

It was a warm day, but the lower regions of the house felt almost arctic after the temperature of the attic. A shower washed the cobwebs from her body, and from her mind, but it reminded her of how tired she was. Perhaps a swim would relax her and loosen her stiffened muscles.

Tim was waiting for her in the hall. He eyed the new bathing suit with candid approval.

"You look a lot better than you did a few minutes ago," he said.

"Thanks. You don't look so bad yourself. Is Michael going with us?"

"Why do women always ask about Mike, when they have me? He's not back yet. I left him a note; he can join us if he wants to."

"Okay, let's go."

As Alan had done, Tim preceded her down the cliff. For some reason, perhaps because she was tired, it seemed steeper and more slippery than before. Carla went slowly, grasping every possible handhold. When she reached the railed section, she was pleased to see that several strips of new fencing shone raw and bright in the sunlight. Its support would be welcome.

"I see you fixed the fence," she said, and reached for the rail as Tim turned a startled face up toward her.

"I didn't have time to—watch out!"

The warning came too late. Carla's hand had barely touched the rail when the whole section disintegrated. Off balance, she toppled out into space.

She had a glimpse of Tim's horrified face, and beyond him, of the fanged rocks at the bottom of the cliff. Then something hit her across the ribs, hard enough to drive out the last trickle of breath in her lungs, and a handful of blunt nails dug holes in her back. It was several long moments before she realized that there was solid ground under her toes. Her face was buried in a surface that palpitated like a drum, and her ribs felt mashed.

"Jesus, Mary and Joseph," said a voice she barely recognized. It was shaking with sincere devotion. "Are you all right? Carla, don't faint, please, because I'm too weak to hold you up."

His arms were locked around her. Carla had to shove hard against his chest before his grasp relaxed, and even then he kept hold of her, as if afraid she would slip off into emptiness.

He was too sunburned to turn pale, but his smile was not up to its usual standard.

"Maybe we should practice that a few more times. You weren't very graceful."

"I don't know how you did it," Carla stammered. "I thought I was gone."

"You almost were. If I had not mighty thews and muscles of steel. . . ." A shudder ran through him, and his smile faded. "No, I can't joke about it. It was my fault. If I had fixed that railing, the way you told me to. . . ."

"But someone did fix it. That's why I leaned on it. Didn't you notice that there were new, fresh boards?"

229

"I didn't pay any attention to it. The only times I've been down here were with Mike, at dusk. I'll have a look. Can you stand alone?"

"Sure."

But she took a firm hold of a rock ledge while he bent to inspect the broken section of fencing. When he straightened up his face was even grimmer.

"I can't tell for sure, but it looks to me as if this was rigged to come apart."

"Sawed?"

"No, a clean break would be unmistakable. Point is, the old rails were set in pockets of concrete. These were simply pounded into the ground; and there isn't much soil here."

Carla said nothing. Tim watched her for a moment, and then said, "Let's get on down before my knees give way. Are you game?"

"I guess I can't stay here indefinitely," Carla said.

It was something of an ordeal to finish the descent, but she managed it. Then she stretched out on the sand, and for a while they lay side by side in silence.

Carla's mind was as active as her body was limp. Like the other incidents, this did not quite justify calling the police; but it was a much more direct attempt to cause injury. At the same time it was a careless attempt, for the carpenter could not have been sure she would use the railing, today or in the near future. Unfortunately there was no way of knowing when the work had been done. She had not been to the beach for over twenty-four hours. Unless Michael had noticed. . . .

But Michael was the most obvious suspect. He had

230

overheard her tell Tim that the railing needed repairing. He could have slipped out to the shore before leaving for the hospital.

She and Tim swam briefly; neither felt like venturing far out. Tim kept close while she was in the water, and he abstained from the ducking and splashing and other horseplay she might have expected from him.

Michael had still not returned when they got back to the house. Tim insisted that she eat something, though she didn't feel hungry, so they went to the kitchen.

The room shone with cleanliness, and the refrigerator was crammed with enough cold food to last for days. Tim hacked a few slices off a roast and Carla forced herself to eat, though his fumbling solicitude was beginning to irritate her. He was at the stove, heating water for coffee, when Carla saw the note. It was lying on the table, pinned down by the sugar bowl, and it was addressed to her.

"Dear Miss Tregellas," it read. "I hope everything will be all right. I feel bad about leaving, so if you ever need me, I will come back, or if you want to come to me you can, any time. I would not go but I know Mr. Michael will look after you. The trifle is in the fridge. Sincerely yours, Ann Polreath."

Carla was touched by this awkward but kindly epistle. So Mrs. Polreath was counting on Michael to look after the last scion of the Tregellases, was she? She had greater confidence in Michael than Carla did.

Tim insisted on going upstairs with her. The way he prowled her room, trying to inspect every corner while appearing not to do so, would have made her laugh if she had not temporarily lost her sense of humor.

"I'll be around," he said, as he left. "In my room. I mean, if you need anything. . . ."

Carla got ready for bed, her fingers fumbling with buttons and straps. It was still twilight outside, but her eyes closed as soon as her head hit the pillow.

 ELEVEN

WHEN Carla awoke next morning, her first conscious emotion was surprise. A whole night in that house without a storm or a midnight alarm? The long sleep had done her good; in fact, she felt fine except for a sore spot in the middle of her back. The memory of the near-catastrophe on the steps was still fresh in her mind, but she could think of it without alarm. It was just another trick, and she had already decided they weren't going to drive her away.

It would be fun to see what the antique dealers of Truro had to say about her cup. Then lunch with Alan, and a good lively fight—for he would certainly nag about selling the house.... Yes, she was looking forward to the day.

When she opened her bedroom door she almost fell over an object that lay across the threshold. Her heart stopped for a moment. In that house, a prostrate form

233

immediately suggested disaster. However, although Tim's eyes were closed, he was breathing placidly. He was rolled in a blanket, his head comfortably snuggled on a pillow. Carla's alarm turned to amusement. She nudged the sleeper with her toe. There was no response. She stepped over him and went on her way to the bathroom.

Tim didn't stir when she passed over him for the second time, on her way back in. Carla finished dressing, without bothering to move quietly. When she was ready, she gave Tim a solid kick in the ribs. This time he responded. Carla watched him grunt and groan and rub his eyes.

"Are you always this easy to wake up?" she asked curiously.

Tim looked up at her dazedly. "I meant to get out before you woke up," he mumbled.

"You're a lousy bodyguard," Carla said. "I've been back and forth several times. Really, Tim—what an idiotic thing to do! Do you want some breakfast?"

"Not if you're cooking," Tim answered. He rolled over, presenting an affronted back to Carla.

"See you later, then." She stepped over him again and started down the hall. A series of explosive wordless complaints, and the pad of bare feet following, proved that Tim had changed his mind about breakfast. After a moment she realized why; she could smell bacon frying and coffee perking. Either Mrs. Polreath had had second thoughts, or Michael was on duty.

Michael it was. He was busy at the stove when she came in. Tim, still wrapped in his blanket and looking like a sulky owl, joined her at the table. Then Michael turned, skillet in hand, and Carla exclaimed aloud.

234

"What happened to you?"

"Brakes gave way," Michael said. "That's why I was so late getting home yesterday. It looks worse than it feels," he added.

The left side of his face, from cheekbone to chin, was raw and scraped. He was holding the skillet awkwardly in one hand. Tim rose, without comment, and relieved him of the heavy pan.

"You had to jump," Carla deduced. "Lucky you weren't going fast. . . . How's the car?"

"Totaled. It's the bus for us from now on."

"Not a good day, yesterday," Tim remarked, serving bacon.

"Tim told me about the railing," Michael said.

"Did he tell you he was planning to sleep across my threshold last night?"

"No, but I'm not surprised. That's Tim all over: chivalrous but impractical."

His mocking tone made Tim blush. Carla rose to his defense.

"He wasn't impractical yesterday. If he hadn't fielded me, I'd have broken my neck."

Michael made no comment. Carla watched with interest as he broke eggs, one-handed. He was good at it. "How bad is your arm?" she asked.

"Twisted, that's all. Are you about ready to pack it in, Carla?"

"No."

"What subject do you teach, when you're employed?"

"Math."

"I'm not surprised. What's on your schedule for today?"

"I'm going to Truro to peddle antiques. Then lunch

with Alan. He'll try to talk me into selling the house. He's had an offer."

"Really?" Michael turned. "How much?"

Carla told him. Michael's eyebrows soared.

"Ridiculous. That's twice what the place is worth."

"More than you were prepared to offer, eh?"

"More than twice as much. Perhaps you had better take it."

"Not unless they are willing to wait six months."

"Think carefully, Carla. There's a fine line between stupidity and courage, and I think you crossed it some time ago."

"Thanks. I thought I'd drop in on Mrs. Pendennis later this afternoon. Can I?"

"Well, they seem to feel she is making a remarkable recovery. But I doubt they'll let you in. No visitors except family, and that briefly. If you were thinking of questioning her, forget it. I tried, obliquely; but she went into a frightful state, and a sister rushed in and evicted me."

"I wouldn't do that. I just want to see her."

"I'll be there later myself," Michael said. "At what time are you expecting to go?"

"Late afternoon."

They finished breakfast in silence, and Tim applied himself to the dishwashing. It was impossible to do this while draped in a blanket, so he hung this article over a chair; and the sight of him washing dishes wearing only a pair of shorts and a fine set of goose pimples—for the early-morning air was cool—was the first touch of comedy Carla had enjoyed for some time.

The bus ride into Truro was fun. The big lumbering vehicle ambled along the back lanes, stopping in obscure hamlets and waiting for long intervals while the driver exchanged gossip and parcels with local residents. As if to make up for lost time, it plunged down the steep slope into Truro at breakneck speed.

Carla arrived at Alan's office some hours later with a smile whose smugness she made no attempt to conceal. Rising to greet her, Alan looked at her suspiciously.

"You look frightfully pleased with yourself. What have you been up to?"

Carla unwrapped the cup from its swathing of tissue paper.

"Delft. Local ware. Early nineteenth century. I've got a whole barrelful of it, at least I think I do. Alan, it's worth lots of money!"

Alan leaned back in his chair and burst out laughing.

"They say the Scots and the Cornish are related. Seeing that mercenary gleam in your eye, I can well believe it. How much money, you little innocent?"

"That depends on how much there is and what condition it's in. But lots. Enough to buy groceries for the winter."

"Whom did you see this morning?"

Carla mentioned a name. Alan nodded.

"He's a reputable dealer. I suppose you're going to let him search the attics? My dear girl. . . ."

"Not just him," Carla said sweetly. "I've also invited the lady who runs that shop on Lemon Street, as well as Cornwall Antiques, Limited."

"I wish you luck."

"Do you really? Darn. I was all worked up for a good argument. Aren't we going to argue, Alan?"

"I have decided," Alan said, "that the more I talk, the more determined you become. I am therefore going to remain silent on the subject. I told you the offer; it will be good for three days, no more. It's up to you. And now, let's have lunch."

They lunched at one of the hotels in Truro, an old building whose former clients had included many eminent Victorians. Alan was at his most entertaining, whispering scandal about the occupants of the other tables and their ancestors; but he fended off Carla's questions about his sister with courteous, smiling skill. She knew he was angry with her, though he was too well bred to display it openly. They parted on the most amicable of terms, but Alan said nothing about wanting to see her again.

It was a long walk to the hospital, but the weather was so beautiful Carla didn't mind the exercise. On the way she bought a bunch of roses; but when she presented herself at the desk, the woman on duty shook her head firmly.

"Mrs. Pendennis is coming along nicely, but she is not allowed visitors."

"Has her grandson come in yet?"

"I don't believe so."

"Well, then, is Dr. Tremuan here? He's a personal friend," Carla added, seeing the woman's face stiffen in incipient refusal. "I'm sure he'll see me."

"I'm afraid I can't. . . . Oh. Are you Miss Tregellas, by any chance?"

"Yes."

"In that case. . . . The doctor did mention. . . . Please take a seat and I will see what I can do."

It was not long before Simon appeared, smiling with pleasure.

"I rang the house this morning and that young chap

—Tim—told me you might be stopping by," he explained, taking her hand.

"I'm glad you thought to leave a message. I guess I would have been thrown out if you hadn't."

"People get officious," Simon said apologetically.

"I guess they have to," Carla said. "Michael warned me I probably wouldn't be able to see Mrs. Pendennis."

"She's an amazing old lady, but she is almost eighty, after all," Simon said. "Leave the flowers at the desk and I'll see that she gets them."

"Has she said anything about what happened?"

"Not a great deal. She becomes so agitated when the subject is mentioned that we refrain from reminding her. It would be best for her to forget the incident altogether."

He hesitated, looking down at his hands as if embarrassed, and Carla said, "I'm not trying to pry, Simon, but you know what has been going on. If there is any clue in what she said. . . ."

"It's all so vague, Carla," Simon said. "One can't distinguish between what she saw and what she believes she saw."

"What does she think she saw? No, don't tell me, let me guess. Did she—did she describe him?"

" 'Seal-dark hair, empty eyes, scaled and webbed,' " Simon said, obviously quoting. "She wasn't all that coherent, you understand. It came out in bits and pieces. She kept saying, 'How did he get in? He couldn't get in.' "

"She read the description in Thomas's manuscript," Carla said. "It's practically word for word. It doesn't mean a damned thing."

"I know. But she must have seen something; she was

most distressed over the fact that something was there, despite the height of her window from the ground. I wonder. . . ."

"Well?"

"One can't interrogate her," Simon said slowly. "But I wonder whether she isn't afraid of something much more solid and real than a family curse. If she saw some person. . . ."

"She would say who it was, surely."

"Not necessarily."

"Oh. I see."

"So do I," said a voice behind them. Carla turned.

"Has she accused me directly?" Michael asked. The bruises on his face had darkened since morning. He was still favoring his right arm. "You're on the wrong track, both of you. If she says she recognized me, she's—let's say she is mistaken. I wasn't even in the house when she screamed."

"Cool down, Michael," Simon said. "She hasn't accused you, or anyone. She's still babbling about fins and scales and—"

"Obviously it was a man wearing a disguise," Michael said in the same soft voice. "It's an old tradition around here, after all. Remember Tennyson's vicar, who used to sit on the cliffs wearing a seaweed wig and a tail made of oilcloth?"

"I didn't realize you were familiar with that story," Simon said.

"Oh, I'm frightfully literate, actually. I simply pretend to be ignorant. May I see her now?"

"I don't think that would be advisable."

"Don't fight," Carla said nervously, for Michael had shifted his weight in a manner she recognized from the days when she had had a boyfriend on the college wrestling team.

"Not in your present condition, at any rate," Simon said with a smile. "What happened to you, Mike?"

"Car went out of control," Michael said.

"Has anyone looked at your injuries?"

"It's not your concern, Tremuan."

"Michael," Carla began.

"Let's go," Michael said. "The next bus leaves at five."

"Wait." Simon extended a placating hand. "I'm sorry if I sounded abrupt, Mike. Let me drive you two home, since your car is out of commission. I was just about ready to leave anyhow." Michael didn't respond, and Simon went on pleasantly, "You can go up for a minute, if you like; but she was sleeping when I last looked in, and they'll be serving tea shortly. That was why I said—"

"Was it? Oh, well." Michael's taut shoulders relaxed. "We could use a lift, at that. Thanks."

"I'll just finish up here. Be with you in a few minutes."

His hand rested lightly on Michael's shoulder for a moment before he walked off. Michael was taller than average, but next to Simon's bulk he looked like a boy, and Carla sensed that he didn't relish the feeling.

They sat in silence for a few minutes. Then Michael said, "Did you lunch with Fairman?"

"Yes. He was pleasant, and I was firm."

"Good for you. Did you happen to ask after Elizabeth?"

"I asked, of course. He said she was fine."

Michael made a rude noise. "Where is she? Do you know?"

"At home, I suppose."

"He didn't say?"

"No, why should he? He's obviously embarrassed about the whole thing. Why are you so curious?"

"He's had her locked in her room since that night."

"Michael! How do you know?"

"The maid is a village girl. She doesn't gossip, as a rule; Fairman has put the fear of God into her, and he pays well enough to be able to enforce his orders; but I have my methods."

"I'm sure you do." Carla was tempted to ask if the maid's name happened to be Vicky, but she decided against it. She said coolly, "I can't see that it's any of your business, Michael."

"It is, though," Michael said, without heat. "I happen to feel that a person with her problems needs professional help, not solitary confinement."

"Why don't you talk to Simon?"

"Because he would agree with you that it's none of my business. Forget it. I asked because I thought he might have said something to you."

Carla didn't ask any more, but she didn't forget it, as she had been told to. Her mind, already heavily loaded with suspicions of Michael, had developed a new one. The car accident had been strangely fortuitous, occurring as it did on the same day she had her near-accident. An alibi, or an attempt to divert suspicion? She felt sure that Michael was perfectly capable of banging himself up in order to add verisimilitude to his story. The marks on his face looked terrible, but they were superficial, and he was actor enough to fake a sprained shoulder convincingly. Now she began to wonder if the injuries had not been incurred in something other than a car accident. If Michael had tried to get into the Fairman house to see

Elizabeth, and if Alan had caught him. . . .

The sprained shoulder was genuine, at any rate. She found that out almost at once when Simon, opening the car door, happened to slip and fall against Michael. A superlative actor, caught off guard, might have been able to simulate the spontaneous gasp of pain, but not even Olivier could turn pale on cue.

Michael was moodily silent during the drive, so Carla chatted busily about her discoveries in the attic, to Simon's visible amusement.

"Good luck to you," he said, as he let them off at the gate. "Perhaps I'll drop by tomorrow and help you count your wealth. No, damn it, I forgot; I've a pretty crowded schedule."

"Come by for a drink anytime," Carla said.

Secretly, she was glad he was going to be busy. She was planning another day-long assault on the attic, and did not want to be distracted.

The antique dealers arrived bright and early the following morning, and for several days she sweated and strained in the dusty attic, making money hand over fist —or so it seemed to her. She developed a surprising aptitude for bargaining, playing one dealer off against another with ruthless skill. The barrel she had investigated had a complete set of delft, in relatively good condition, that all three dealers visibly drooled over. Carla sold it, several pieces of furniture, and two boxes of old clothes. Then she called a halt. Golden visions were swimming in her brain: London dealers, Sotheby's. . . . Her decision merely whetted the appetites of her victims, and they left with reluctant backward glances. Carla felt sure she could go on for some time with the money she had made thus far. Why on earth hadn't Walter exploited the attic treasures? Laziness, perhaps. He was not a young man; probably he had snatched the things that came first to hand, knowing he would not live long enough to empty the house altogether.

It was as if the house cooperated with her in her efforts to remain with it as long as possible. After the disturbing episodes of the earlier days, there was a complete absence of trouble while she was on her selling spree.

"Not even a stubbed toe," as Tim put it, while they were eating a hastily assembled cold supper on the evening of her final day of selling.

"Maybe we've come to the end of a streak of bad luck," Carla said, foolishly euphoric after a successful afternoon with Cornwall Antiques Ltd.

Tim looked at her scornfully.

"Bad luck, hell. Bad luck doesn't jinx fences, or cut brake cables."

"Was that what happened to Michael's car?" Carla glanced vaguely around the room. "Where is he, anyway?"

"He's at the hospital," Tim said disgustedly. "Not that you would notice; you even missed the fight last night."

"What fight?"

"With Fairman." Tim laughed. "Mike's got a fat lip on top of his other bruises. But he says Fairman looks worse."

"Oh, God." Carla came back to earth with a bump. "Did he go over there and demand to see Elizabeth? What's the matter with him?"

Tim considered this question seriously.

"Plenty. If you gave a damn, I could tell you about some of it."

"You'll have a fat lip yourself if you don't shut up,"

Michael said from the doorway. "What's for dinner? Not that mutton again! Can't either of you cook?"

"I can't, and Carla won't," Tim said. "She's been upstairs all day cheating the natives. How's your grandmother?"

"As well as can be expected," Michael said. He got a plate from the cupboard and sat down. His bruises were fading, but the swollen lip was very much in evidence. He chewed carefully on one side of his mouth.

"Don't tell me you visited your dear old grannie today," Carla said. "I know that look; you've done something awful, and you're proud of yourself. What?"

"I can't imagine what you are talking about," Michael said.

Carla never had time to frame her next question. The kitchen door burst open, and crashed back against the wall. She started up, and then sat down again, inadvertently, as Michael's hand tugged at her shoulder.

"Don't move," he said tightly. "Can't you see he's flipped?"

Then she recognized Alan. At first she had seen only a wild, disheveled figure holding a gun. His normally elegant clothing was rumpled and his hair stood on end. His eyes, and the shotgun he carried, were fixed on Michael.

"Where is she?" he asked.

"Hold on, relax," Michael said quickly. "If you shoot me I can't tell you, can I? For God's sake, Fairman, that gun is big enough to blow away everything in the room. Let Tim and Carla move back out—"

"Nobody is going anywhere," Alan said. "I don't care who else gets hurt so long as I don't miss you, Pendennis. She could not have left her room without help, and you are the only one who would have the effrontery to interfere in this matter. What have you done with her?"

Michael didn't glance at the others, but Tim must have received some message from him; very slowly, almost imperceptibly, he began edging his chair away from the table.

"She's on her way to London," Michael answered. "To see a specialist. Harley Street—one of the best—"

"You had no right! I was helping her—"

"Stop deluding yourself, Fairman. You can't just . . . dry her out, and turn her loose. How many times have you done it before? She needs professional help, not your version of cold turkey; she'll never get clear of the stuff until she finds out why—"

"Talk," Alan said, with a travesty of a laugh. "That's all any of you do—talk. I'm the only one who can help her. She trusted me, until you took her away from me. I could kill you for that; but I'll let you live if you give me that address. I'll get her back. They can't keep her without my permission."

"She's an adult," Michael said incautiously. "You can't—"

"I tried twice to kill you," Alan said, as if Michael had not spoken. "Clumsy attempts, both of them; I was in a state of panic, afraid you'd speak. To think I worried about such a trivial matter! I must have her back. Where is she?"

"I'll have to look up the name," Michael said, starting to rise. "I don't remember it. I was referred by—"

"Sit down!" The gun reinforced the order, and Michael dropped back into his chair.

"I have it here," he said quickly, fumbling in his pocket. "Somewhere. . . . Fairman, it's not too late to give

246

up this business. Elizabeth needs you. You can probably get off scot-free in exchange for the names of—"

"Give up?" Alan laughed again. "No one gives it up. Ever. I may as well cut my own throat, it would be quicker and less painful. Do you think I'd risk those thugs getting hold of Elizabeth?"

"They can't hurt her if they're in prison," Michael argued, as Carla stared in bewilderment. Tim was away from the table now. She wondered what he was trying to do. It would be suicide to try to jump Alan.

"Give me one name, in exchange for the name of the doctor," Michael went on persuasively. "You could emigrate, Fairman; change your name, get clean away. Look here, I'll give you a week—longer, if you like—before I go to the police. You can trust my word; you know I wouldn't hurt Elizabeth."

For a moment Carla thought he was getting through. Alan's face changed. He appeared to be considering the proposition. Then, quite suddenly, his lips stretched out in a snarl and he swung the gun barrel up. Michael let out a yell and something hit Carla a smashing blow on the left side, knocking her to the floor. The sound of the shot deafened her.

When her ears had stopped ringing she shoved frantically at Tim, who was lying on top of her.

"Did he shoot you? Tim! Get up, will you, you're mashing me."

Tim was so slow in responding that for a moment she was afraid he had been hit. But when she lifted herself off the floor, she did not look at him. Her heart gave a great leap and began beating again when she saw Michael crouched by the fallen figure.

"God damn it," he said. "You've killed him."

247

"I had to. He was just about to fire."

The response came from the butler's pantry. Simon, leaning against the doorframe, passed a shaking hand over his eyes. "I didn't mean to kill him. I aimed at his arm. Never was much of a shot. . . ."

"Good enough," Tim said. "Thanks, Doc."

"He was going to tell me. . . ." Michael broke off. "Give me that gun, Tremuan, you're too shaky to be trusted with a loaded weapon."

Simon looked at the pistol as if he were surprised to see it. He did not resist when Michael took it from him.

"I've never killed a man before," he muttered. "Not intentionally, at any rate. . . . Sorry. Sorry if I did the wrong thing. What was he about to tell you? I didn't understand what you were talking about. He called me a while ago, raving about Elizabeth's having disappeared, and cursing you. I thought I had better get over here. Good thing I did."

"It sure is," Carla said. "Michael, I don't understand either. What was wrong with Elizabeth?"

"Drugs," Michael said shortly. "Heroin, to be precise. What kind of innocent are you, not to have seen it? I've suspected for some time, but when she wandered in here the other night, it was obvious what was wrong with her. I had hoped Fairman would give me the name of her supplier."

"I doubt that would have done much good," Tim said. "I don't know how things work here, but usually the local supplier is small-fry. They never catch the big ones."

"Come on, we'd better ring the police," Michael said. With an apologetic shrug, Tim followed him out.

248

Carla looked at Simon, who was leaning against the door.

"Don't feel bad," she said. "You couldn't help it; you almost certainly saved our lives, Simon. And Tim was right about the supplier, they don't—"

"What sort of weakling do you take me for?" Simon demanded. He took a long stride toward her and pulled her roughly into his arms. Carla was too surprised to object. She had never seen the mild doctor in this mood.

"I didn't intend to kill him, but I'm not broken up about it," Simon went on. "That isn't why I. . . . Do you realize how close you came to dying, Carla? My God, if I hadn't arrived when I did. . . ."

His lips closed over hers.

"Excuse me," said Michael, from the doorway. "Don't you think you could find a more appropriate place for that, Tremuan? Practically over the body. . . . I mean, it isn't quite the thing, is it?"

When the police had come and gone, with the body, Carla collapsed limply into a chair in the drawing room.

"I could use a drink," said Tim. "And I don't mean beer. Is there anything in that cabinet besides fine old Madeira?"

"I don't know," Carla mumbled. "Have a look. And pour me a double."

Michael returned from seeing the police on their way. Carla winced as she heard the wail of the ambulance siren retreating into the distance.

"What's their hurry?" she asked rhetorically. "It doesn't matter to him."

"Where's the doc?" Tim asked.

"Where do you think?" Michael answered. "He just killed a man, in case you didn't notice."

Tim handed around glasses of brandy, and lifted his own.

"Yes, I noticed, and I propose to drink his health. Here's to Simon, and to June sixteenth—a date I shall celebrate in future years as a second birthday. I like being alive."

"So did Alan," Carla said. "I can't help it, I feel sorry for him."

"You're so damned noble you make me sick," said Michael, who seemed determined to see how disagreeable he could be. "Save your sympathy for Elizabeth. What he's done to that girl. . . . No," he added as Carla looked inquiringly at him, "I'm not talking about incest, or anything as prosaic as that; though in a way I suppose it was a kind of spiritual incest. He's never really looked at another woman, and he's kept her bound to him by undermining her confidence in herself, and by demanding her love as a duty."

"Did he turn her on to drugs?" Tim asked.

"I rather imagine she found that means of escape all by herself. Of course it wasn't an escape, it was another chain around her, once he had found out about it and nobly forgiven her. The drugs were only a symptom, as they often are."

It was a tragic story, but to her shame Carla was able to feel only formal sympathy for Elizabeth. She had never been more than a wraith, an ephemeral figure; and the look of passionate anger on Michael's face when he spoke of the woman made her conscious of an emotion that was even more contemptible than disinterest.

"Then Alan was the one who was playing the tricks?"

she asked, sipping her drink. "Working on Mrs. Pendennis until she came to believe in that idiotic story, hanging up the seaweed. . . . No, that must have been Elizabeth; Alan was with me. He sent her out again another night, but that time. . . ."

"She was too far gone to remember what she was supposed to do," Michael said grimly. "I wonder what he had planned for that episode."

"He said he had tried twice to kill you," Carla said. "The car—and the railing that collapsed must have been aimed at you too."

"We should have realized that," Tim said. "Mike was the one who used that path most often. You'd never go down alone."

"But why?" Carla demanded. "I can see why he might want to kill Michael. . . ." Tim started to laugh. Michael's expression didn't change. Carla said, "I didn't mean it that way. I mean, he did have a motive. But why did he want to get rid of me? I wasn't any threat to his precious Elizabeth."

"I don't know why he bothered either," Michael said nastily. "You're so dim he could have carried out his plans right under your nose, and you'd never have noticed. Think, woman. What has been the chief occupation of the Cornish since time immemorial?"

"Mining," said Carla. Michael snorted.

"Smuggling, you nitwit. That little cove down there is a fine harbor, one of the few on this coast that is privately owned and virtually unused."

Carla's jaw dropped. Michael went on, "You ruined his plans by coming over here, when he expected he could sell the place to his unknown employers with no questions asked, after Walter died. It's a perfect spot for running in an illicit cargo."

"Drugs?" Tim asked.

"And other contraband. It isn't as easy to get illegal merchandise into this country as it is in a big, sprawling, open-bordered place like the States. We're an island, remember. The customs people do a decent job. When they close down one route, the big boys have to find another. I suspect, from the frantic measures Alan was resorting to, that they are presently in need of a new method. This must have looked ideal. They could pressure Alan through his sister, and offer him a substantial bonus for making the deal."

"That company that offered me so much money for the house," Carla exclaimed. "Do you think they—"

"Yes, probably. Not that it will do the police any good to check them out; they'll be a perfectly reputable firm, with a good cover."

"But suppose they still want the place?"

"Not to worry," Michael said quickly. "There's been too much publicity now—in our own small circle, at least. Anyhow, crime is big business nowadays. They don't pursue a lost cause for the fun of breaking the law. They'll write this off and forget it."

"Then we can relax and enjoy life," Carla said, hardly daring to believe it.

"And wax rich on the junk of your ancestors," Michael said sarcastically. "Here's to them—junk and ancestors." He drained his glass and went to the sideboard for a refill.

II

The ensuing days should have been idyllic, now that there was no longer any need to expect midnight alarms and dangerous "accidents." The weather continued fine, the attic yielded up treasure after treasure, and Tim's cooking improved. The vicar came to tea; and Carla spent several enjoyable hours surveying the tombs of the Tregellases in the church. She might not have found this outing enjoyable a few months earlier; now, immersed in family lore, and pouring over Walter's genealogy, she reveled in local history.

Everything was fine except the most important thing. Carla was reluctant to admit it even to herself, but a few days after Alan's death matters came to a head, when Simon Tremuan asked her to marry him.

They were picnicking on the moors, which are so reminiscent of the Brontë country of the far north, and Simon had been entertaining her with wild tales of pixies and hobgoblins.

"This country seems to breed fairy tales," Carla said. "What is there about it?"

"There are plenty of folk legends in your own country," Simon said. "Not as many as we have, they haven't had time to grow—but quite a few. You simply weren't interested in the subject before."

"I know." Carla grasped a handful of the tough, springy gorse. "I love this place. I'm going to hate to leave."

"You needn't leave, Carla. Stay. With me."

Carla wasn't surprised. She had seen it coming on, and had not known what to do about it, because she wasn't sure in her own mind what she wanted to do. Now the knowledge she had tried to deny crystallized. She sat in silence, her head bowed, and sought words that would not be too hurtful. But there was no need. After a moment Simon said quietly, "It's Mike, isn't it?"

"Am I that obvious?"

"Not to anyone except me. Loving you gives me an extra touch of intuition. I don't want to sound dog-in-the-mangerish, my darling, but a lot of women have fallen in love with Michael. He's got . . . I suppose 'sex appeal' is the term."

"It's one term," Carla said, with a faint smile. "And I suppose it's one of the reasons why I. . . . He doesn't care about me, Simon, I know that. And I've no intention of letting him know how I feel; I couldn't stand either contempt or kindness from him. But I can't think about anyone else till I've gotten over him, and I can't get over him when I see him every day. . . . I'm going to let Michael have the house."

"And go home?"

"Yes. As soon as I finish looking through the attic. I may as well have a few keepsakes, to remind me of my one wild adventure."

"But you'll come back."

Carla threw herself onto her back, her hands under her head, and stared up at the wide blue bowl of the sky.

"I'd like to be dramatic, and say, 'Never.' But I'm too old for sentimentality. Yes, maybe I will come back for a visit someday. I'll get over this. That's the saddest thing about growing up, learning that nothing is forever, not even love."

"Sometimes it is," Simon said quietly. "I'll wait, Carla. I'll wait a year, then I'll come to you. That should be long enough to get even Michael out of your mind."

Carla smiled at him. She saw that his hands were tightly clenched. He knew better than to touch her, and she appreciated his intuitive sensitivity.

"So," he went on, returning her smile with a visible effort, "you'll leave without ever discovering what happened to Lady Caroline."

"I won't be leaving for a few weeks. Maybe I can crack the case before then. Really, Simon, I wonder if we aren't making a mystery where there is none. I can think of a dozen things that might have happened to her, all perfectly reasonable, and no way of ever checking on them. And we know how the legend arose. . . ."

"We don't, though, do we? Certainly Alan seems to have used it with Mrs. Pendennis, but he didn't invent it."

"No, that was Squire Thomas. He must have been demented."

"Didn't you say he got the story from an older manuscript?"

"So he claimed. But the old parchment was destroyed, and Thomas's quotes from it sound exactly like the rest of his manuscript."

"So our mystery is only the invention of a crazed old man."

"I certainly hope so."

"Yes, of course. All the same. . . ."

He looked so wistful that Carla began to laugh.

"Simon, you are impossible. You still believe in pixies and ghosties and ghoulies, don't you?"

"Life is so dull," Simon said, with a half-comical grimace. "I'd dearly love to see an honest-to-goodness ghost. And your legend is particularly delicious. The Bane of the house of Tregellas. . . ."

255

"It's not a very demanding Bane, come to think of it," Carla said, entering into his mood. "One sacrifice every two hundred years. And the poor merman isn't really a demon, he just wants his bride."

Simon's eyes brightened.

"A Luck rather than a Bane? The two are not mutually contradictory, actually. The fortunes of the house are guaranteed by the sacrifice. . . . It's quite a common theme in folklore."

"Well, the family fortunes are definitely in decline right now," Carla said. "I suppose I ought to give myself up for the good of the house. But I'm not that noble."

"You're sure you aren't having any eerie sensations of being taken over by another mind?" Simon asked jokingly. "Lady Caroline entering in—yearning for her lover—"

"Not a qualm."

"That's a relief. Much as I'd love to encounter a creature from the depths, I'd not like it to be at your expense." He was silent for a moment. When he continued, his voice was quite serious. "It's an interesting idea, you know. I hadn't thought of it before. A combined Luck and Bane. . . . It might be regarded as the Bane of the Tremuans; Sir William's encounter with it was fatal enough."

Carla was about to making a joking reply when she realized what he had said.

"Sir William? You don't mean to tell me he was your ancestor?"

"Hardly," Simon said, smiling. "He died without issue, if you remember. He was a cousin of my many-times great-grandfather. Didn't you know?"

"No. I don't think I ever heard his last name. He

256

wasn't in the genealogy, since he never married into the family. How amazing!"

"Not really. My family has been here as long as yours. The title passed on to another branch of the family; that's why I'm a humble commoner."

He continued to talk about his family, and its involvement in county history. Carla was unresponsive. She could not have explained why this revelation should have surprised her so, but it did. Good thing I'm not superstitious, she thought. But Simon is; I wonder if one of his reasons for proposing to me.... No, that's too silly.

Still, she felt badly about having refused him, and when he left her at the door, with a long meaningful look as he pressed her hand, she went in loaded with guilt.

Her feet turned automatically toward the kitchen. They had fallen into the habit of sitting there in their leisure hours; it was by far the most cheerful room in the big, echoing house, and Tim liked to be near the refrigerator. The door was open, and as she approached she heard voices. So Michael was back. She was still in the darkness of the butler's pantry when she heard a sentence that stopped her in her tracks.

"I won't have her told, I tell you. It's none of her business. Nor yours, come to that."

It was Michael's voice, flat with anger. Tim started to speak, but was cut short.

"I don't want to talk about it. Why the hell did you let her go out today?"

"How the hell was I supposed to stop her?"

"I told you—"

"All right, all right," Tim snapped. "I goofed. I'm not cut out for this sort of thing. If I'd known what I was getting into—"

"Drop it, I said."

Carla waited, but nothing more was said. She cleared her throat noisily and went in. Tim started. He had a hopelessly transparent face; she would have known from the way he looked at her that she had been the subject of their conversation, even if she had not overheard. As always, Michael was in perfect control.

"Did you have a nice day?" he inquired politely.

"Yes, thank you. Did you?"

Michael considered the question.

"No," he said, "not particularly."

"How is Elizabeth?"

"Elizabeth? Oh, these things take time, you know. One doesn't measure progress, if any, by the day or week."

"Want a beer?" Tim asked.

"No, thanks. I had a late and ample lunch. Simon's housekeeper must think he's keeping a harem, she gives us so much food."

"And how is our friendly neighborhood murderer?" Michael inquired.

"Well, really! Of all the ungrateful—"

"Oh, I'm grateful. I'm very grateful. You're grateful, Tim is grateful. The police aren't so grateful, but they couldn't complain after you two had poured forth your gratitude. . . . What did dear old Simon say today?"

"He asked me to marry him."

Carla hadn't meant to mention that. A perfectly explicable motive made her do it, and she got the reward people usually get for spite. Michael's scowl relaxed.

"Did he really? How nice."

Carla knew she had to get out of the room before tears or anger—or both—boiled over and humiliated her. With an incoherent mutter about wanting to take a

258

shower, she turned and fled.

Tears came to her eyes as she ran down the hall and up the stairs—tears of rage, she told herself. Not that she had any right to be angry. Michael had never given her the slightest encouragement. No doubt he had noticed her infatuation, and was relieved that he wouldn't have to suffer it any longer. He had taken it for granted that she had accepted Simon's proposal—and that was almost the worst insult of all.

Carla flung herself on her bed and abandoned herself to a raging attack of self-pity. The fact that she recognized this disgusting emotion for what it was did not prevent her from wallowing in it briefly; but after a while she sat up and blew her nose with stern determination. No more of that. It was time to act, not feel sorry for herself. She had to get away. It was sheer masochism to hang around watching Michael as he fussed over Elizabeth and expressed a kindly fraternal interest in her happiness with another man.

She would sell him the house. Spite shouldn't enter into a major decision of that sort. She still couldn't understand why he should want it. His reasons had never been convincing, and the conversation she had overheard intensified her former suspicions without clarifying them. How had Michael been able to figure out Alan's plots so readily? Perhaps he had plans of his own —a cut of the profits in return for silence. Ugly theories sprouted and spread in her mind, like rank weeds.

She started violently as her bedroom door swung slowly open. Then she saw a long tail, swaying as it moved, and King came into sight around the bed.

He greeted her with a rusty purr. It was the first time he had come to her room, and Carla was surprised and pleased. She hadn't seen him for some time, though the food dishes she filled each morning were always licked clean by nightfall.

"What brings you here?" she asked.

King sat down and looked at her intently.

"You can't be hungry," Carla told him. "Did you come to keep me company? I appreciate it. I'm so down I'm ready to babble to any sympathetic face, even one with fur all over it."

The cat cocked its head interestedly, and Carla went on talking. She felt slightly ridiculous, but her need for catharsis was strong.

"I guess talking to a cat isn't quite as bad as talking to yourself. . . . I was just about at that point, I can tell you. Don't worry, King, I'll survive. 'Hearts do not break; they sting and ache, for old love's sake, but do not die.' "

This profound sentiment made King narrow his eyes in disgust. He shook himself and stalked across the room and out through the French windows. With an easy lift of his hindquarters he sprang onto the balcony rail. The graceful power of the movement reminded Carla of Michael. She laughed, jeeringly, at herself, and went to join the cat, who was silhouetted against one of Cornwall's spectacular sunsets.

"All right," she mumbled. "Tomorrow is the day. I'll go to Truro, to a travel agency. It's tourist season, and I may not be able to get a plane reservation right away, but I'll get to work on it. And I'll see my new lawyer, tell him what to do with the house. He can deal with Michael after I've left."

King meowed approvingly.

Carla was still on the balcony, trying to get her thoughts in order, when there was a knock at the half-open door and Tim's head came into view.

"Want to go to Penzance for some fish and chips? Mike is on strike. Says he's tired of cooking."

"No, thanks. I'll make myself a sandwich later."

"Okay. Oh, I forgot, you had a telephone call. From the vicar. He said, would you call him back."

Carla waited until she heard the front door slam before she went downstairs to the telephone. Once she would have been afraid to be alone in the house. Now she welcomed it. The less she saw of Michael, the better.

Her emotional turmoil, and the decision that resulted from it, had left her drained of emotion. She had to force herself to pick up the phone and make cheery conversation, although John seemed pleased to hear from her.

"I'm so glad all is well with you, Carla. You seemed rather distracted the last time we met. You mustn't brood, you know."

"Brood?" Carla repeated blankly. He couldn't possibly know about her decision. She was in no mood to talk about it, the idea of going away was still too painful. Then, belatedly, she realized what he was referring to. She had forgotten the major tragedy of the recent past in her own selfish unhappiness.

"Oh, that. I'm ashamed not to be more concerned, John. I was fond of Alan, but I hardly knew his sister, and I. . . . I guess I'm more callous than I had realized."

"No, no, it's perfectly natural that you should feel that way," John said soothingly. Carla had a feeling he would have produced the same professional bromide if she had expressed a weakness for cannibalism; but it was nice to have someone approve of her.

"I rang you earlier to tell you I've discovered some rather interesting facts about your legend," he went on.

"It's no longer of imminent importance, of course; but I found it most provocative. I'm anxious to hear your reaction. Perhaps you could come to tea tomorrow."

"I suppose there's no use asking for a hint," Carla said.

"You know my little weakness. I had hoped to tell you today, that would have been most appropriate, but I've a parish meeting this evening, so it will have to be tomorrow—if that suits you."

"Thank you, I'd like that. Just a *little* hint, John?"

"That would spoil the surprise. Till tomorrow, then."

With a sigh of relief, Carla hung up. Perhaps by teatime next day she would have gotten a grip on herself and be able to take polite interest in John's revelation. He had sounded so pleased about it.

As she trailed disconsolately back up the stairs, a faint spark of interest stirred. She had almost forgotten about Caroline during the excitement of the past week. Odd, that both Simon and John had brought up the subject on the same day. . . . Well, it would be mildly interesting to hear what the vicar had discovered, but she had no intention of spending any more time on the story. She had poured over poor Caroline's diary till her eyes and brain ached with boredom. Instead she would spend the evening sorting some of the family things she planned to take home with her. They would have to be shipped, and packing would take time. She might as well get started. Nothing was better for self-pity than hard work.

To her surprise King was still in her room. He had moved from the balcony to the bed. Curled into a ball, his tail tucked in, he looked lazily comfortable, but his eyes were wide open. He was staring fixedly at something on the wall. Carla's eyes followed his, but there was nothing moving that would account for his interest.

Then she realized that he was looking at the spot where the portrait had hung.

The shadows lengthened as the red ball of the sun slid down toward the sea. Carla was suddenly conscious of the silence. She was not afraid, but she found herself cocking her head, as the cat had done, straining to hear some sound that was as yet only a faint vibration of the air.

How silly she had been, to hide Caroline's portrait. She was tempted to take it and the diary back home with her. After all, she was the last of the family. If she had children, one of them might one day find the old story as absorbing as she had done.

She went to the wardrobe and took the picture out. It was the work of a moment to restore Caroline to her place. A long ray of deepening sunlight fell across the canvas, giving the blurred features greater distinctness than they had ever had. Or were her eyes playing tricks on her? Carla rubbed them and looked again. The face did look clearer.

Caroline had had gray eyes. Strange that she hadn't noticed that before. Carla put out her hand and brushed the painted hair with the tips of her fingers. For a moment she could have sworn she felt, not hard canvas, but a softer, more pliant substance. The sensation did not recur, though she brushed her fingers across the painting again. Behind her, King gave a sudden, sharp growl.

"I wonder what happened to you," Carla murmured. There was no answer in the painted face. The silence deepened around her. Even the cat's growl sounded echoing, and far away. "You'd be dead now anyway," Carla went on. "It doesn't really matter."

But it did matter to her. The dead girl had cast a spell

over her—not the fantastic supernatural possession the legend had suggested, but a more subtle influence, born of sympathy and kinship. The most frightening part of the whole affair, to Carla, was the change in herself. Her parents had been affectionate, easygoing people, but there had never been any profound depth of sentiment in their attachments. Her mother had gone without regret to the plastic, artificial shelter of her retirement town, and none of them had ever had the least interest in the past. She couldn't remember her father speaking of his family, or wanting to visit the country where his people had lived so long. And here she was, helplessly entwined with old memories—the call of the blood and the soil? Sentimental twaddle she would have called it once, and yet her departure from the old house would hurt only a little less than leaving Michael.

She would not take the portrait with her. It would stay where it had been from the first. There were too many influences radiating from that painted face to be quite comfortable.

The diary was different. It had never caused her any qualms of strangeness, and it could be hidden away for a future day. And the wedding dress. It was of no interest to anyone else. She couldn't let it be sold to some sophisticated young modern, who would giggle over its quaintness and wear it to costume parties.

Carla opened the wardrobe. The dress hung there, shimmering softly in the gloom. The satin felt stiff and dusty under her fingers as she drew it out. She spread it across the bed. With a muffled yowl of protest the cat sprang away as the heavy folds approached him.

Carla stepped out of her shoes, untied the bow of her wraparound skirt, and let it fall to the floor; pulled her blouse over her head and dropped it. The rustling satin folds enveloped her.

For a few seconds she couldn't breathe. Then her arms found the sleeves and the dress fell into place around her body. It was a perfect fit. Even the length was right. Her fingers moved quickly over the laces and ties. Rotten thread gave way as she tugged, but the gaps didn't matter; the satin molded itself to her breast and waist as if the dress had been made for her.

The last thin paring of the sun dipped under the horizon. Carla was unaware of it; she saw only her pale reflection in the mirror. For a moment she saw it clearly —the wide gray eyes and dark hair blending into shadow, so that it appeared longer, thicker, than her own hair. Then, as suddenly as if she had dived down into deep icy water, darkness swallowed her. It was an inner darkness, a horror of the soul. She was choking with revulsion, all the worse because it had no cause.

Blindly she turned from the mirror. All her senses felt clouded, as if she strained to see through fog, tried to hear through thick walls. She was dimly aware of the cat's shriek as he threw himself against the door. The howls rose to a crescendo as she walked stiffly toward the animal. Then the latch yielded, and King fled. Carla followed. She began to run, stumbling over the long skirts, down the stairs, through the front door, along the path. She was running away from something; but the terror went with her, step by frantic step, deepening as the shadows deepened around her.

Her own identity was not overlaid by another; there was no individuality in the thing that gripped her body. It was pure fear, naked and unspecified. Beneath it her mind writhed and twisted, trying to regain control, as her muscles might have strained to guide an imperfectly functioning machine. At the last possible moment some shred of will surfaced long enough to turn her stumbling feet away from the path they had taken—the path toward the western gate.

Thorns ripped the satin skirt and the skin of her hands as she fled through the gardens, but she couldn't stop herself anymore than she could have stopped a car whose brakes were gone. Her own personality was still aware and thinking; even as she wrestled futilely with the controls of her body, isolated pieces of information began to fall into place. She had lost track of time in the past few days. There had been no reason to note dates or days of the week. But now she knew why the vicar had said this would be an appropriate day for his revelations, why Simon had remembered the legend on this afternoon. This was Midsummer Eve. The sun was gone, and it was twilight, and she was approaching a rendezvous that had awaited her for over ten centuries. Yet she knew she was running, not toward some awaited end, but away from a greater terror than anything suggested by the legend.

The sky in the west was pale blue, with a single star pinned like a diamond on its breast. . . . Had she written those words, not long ago, in her diary—the diary where she had not dared to write about the thing that drove her . . . not toward the western gate, it lay behind her now. Ahead was her goal: the tall, leaning stones, like charcoal outlines against the sky. A source of knowledge older than Carla or Caroline Tregellas told her the truth; for this had once been a gate too, a gateway to forces that had ruled the world long before the saints brought Christ to the heathen Cornishmen.

Her bare feet hurt. She had run unheeding over stones

266

and brambles. Then a deeper, tougher set of thorns wound around one ankle and held, biting deep; she fell headlong on the threshold of the ancient stone circle.

The impact was hard enough to drive the wind out of her, and perhaps it drove something else out, too; for when she raised herself on her elbows she realized that the gripping horror had retreated. It was not gone, not altogether, but she could command her own limbs again, though they moved rustily and reluctantly. She rolled over and clutched at her ankle, which was pulsing with pain. Her fingers slipped in a sticky flow of blood. Then she realized that the rustle in the tall grass behind her was not the wind. The cat had dived at her feet; that was why she had fallen. He was hiding in the grass, but she could hear him growling.

She pulled herself slowly to her feet. Her strength was gone. She would have fallen without the support of the rough stone at her back. The pointed arch loomed over her. Her hands went to her breast and pulled, wrenching at the fastening of the dress. With the perversity of the inanimate the fragile thread held.

"No, don't do that," a voice from within the circle said. "Come through, Carla. Come all the way in."

He was sitting on the fallen stone, as he had the first time she met him. There was not enough light for her to see more than a shapeless outline; some other sense than sight showed her the tumbled golden head and broad, powerful shoulders.

"I've been sitting here for the longest time," the quiet voice went on conversationally. "I knew you'd come. I don't know how I knew, but I did. Strange, isn't it? You came so close to ruining all my plans. You and that wretched bastard of old Walter. . . . Oh, yes, he's Walter's son; my father delivered the brat, he knew the whole story. Our two families seem destined to be rivals. But the rivalry will end here, tonight. Do you know I was almost ready to give the thing up? I don't like killing. I had to kill Fairman; he'd have spoken in another minute, and exposed me. I couldn't allow that. But I had almost made up my mind not to harm you. I'm fond of you, actually. He was fond of her, too."

Carla's head was clear now, but she still couldn't move. It was as if the ancient stone held her fast in its magnetic grip. She cleared her throat, and Simon said quickly,

"Don't scream, Carla. I don't like loud noises. It's so quiet here, so peaceful. Screaming won't help you. This is the way it was meant to be. It came over me, quite suddenly, this evening, after I had taken you home. I knew that if I came here and waited, you would come, just as she did; and then I could do what had to be done. Come here, Carla. Don't try to run, you can't get away, you'll only suffer. I won't let you suffer. It will soon be over."

Less than half of what he had said made sense to Carla, but she was not inclined to waste time and energy puzzling over incongruities. She forced herself to move, sliding along the surface of the leaning stone, away from Simon; but even as she did so, despair gripped her. Even if she had the full use of her legs she couldn't hope to escape him. The dress would hamper her, and its rustling paleness would betray her slightest movement. Caroline's wedding dress would be her bane.

Still, she had no intention of giving up without a struggle. She threw back her head and screamed at the top of her lungs.

Simon moved. She saw his dark bulk lift up and drop. A lovely clear light still lingered in the west. The tall grasses along the edge of the cliff looked like a Chinese pen-and-ink drawing, and she stared at them, mesmerized, wondering if they were the last things she would ever see. She screamed again, hearing the grass rustle as Simon walked toward her. He was in no hurry. There was no reason for him to hurry.

Then the silhouette lifted up over the rim of the cliff. The seal-round, seal-dark head and long, wiry arms, the wide shoulders and tapering body. . . . It made no sound; or perhaps the sound of its passage over the grass was hidden in the noise of Simon's movements. Its shape was hidden too, blending with the darkness as soon as it left the cliff edge. But Carla's other senses, sharpened by the failure of sight, worked only too well. Muffled sodden thuds and hoarse breathing followed Simon's first cry of startled surprise. Then a voice rose in a piercing, inhuman shriek, and Carla's stretched nerves finally gave way.

She awoke with her head on Michael's shoulder and his arms tight around her. It was pitch-dark, but she did not need to see him; the feel of him was identification enough. She stirred and murmured pleasurably, and Michael said softly, "Everything is all right. Rest a minute."

His heart pounded like a hammer under her cheek, belying the calm of his voice. Something brushed against her bare feet, and she started.

"It's the damned cat," Michael said, his control giving way momentarily; she couldn't decide whether the break in his voice was amusement or relief.

"He's not a cat, he's a guardian angel," Carla murmured. "Michael, if you hadn't gone swimming to-night. . . ."

"Swimming? I don't know what. . . . Never mind, we'll discuss that later. Can you walk?"

"I think so. If I could just get this horrible dress off. . . ."

"Not just now, please," said Michael, with the same quiver of amusement in his voice. "Here we go—upsy daisy, that's a brave girl."

"Oh, my feet hurt," Carla moaned. She balanced gingerly on them, with Michael's arm supporting her.

"Thank God that's all that hurts," Michael muttered.

"Is he—"

"He won't bother you again."

Leaning on his arm, Carla turned. There was nothing beyond the stones but silent darkness. The tall gateway framed a sky emblazoned with stars, and a cool wind carried the smell of the sea.

III

The dress was ruined. Stained with dew and dirt, shredded and torn, it was beyond repair. Carla held it on her lap as she sat enthroned in state in the drawing room, her bandaged feet on a stool.

The police had come and gone. Carla hadn't seen them. Michael had shoved her into her room and told her not to come out until he fetched her.

"We've got to get our stories straight," he explained. "No, don't argue with me; get into some decent clothes. You look like the madwoman out of *Jane Eyre*."

When he finally came for her she had changed, and worked on her abused feet, but she had not done much about makeup; she was rather avoiding mirrors. She took the dress downstairs with her. As she entered the drawing room, John came to meet her.

"Michael rang me as soon as he had notified the police," he explained, his fine face haggard with shock. "This is absolutely frightful! Carla, my dear, what can I do for you? Michael, I think a glass of warm milk, and a sleeping pill, don't you?"

"She doesn't need a sleeping pill, she needs to talk," Michael said. "Vicar, you don't realize what a spot we're in. Neither does Carla, and she had better get with it before she talks to the police."

"What do you mean?" Carla demanded.

"Sit down," Michael ordered. "You too, John. Tim—I know you're there. Come take your medicine like a little man."

Tim appeared in the doorway, trying to look nonchalant.

"What are you mad at him for?" Carla asked.

"Because he's a rotten bodyguard. He's never around when he's needed."

"You told me I could go to Penzance," Tim protested.

"And I told you to come straight back. Well, never mind; it's true that I was supposed to be on duty tonight, and I came damned close to—"

He broke off, and for the first time Carla saw his face without its trained mask. The look he gave her compensated for most of what she had gone through that evening.

"But you did get there in time," she said. "My hero."

Michael shook his head.

"We'll get to that later. First tell me what the hell you were doing out there in the dark in Caroline's wedding dress. I assume it was hers?"

"*Was* is right." Carla lifted the tattered folds. "I'm going to burn it. It's beyond repair, and after tonight. . . . It was natural enough for me to try it on, wasn't it? I don't know why I decided to do it tonight. I had forgotten the date." She turned impulsively toward the vicar, who was leaning forward in his chair, his mouth ajar. "John, I know now what happened to Caroline. She was running away from him—her handsome dream lover. She was terrified of William. She couldn't refuse to marry him, when her family was so keen on the match, but she hated and feared him. That night, when they sat whispering together in the drawing room. . . . He was saying terrible things to her. Suddenly she couldn't stand it anymore. She got up and ran, mindlessly. I don't know what happened to her after that; probably she jumped from the cliff. But I know how she felt. I felt the same thing when I put on her wedding dress."

She expected incredulity. Instead John nodded.

"That was the theory I meant to put to you tomorrow, as a result of my investigation of the parish records. I've never had time to look through the older ones, but I felt that this matter was more than a question of purely antiquarian research. Well, you'd be amazed at some of the things I discovered about our oldest and most distinguished families! That particular branch of the Tremuans were a wild lot. Bad blood, they used to call it, before scientists told us we mustn't believe in such things.

"Mr. Martinson, the vicar at that time, was a garrulous old soul, and he recorded a considerable amount of gossip. Nothing definite, you understand; the Tremuans were the leading family, and a clergyman in the eighteenth century held the living at the discretion of his noble patrons. All the same, he dropped certain hints, and I began to see Sir William as quite a different person from the hero of romance tradition had made of him. He was the ringleader of a gang of young blades who tried everything from rape to desecrating the church in order to relieve their boredom. It is quite conceivable that a sensitive, delicate girl would find him loathsome; and equally conceivable that he would enjoy 'teasing' her."

"That was what I felt," Carla said. "Her loathing of him."

"Very spooky," Tim said appreciatively. "The haunted dress. Sounds like a Hardy Boys' mystery."

"I cannot accept that," the vicar said firmly. "I don't rule out the possibility of an attack of . . . call it ancestral memory, even clairvoyance. Such things do happen. Carla had been thinking about the girl, brooding on her fate; the dress might act as a catalyst to a sensitive mind like hers. But please let's not have ghosts. If our theory is correct, we have just solved the family mystery."

"And Sir William's horrible fate?" Carla asked. "Can you account for that logically, John?"

"Certainly. He was not really a monster, only a vicious, unimaginative young clod. In his own strange way he loved the girl. He found her that night, but too late; in her attempt to avoid him she went over the cliff. It must have been a horrible shock to him. Searching for her, or her body, he injured himself on the rocks and acquired those strands of seaweed which figure so dramatically in the legend. Belated remorse and guilt affected his mind. Because he could not accept the responsibility for her death, his crazed brain invented demons."

He looked at the others triumphantly.

"Not bad," Tim admitted. "Not bad at all."

"Never mind all that," Michael said. "Our chief concern now is to invent a story that will account for Carla's presence there tonight, without dragging in ancestral memory and clairvoyance and all that rot. What about it, Carla? Did you go for an innocent evening stroll, or were you lured to your doom by a note from the villain?"

"Just a moment," the vicar said, before Carla could answer. "Lying is a sin, of course, but. . . . Is it necessary to make anyone a villain? Couldn't Simon's death have been an unfortunate accident? I'm thinking of you, Michael. We all know you acted in defense of Carla, but the case will be a cause célèbre, and it may involve you in a great deal of unpleasantness. If—"

"Hold on," Michael interrupted. "You don't know what you're talking about, John. You've only heard part of the story. There is no way in which Simon's death could have been an accident, and no way of saving his reputation. He deliberately murdered Alan Fairman to keep him from talking. Fairman and he were partners in the smuggling business—in fact, Simon was the senior partner. He meant to continue the original agreement after a reasonable time had elapsed. Six months, a year —people would have forgotten my rude accusations by then, especially if Carla and I were no longer around to remind them."

"I can't believe it," John exclaimed.

"You find it easier to believe Simon turned homicidal maniac and tried to kill Carla for the fun of it?" Michael inquired. "It was obvious to me from the first that Alan wasn't the master crook. The police mightn't see it; they didn't know the people involved, or the details of the

274

plan to drive Carla away. But you, John—how could you possibly think Alan capable of inventing that scheme? It was so typical of Simon! And he was one of the few people who could have talked Gran into buying it. Not only did she trust him implicitly, but as her medical adviser he was able to distort her moments of confusion and absentmindedness into something really sick." He turned to Carla. "I thought surely you'd catch on that day at the hospital, when he was relating his highly colored version of what Gran saw before she collapsed. He had read Squire Thomas's manuscript, of course. A student of local folklore wouldn't pass over a juicy source like that. He had free access to everything in the house, including the cupboard in the library. When he decided to use the legend to frighten you away, he ripped out of Walter's genealogy the pages that exploded the myth."

"You believe Walter had discovered the true story?" John asked, looking slightly crestfallen.

"He had the same sources at his disposal that you did, and a much more personal interest in the story," Michael said.

"Then why didn't he tell people?" Carla demanded.

"Because nobody really gave a damn," Michael said. "Who cares about an antique ghost story? Only horror buffs, who would much rather repeat a good yarn than have it explained rationally. I suspect he did tell Simon, the only person in the neighborhood who shared his interest in the subject. It was Simon's family that was involved, remember—not very creditably. His regard for Simon might have been another reason why Walter didn't make the story public."

The vicar nodded. "You are quite right. Walter had

completed most of his research when I arrived. I never knew him well. And who could possibly imagine that the old legend would ever take on such importance? I still can't imagine how Simon did all the things he did. I take it he was responsible for Mrs. Pendennis's stroke."

"Indirectly, yes," Michael said. "We'll never know precisely what happened that night. Thanks to Simon's tampering with her mind, Gran is no longer a reliable witness. That's why she was never in danger from him; he knew quite well she could never testify against him. I think I can guess what he was up to, though. He planned to drag his bag of seaweed across the room and down the hall, toward Carla's door—"

"Why not simply come in my window?" Carla asked, shivering at the idea.

"That would not have been mysterious and supernatural," Michael retorted. "Your balcony is accessible to a good climber, but Gran's window is two floors above the ground. He simply walked into the house, of course; locking up that place is a waste of time, there are too many means of entry. But first he threw a handful of pebbles at my window. When I looked out he treated me to a pretty little tableau—a shadowy figure wearing some sort of weedy-looking wig, slithering around in the shrubbery. Of course I went tearing out to investigate. Then he went upstairs. He must have had a shock himself when Gran woke up. He had been doping her for days, as you recall. That night she didn't take her pills, or else they failed to work. She saw him. She probably wouldn't have recognized him, in his disguise, but the mere sight of a man in her room in the middle of the night brought on an attack. He had barely time to get out and down the back stairs before Carla came to the rescue."

"It all seems so silly," Carla said. "So childish."

"It was, rather," Michael agreed. "But that's the way his mind worked. I fancy he enjoyed it. If the plan to frighten you didn't succeed, he could always resort to more drastic methods, as he did tonight. The portrait was his best effect, and yet it was a dead giveaway. I was certain of him after that."

"Why?"

"Do think logically, if you can," Michael said rudely. "It was obvious, wasn't it, that you were under the influence of some drug that night? It couldn't have been in your food or drink; with that method there was no way of predicting when it would take effect. So I thought to myself, what if the portrait had been moved in order to maneuver you into a position where you would be vulnerable to some kind of gas? It sounds like Fu Manchu, but doctors do have access to anesthetic gases, you know —just as they have access to drugs like heroin. He had to open the window afterwards so the stuff would dissipate."

"It's the most complicated thing I ever heard of," Carla protested.

"He had a complicated mind. There was another reason for moving the portrait to that dark corner. You didn't get a good look at it. What you saw, of course, was a mirror. It reflected your own face, and it's not surprising that your expression was horror-stricken. He could remove the mirror with a flick of the wrist, it was simply wedged in under the frame. It wouldn't have taken him sixty seconds to set the thing up. He simply waited on the iron staircase until you left the room, which you were bound to do at some point during the evening."

No one spoke. Carla was struggling to assimilate the mass of information. The vicar looked stunned.

"I've known Simon for years, you know," Michael went on. "Long enough to realize that under his affable smiling facade he was a mean bastard with a lot of emotional problems. He was my bête noire when I was growing up. He outweighed me by several stone and he used to beat the daylights out of me every time we met. But I couldn't seem to get any evidence against him. None of you would have believed me if I had accused him without evidence; I was a suspicious character myself. I hoped to persuade Alan to accuse him, but he got here in time to save himself. I didn't think he'd given it up, though, and I've been worried sick about Carla. When she told us Simon had proposed to her, I thought, marvelous, he's decided to try another method of getting the house. At least she'll be safe while he does his courting, and if she is fool enough to accept him, I'll think of something to stop her before she actually marries him."

Carla had forgotten there was anyone else in the room.

"What would you have done to stop me?" she asked.

"Killed him, if I had to."

"I was going to give you the house."

"You might have said so. Simon would have turned his attentions to me if I had been the owner."

"I couldn't imagine why you wanted it. All that stuff about a hotel was singularly unconvincing."

"It was true, though."

"But your career—"

Tim, whose head had been swinging back and forth

following the conversation, like a spectator at a tennis match, now interrupted.

"I told you you were a jerk not to tell her the truth." He turned to Carla. "He's got a trick shoulder. Threw it out of whack last year playing soccer with the boys. It's never been right since."

"So that's why. . . ."

Michael shrugged.

"A dancer's legs aren't the only parts of his anatomy that count. Imagine me dropping the prima ballerina when she leaps into my arms. It wouldn't do."

"Then you really do want to turn the place into an inn?"

"Why not? It might be fun."

"Yes," Carla murmured. "It might. . . . Tim, who the hell are you, anyway?"

"Exactly who I said." Tim looked hurt. "Mike and I have had this deal in mind for months. We met in London last year while I was seeing the world. . . . I did lie a *little*, Carla. I'm not quite as broke, or as new to the Old World, as I said. I majored in hotel management at college, and when I inherited a little money from an uncle of mine, I started looking for a good investment. Mike told me about this place. We figured we could get it cheap. The only thing I didn't figure on was getting involved in a real-life thriller. Mike sent me an SOS after he started to suspect that someone was out to get the girl of his dreams—"

"That's enough of that," Michael interrupted. "Is the deal still on?"

"Sure. We'll turn the place into a combination Haunted House and posh hotel. It can't miss."

"But my dear friends!" The vicar waved his arms help-lessly. "All these plans. . . . I'm afraid we have a troubled period before us. Michael, how did Simon Tremuan die?"

"I didn't kill him. The sergeant knows that; that's why I'm here among my friends and admirers instead of being charged."

"How did he die?" the vicar repeated.

"His neck was broken," Michael said reluctantly. "And there were other injuries. . . ." He turned to Carla. "I heard you scream. I had realized by then that you weren't in the house, and I was getting frantic. I ran out into the garden, and then you yelled again. When I arrived on the scene. . . . This is the part you won't believe."

"I already don't believe it," Carla gasped ungrammatically. "I thought you'd gone to Penzance with Tim. Then, when I saw you climb over the cliff—"

"But I didn't. I came from the house. I found you on the ground, out cold. Simon was lying on his face next to one of the fallen stones. I had a torch with me. I didn't turn it on later because I didn't want you to see. . . . A man might have inflicted those injuries. A karate black belt. Maybe."

There was a brief, horrified silence. Then Michael said thoughtfully, "I should have heaved him over the cliff, I guess. I wasn't thinking clearly. But the sergeant agreed with me that it was probably a professional killer who did the job—a hit man hired by Simon's criminal colleagues, perhaps because he was threatening to blackmail them. Lucky for me, though, that I haven't any fresh bruises. I'd take it as a favor, Carla, if you wouldn't put any nasty suspicions into the good sergeant's mind.

I don't know what you saw, but it wasn't me."

"I must get over these crazy ideas of mine," Carla said slowly. "I couldn't have seen anyone; it was too dark. I heard the sounds of a fight. And, being a poor timid female, I fainted dead away."

"The police will probably buy that," Michael said.

"So will I," said Tim. "I don't want to know anything else. That's a nice story, Carla. Stick to it."

They all looked at the vicar.

"It seems clear-cut to me," he said calmly. "What else could have happened? If I must, I'd rather accept a highly unlikely and hypothetical—er—hit man, than an even less likely. . . . Well. It has been a trying evening, and Carla should get to bed. Good night, all of you. I'll see myself out."

After he had gone, Tim effaced himself with loud significant clearings of his throat and glances at Michael. Carla got up, wincing as she put her weight on her sore feet, and hobbled to the window.

Darkness and stars, nothing more. She felt, rather than heard, Michael come up behind her with his light dancer's step.

"You're wondering what's out there, aren't you?" he said softly.

"We'll have to talk about it someday," Carla said. "Even Walter's will. . . . What prompted him to express it in such a way that I was the only one who qualified?"

"It can all be explained rationally, Carla. Coincidence. . . . Even that damned jingle Simon faked and inserted in the diary."

"What about it?"

"I do believe you're only semiliterate. He's an American poet, too. Edwin Arlington Robinson. 'Come to the western gate, Luke Havergal. . . . And in the twilight wait for what will come.' "

"I don't care how much of it was faked," Carla said. "There are still things. . . . But you don't have to rationalize everything in order to make me feel better, Michael. I'm not afraid. Simon was right after all. It's a Luck, not a Bane."

Michael's arms went around her.

"Shall we try it, then? It's a crazy scheme, Carla; almost as crazy as you are, my poor superstitious darling."

Carla thought about it. They would have to work their fingers to the bone, all of them, and the scheme might not work. They were young and inexperienced. All the odds were against them.

Practical considerations on one side of the scale. On the other. . . .

"Oh, yes," she said. "Yes, please. Let's try it."